RANK

TESS MERLIN

Published in Australia 2023
www.tessmerlin.au

Print ISBN: 9780645664911
Ebook ISBN: 9780645664904

Disclaimer
This book is written as an autobiographical novel. Whilst the contents are predominantly factual, it is not a memoir and therefore there are elements of fiction throughout. The depictions of workplace harassment and assault are based on the author's personal experiences. The stalking is also based on the author's personal experiences, however, the level to which this escalates has been fictionalised.

The majority of names, characters, businesses, organisations, places, events, and external incidents have been presented in a fictitious manner. Any resemblance to actual persons, living or dead, or actual events is purely coincidental.

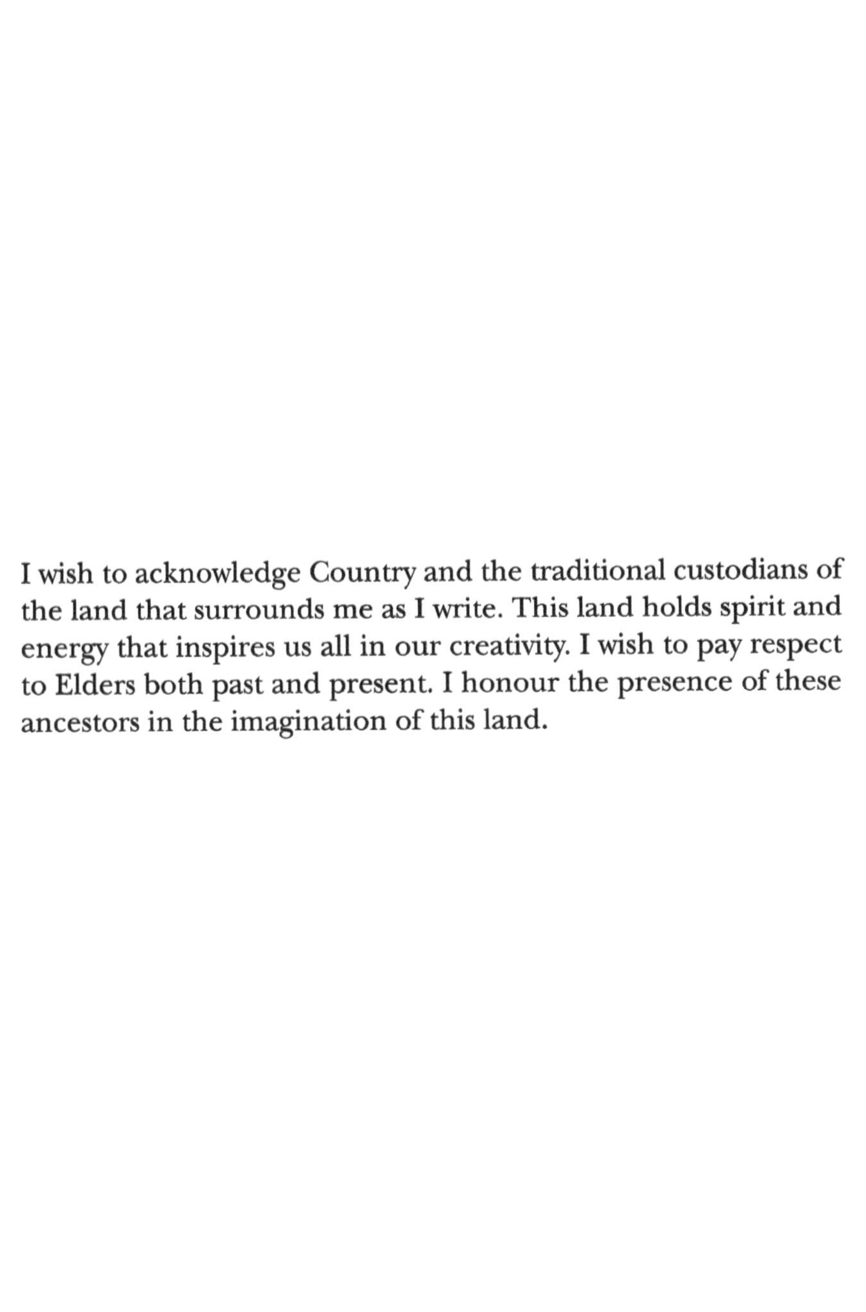

I wish to acknowledge Country and the traditional custodians of the land that surrounds me as I write. This land holds spirit and energy that inspires us all in our creativity. I wish to pay respect to Elders both past and present. I honour the presence of these ancestors in the imagination of this land.

For Hannah

You inspired me to write

You inspire me daily by just being you

A Brief History of the Introduction of Female Officers into the Queensland Police Force

1931 > First two policewomen appointed but not sworn in – no uniform and no power of arrest

1965 > Female officers sworn in and given the same powers as men

1970 > Equal pay for female officers. A total of 27 policewomen.

1976 > Female officer numbers increase to 308

1987 > The number of female officers drops from 8 percent to 5 percent of total force

1990 > Queensland Police Force becomes Queensland Police Service. Motto changes from Constantia ac Comitate (Firmness with Courtesy) to With Honour We Serve

1990 > First female Inspector

1992 > First female Superintendent

2000 > First female Assistant Commissioner

2008 > First female Deputy Commissioner

2019 > First female Commissioner

Stalking was not legally recognised as an offence in Queensland prior to 1993 when *Unlawful Stalking* was introduced into the Criminal Code. Prior to this, someone who was being stalked was unable to receive social or legal assistance and the stalker could only be pursued under broad anti-harassment laws that were difficult to enforce and did little to deter offenders. Stalking would often escalate to assault before an offender could be arrested and charged with a criminal offence.

CHAPTER 1
Night Shift

My apprehension mounts with each word that emerges from his darkly bearded mouth. "You're not allowed to say, right? Like priests and doctors?"

I attempt to speak but my throat is suddenly a desert. I cough to clear it and try to match his neutral tone in reply. "Well, it's more a matter of being discreet rather than a Hippocratic oath or solemn vows."

He glances at me with his cold blue eyes then continues to print in big generic letters on the card. I read it upside down. *MINE FOREVER.* I sense cold fingers pinching the back of my neck, nerve endings tingling.

I hoped to find a hint of playfulness in those eyes, an assurance that this is just a spontaneous and affectionate message. That the anonymous flowers wrapped in black are from a secret admirer, a declaration of love or a flirty floral gift. The steely eyes meet mine again, fleetingly, but give no hint of his motives or intentions.

As I finish writing the order into the diary, he places two fifty-dollar notes on the counter in front of me. "Here, I'll pay by cash," he says.

Pushing aside the emerging, intrusive memories I find myself rushing to complete the unpleasant transaction. I just want this person gone. I imagine that he's paying by cash so that I can't check whether the name that he's given me matches that on his credit card. I suspect that *Jack Brown* is not likely to be his real name. I open the till and hand him his twenty dollars change, almost choking on a thank you, as he pockets the bill and turns to leave.

I close the till and watch as he exits the store; the door closing softly and innocently behind him, just like any other customer. *Maybe he is just any customer.* Maybe he's just shy, or could he be someone famous–wanting to hide his identity? Somehow, I think not. My gut tells me differently. I worry for this Veronica Hart, the recipient of his dozen red roses with the black paper and black ribbon. I imagine her as a trapped and downtrodden wife or lover, who perhaps has voiced her plans to leave an abusive relationship, or who has just made that brave move, believing she has succeeded, only to receive this seemingly beautiful but subtly threatening reminder of his control over her. *Mine Forever – You can't escape me.*

During my past career as a Queensland Police Officer, I had met and tried to help many women in abusive and controlling relationships. I had also at times been frustrated and confused by some women who refused to leave these situations even when offered assistance to do so. Only later did I understand their fear.

A hand on my elbow rouses me from my thoughts. "Tess. Are you ok? You've been standing there like a statue for a couple of minutes now." Ros has a bunch of white delphiniums in her other hand, reminding me of the work that still needs to be done today. The afternoon ahead is going to be hectic, and we will most likely be working well into the night.

"Yeah, it's just that guy–he was so creepy, and look what he ordered for delivery tomorrow." I show the card and instructions to Ros. "Is it just me?"

Ros reads through the order, nodding and raising one side of her mouth into a half-grimace.

"Yeah, we get some pretty weird requests as florists, but hmm, I suppose that could be a bit sus… or it could just be their way. You know as well as I do that relationships are like snowflakes–no two are the same."

Of course she's right. I could just be over-reacting, over-sensitive and harbouring too many memories of what my earlier career had exposed me to. But deep down I know it is my own unpleasant experiences and what *he* subjected me to that is making me so uneasy.

I sweep the creeping tendrils of dark memories from my mind and bring myself back to now. I need to concentrate on the job at hand. The happy event–tomorrow's wedding.

* * *

Weddings and funerals are the biggest income earners for a florist. Of course we prefer the weddings for obvious reasons, but in reality, the flowers are much more of a focal point at funerals–everyone needing somewhere to look that isn't the coffin or the eyes of the bereaved. For weddings, the workload is intense and because of the nature of fresh flowers there is a limited timeframe to prepare the bouquets. Once their stems have been cut off in order to wire them, the flowers can't last long before wilting. Even after suggesting and displaying multiple examples of beautiful, natural options, some brides still want very formal and structured shapes that require wiring.

This is one such bride. She's mid-thirties, second time around and this time she wants all the bells and whistles. Of course, *what the bride wants–the bride gets.*

As soon as I walk through from the showroom to the workroom, Sally pounces on me. "We're not going to have enough stephanotis and it's too late to order in and get it delivered before tomorrow."

"It's fine Sally, if we run out, we can start to use those white freesias to fill in here and there," I reassure her. She seems happy enough with that, but soon finds something else to worry about. I manage to come up with quick answers to all of her perceived problems and she seems happier as she returns to her work bench.

Ros turns to me and gives me a look that suggests that this is just the start of Sally's fretting, and as usual, it will continue until the job is finished. Ros is a lass of few words, and a great counterfoil to Sally who is rarely silent and believes in sharing her thoughts–sometimes it seems, without even thinking them first.

The three of us have been working together at Bloomin' Perfection for the past four years and in that time, we have come to know how each of our personalities plays out under pressure–and we work well as a team. Sally is the worrier, Ros is the head down bum up silent concentrator, and I'm the organiser and spot-fire douser.

Before starting the business, I worked for three other florists, learning everything I could from them, always with the hope of going out on my own. Then when I first opened my own shop, I worked on my own for a few years before hiring Ros, and then Sally a few months later when business boomed.

Becoming a florist was a bit of a rebound after leaving the Police Force. After 10 years of walking the beat, attending traffic accidents, wading into domestic disturbances, arresting all sorts of offenders, and dealing with some unpleasant people and horrendous situations, I just wanted to do something pleasant and pretty and go home at night feeling good. In the force, I increasingly found myself working with people who seemed to have lost the capacity to care and show empathy. Some worse than others.

This was not surprising, considering what we were confronted with on a daily basis, but it did start to ring alarm bells with me. I almost resigned at the five-year mark after a horrible period in my life–both work and private–but I stuck it out for another five after that. The last straw was on a night shift where the sergeant I was working with somehow decided it would be ok to put his hand on my leg while I was driving the patrol car. He was older, in his mid-forties and married. He had never received even the slightest encouragement from me in that regard. When I rejected him, he set about spreading nasty rumours about me. I'd already been through some tough times with unwanted attention, physical assault and downright prejudice, but that last experience came on the back of a very confronting month, and it proved too much for me.

A few weeks earlier, I had been seconded to work in the city in Brisbane for two weeks, so I was working with people that I hadn't met before. As always in the force, this was mostly male colleagues. During the second week, I was rostered on with a Senior Constable on a 4pm to midnight shift. From the very start of the shift, I felt uncomfortable with the way he kept looking at my legs in the standard issue A-line dress that we were required to wear. We shared little conversation during the patrols in the afternoon section of the shift and then we took a break for dinner, which we ate in separate areas of the station, before heading out for the evening patrols.

As we drove around the now darkened streets, responding to jobs as they were allocated via the Police radio in the car, my partner insisted on doing the driving. He spoke rarely but when he did it was to question me about my private life. *Did I live with my parents? Did I have a boyfriend? What was he like?* I could clearly see his wedding ring glinting in the glow from the dashboard. Sadly, this was not the first time that I had felt uncomfortable on a night shift where I had been rostered to work with someone that I had never met before.

In fact, I *didn't* have a boyfriend, but I had made up an imaginary one for just this type of situation. He was a truck driver called Bruce and we'd been going out for about a year.

Anyway, Bruce didn't deter him. Around 10.30pm, when we should have been thinking about heading back to the station to finish up our paperwork and prepare to sign off, he silently drove to the wharf area at Newstead. I asked where we were going, and he said he had a summons to serve on someone out there. Then he drove around behind some shipping containers where there couldn't possibly be anyone to serve the summons on and stopped the car. I asked again what we were doing there. He unclipped his seat belt and thrust himself at me while I was still pinned in position by my belt, one hand on my thigh and the other behind my head. "I can read the signals," he said pushing his face close and trying to kiss me. I turned my head away and elbowed him in the ribs, then fumbled to undo my seatbelt. I told him to stop and yelled that there *were* no signals. I got out of the car and ran between some shipping containers. It was very dark and my bag was still in the car, so I didn't have my torch. Still, I thought about just running for it until I reached the road, but the navy court shoes that we were issued with did not make running easy.

I took a breath and waited until I heard his footsteps as he got out of the car and took a few steps. There was no sound of the door closing so after a few seconds I made a dash for the driver's side in the hopes that he'd left the keys in the ignition. He had. I jumped in and started the car, watching in the rear-view mirror as his shape emerged in the tail-lights and made for my door. I could hardly reach the pedals with the seat adjusted to his height but had no time to fix it. I floored the accelerator and left him standing there.

When I reached the road, I stopped and thought about what I should do. Although I would have liked to, I couldn't really leave him there to make his own way back. Now that I was in the driver's seat, I felt more in control. I knew I could drive us back to the station and felt pretty sure that he wouldn't try to do anything while were driving around quite visibly in a marked Police vehicle, so I parked under a street light, locked my door and waited until he emerged.

While I waited, I considered my options. I was shaken by what had just happened, but I had experienced something much worse than this five years ago, in my private life outside of working hours, and I kept telling myself that if I could get over that, I could handle anything. I steadied my breathing and took strength from that knowledge. I could handle this.

Less serious assaults than this had also happened to me at work on other occasions, but I had learned to deal with them and not let them get to me. I could not help feeling disappointed that this kind of thing could happen in my workplace and that I and other female colleagues felt helpless to change that. I had friends–other policewomen–who had experienced the same and had dealt with it in various ways. The ones who reported this kind of behaviour to senior officers rarely had a good outcome, with many finding that resignation was the only way out and others trying to persevere but having their reputations ruined by the gossip that followed. We all learned that the Boys' Club was rife, and it was powerful. To be labelled a 'dog' was the worst thing for a police officer. Regaining respect and reinstating a reputation were nigh on impossible.

I decided to add this one to the pile and just be strong and persevere with my career. I'd joined because I wanted to make a difference. Quitting, although I had thought about it many times, just seemed too much like giving in.

I knew there were good cops as well, and I'd worked with them and learned from them, but sadly, I had almost come to expect this type of behaviour from a percentage of the guys, usually the older generation. The ones who seemed to be only capable of seeing a woman as either a relative or a lover. They had no concept of how to work with a woman as an equal–a colleague or partner.

* * *

He walked up to my door and tried to open it. Finding it locked, he banged on it and yelled, "Get out. I'm driving."

I opened the window slightly and said as calmly and firmly as I could, "You're not. You're a passenger, or you walk. Take your pick."

Once he was in the passenger seat, I took off while he was still doing up his seatbelt. "Don't speak," I said, and he didn't–for a while. When he spoke, it was to admonish me for leading him on–not to apologise. I told him to shut up and drove back to the station in silence.

So when I returned to my normal station and this experience was so quickly followed by the next, where my sergeant, who I knew and had worked with on many other occasions, grabbed my leg, it just really was the last straw for me.

I'd also come to the realisation that after all of those years doing police work, I was either going to become like a lot of officers that I worked with, with hardened outlooks and a cynical and dark humour that they had developed to protect themselves–like an armour; or like others on the opposite end of the spectrum, who had let the job get to them and felt it all too deeply. A lot of them were on stress leave. I even questioned whether I was already cynical and just didn't know it. Ultimately, I felt it was time to make the decision to leave.

So, exactly ten years after being sworn-in and six weeks before Christmas I submitted my resignation, giving four weeks' notice. I'd given myself a Christmas present of unemployment and uncertainty, but I felt a great sense of relief as well.

My friend Marta has stuck it out and is now only a couple of years away from retirement. We used to walk the beat in the Valley together; back then it could often be a rough place to be late at night. Those 7.30pm to 3.30am shifts were mostly busy and full of all kinds of unfortunate human behaviour, along with the usual drunks and other night-dwellers, but the quieter moments, and hours, gave us lots of time to get to know each other very well.

Marta has spent the rest of her career in the Police Photographic Section, where she transferred to after six years in general duties, requesting the transfer for similar reasons to those that prompted me to resign–the attitude and behaviour of some of her colleagues, but not just toward women. A disturbing incident that she cites as the catalyst for radical change happened one night shift, where she was rostered on car patrol with a particularly unpleasant Sergeant as her partner. She saw him steal $20 from a drunk that he was searching, and whom he was about to take to the watchhouse for the night. She was mortified and so shocked that she didn't know how to react. She started to say "Sarge…" but he pointed at her and then put his finger to his lips in a shushing motion. He was a threatening kind of guy and as a young constable, Marta felt alone and helpless to do anything to stop him.

Later, when she told me the story, I tried to put myself in her shoes. I knew her partner for that shift. He wasn't easy to talk to and he usually smelt like a mixture of stale alcohol, body odour and bad breath. Sitting in a car with him for eight hours was a nightmare to even contemplate.

But to risk his career for *twenty dollars?* It was inconceivable that someone would take that risk for such a small amount of money. The fact that he had the temerity to do it showed his arrogance, and a belief that he was untouchable. It made me wonder how many times he'd done it before.

I decided that I probably would have done the same as Marta in her situation and then, like her, wondered if I should report the incident to the Officer in Charge of the station. We'd both seen how these guys would stick together, which is something that you need in a dangerous situation, but sometimes extended as far as covering up as well. I had experienced the extent they could go to in that regard, first-hand.

She had no proof and no other witnesses, so she kept it quiet. After a long and unpleasant six month wait, she got her transfer.

She has to confront and photograph some horrendous sights, but she likes the team she works with now, and she has more autonomy in her role. Plus, having studied photography, she has the opportunity to use her skills and knowledge. She really has found her perfect little niche within the Force. She also does the occasional private assignment as a wedding photographer and is a great back-up when any of my brides have a last-minute problem with their photographer.

So, with a night shift of a very different kind ahead, and a different crew by my side, we set to work, wiring a sea of flowers and a forest of leaves.

CHAPTER 2

Green-eyed Monster

"Can we stop and give our fingers a rest now, and have some dinner?" Sally asks while stretching her arms and rolling her head from side to side.

"Sure," I reply. "We're more than half-way through the wiring, so yes, we definitely deserve a break." As they down tools, I do a rough count and let them know the list of items still to wire and arrange.

We let out a collective sigh as we survey the workbenches in front of us. Flower heads, petals, leaves and stems are strewn in a seemingly random fashion, creating a beautiful abstract artwork of pinks and greens. This is contrasted by the growing piles of completed works in neat rows, waiting to be intertwined with their unruly neighbours.

"Thank goodness Joe is coming in to do all of the arrangements for the church and reception. He's so quick and so creative," Sally says.

"What time's he getting in?" asks Ros.

"He said around eight, so he should be here soon."

No sooner are the words out of my mouth than we hear Joe's key in the front door of the shop. He wanders through to the back and greets us with his usual big grin and double hand waves.

"Wow, you ladies have been hard at it I see," he says as he picks up a few of the buds with their newly wired stems and surveys the scene. The buds look so tiny in his big hands, and I marvel again at how a big guy like him can create such delicate and intricate arrangements.

I found Joe after I'd put a notice up on Facebook looking for someone who wouldn't mind just being on call for busy times. When he walked in for the interview, I felt like perhaps he'd gone to the wrong shop and was applying for a job at the gym three doors down. His frame filled the doorway and cast a giant shadow over me. On first impressions, I had my doubts about whether he was going to be right for the job, but his personality won me over straight away, and his demo arrangement of peonies and gum leaves was spectacular. He also regularly provides us with hilarious stories from his other job as an aged care nurse.

His gaze moves to the wall above the microwave and kettle, and he walks over to read the latest of Sally's little affirmations. Sally is always trying to share some deep and meaningful message, Blu-tacked to the wall above the kitchenette bench, where we might have a second to stop and read it while we have a bite to eat or a coffee. Joe is her biggest fan and always takes a minute to read her latest missive before he starts work.

After a moment he says, "Sal, you outdid yourself with this one. I love it!" He begins to read it aloud for us all as Sally sits herself down with a proud smile.

Imagine you see a dog sitting alone and looking sad and you go up to it to give it a pat to cheer it up, but it tries to bite you. You feel disappointed and angry, but as you walk away you see that the dog has its leg caught in the teeth of a metal trap. Now you can see why it was aggressive. Next time someone is unpleasant to you, realise that ***their*** *leg is probably caught in a trap.*

Silence follows for a few seconds, and we all look at Sally. It's obvious that none of us had bothered to read this earlier.

"That's so deep, and so true." I break the silence, trying not to show my amazement that Sally has come up with this insightful metaphor. Her usual offerings are something like, 'Smile and the world smiles with you', or 'Today is a gift, that's why it's called the *Present*', but this is something else. I have to admit that I'd stopped reading them because they were so bland.

"Well, I can't take all of the credit for that. Jim wrote it out for me when I told him that I've been putting these up at work," says Sally through a mouthful of sandwich.

"Ah… Jim?" Ros gets in first with the question we all want to ask. "Who's Jim?"

"Oh, a friend of mine," she replies coyly and looks at her feet like she's just discovered them at the end of her legs for the first time.

"Ok. Spill it girl," prompts Joe. "Where'd you meet this Jim and what's he like?"

Sally has gone quite red in the face and looks a bit like a deer in the headlights. She'd have known she would come under this scrutiny if she mentioned Jim, so I figure she must want to share.

"Well, I met him online, and he's so lovely. He's actually spiritual and intelligent and really cute."

"What? You went on an online dating site?" I ask, unable to picture it. Sally is not great with IT at the best of times, so I'm amazed that she's figured out how to do this. "Did someone help you set that up?"

She puts her hands on her hips and feigns offence that I should suggest that she couldn't find her way around a dating site, but then readily admits that her friend Jill helped her. Jill's husband died six years ago and recently she has started trying to match-make for Sally and trying to get her to go to singles events so they can both meet someone.

"So, tell us more. Where's he from? What's he do, and what's he look like?" Joe asks.

Sally pulls her phone from her pocket and taps away for a minute, while we all gather in closer. She holds up the phone triumphantly and angles it from Joe to Ros to me so we can all get a look at her Jim. In the photo, he's got his arm around Sally's shoulders in a protective way, and they're both smiling broadly into the camera. It looks like it was taken at a restaurant, probably by the waiter or waitress.

Jim looks around 60 with not a lot of hair left but thankfully without a combover. He's quite fair-looking with pale eyebrows, and his smile has carried right through to his blue eyes which are crinkled up at the corners. From first impression he does look nice. Sally hasn't scrubbed up too badly either. She doesn't normally bother with make-up or body image, but she has obviously made an effort for the date that they're on in this photo–her short dark hair is looking styled and shiny and she's wearing eyeliner and mascara.

"That was our second date," she explains. "I already knew how special he was after the first date."

Sally looks longingly at the photo and can't hide a smile. "He only lives a few streets away from me, but I'd never seen him around. He's divorced and used to own his own publishing company until he sold up and retired last year. He even published a book of his own writings on inspirational stories and quotes. That one is from his book," she says, indicating the words that Joe has just read. "There's a lot more I still don't know about him but I'm looking forward to finding out."

"Wow Sal, that's amazing. Good on you." Ros sounds genuinely pleased. "How long were you on this site before you met him? Did you meet a lot of weirdos along the way?"

"No! I only had a chat with one other bloke and then Jim sent me a *kiss*. We met up after a couple of days of sending each other messages. It only took about two weeks."

"Two weeks? That's so quick! Hasn't your friend Jill been on those sites for about four years?" asks Ros.

"Yes, and I feel so bad that I've met Jim just like that," she says snapping her fingers, "so bad in fact that I haven't told her much about us yet."

I hate to crack the whip, but I know from experience how time gets away and considering we're preparing for a 10am wedding, we need to have everything finished by 8am at the latest–and grab some sleep in there somewhere as well, so after a couple more questions I encourage everyone back to work.

While I'm washing up my bowl from my dinner of leftovers, I glance up at the notice that sparked this whole conversation. It really is thought-provoking. I remember hearing someone quoting or maybe mis-quoting some actor saying something similar but much more direct like, *Be kind because everyone's got some shit going on in their lives.* I can't help but think that Veronica Hart has. Maybe hers even has a name–*Jack Brown.* I decide to deliver her dark and mysterious flowers personally tomorrow afternoon–maybe get a chance to gauge her reaction when she receives them.

I also can't help feeling a little pang of jealousy about Sally's good fortune. I think back to around eight years ago when I was still married, with all the kids at home and the belief that I was happy and that the relationship with my then husband would last forever. But in the end, we realised that we were heading in different directions and wanted different things from life. When the kids had finished school and become more independent, there seemed to be nothing left to hold us together. Also around that time, I found out that he'd been keeping a separate bank account where he syphoned money off into so that I wouldn't know that he was gambling again. It wasn't a fortune, but the dishonesty worried me.

Since then, I haven't even considered finding a new partner and have honestly enjoyed the peace and a chance to concentrate on myself and building my own business–and re-building my confidence as a single person again. But sometimes when I see a couple who seem to have a real connection, I do wonder what that would be like.

I'm surrounded by weddings at work, but I often think marriage is a folly. I wonder why we expect that just because we love someone the way they are now, that we're going to still love them in *x* number of years' time. Surely, each party is going to change–people do. How incredibly unlikely is it that two people would change in the same direction?

I shake off my cynical thinking and let that jealousy creep in a little further. My mind is telling me that I'm more attractive than Sally. She's older, with an addiction to Krispy Kremes and an aversion to exercise, the results of which she's been covering up with an expanding array of brightly coloured caftans. I think about my thick, long auburn hair versus her greying, short bob and I know I'm still trim and reasonably fit. I tell myself that if she can find a nice, half-decent looking guy online, *in two weeks*, then I should have no trouble. Another part of my mind also has the good sense to tell me that Sally is sweet. She'd do anything for anyone and doesn't have a nasty bone in her body. One thing I've never been accused of being is 'sweet'.

Also, that sensible part of my mind asks me if I even *want* to find someone. *Can I be bothered?* I don't think about it from one day to the next but when I see how happy Sally seems… then another thought hits me out of nowhere. *Sex.* Are blokes in their 50s and 60s still obsessed with sex? My ex was one of those guys who thought we needed to meet a quota–or exceed it. He would often remind me that the average Australian couple had sex twice a week and even make me feel guilty if I didn't meet that expectation. The last thing I need in my life now is that kind of pressure to perform.

From the rare conversations I've had with girlfriends on the topic, it seems like sex becomes a lower priority for a lot of women as they get older, although most of their guys aren't showing signs of slowing down or losing interest.

But am I game enough yet to put myself out there in the public eye? To be visible? To be vulnerable–after Burmont?

That's a Pandora's box I really don't want to open and immediately I can feel the old, disturbing memories rise up again and fear quickens my heartbeat. *Think about something else,* I tell myself and my mind switches back to Sally. I wonder just how close they already are, emotionally and physically. Then a visual image pops into my head before I can stop it.

I glance at Sally, feeling a little embarrassed and ashamed. I turn my attention to Joe. "Hey Joe, let's get the party started in here." He loves his music and I like his taste. Modern but not too shouty with an old classic thrown in now and then. I think a good blast of one of his playlists is just what I need to clear my mind and get us all moving again.

The Jungle Giants' *On Your Way Down* replaces the subdued corporate music that had been playing in the background. We all start singing along and the pace of work seems to pick up to match the change in tempo of the music.

* * *

10pm was going to be the cut-off, but that was almost an hour ago. I'd planned to send everyone home by then and have them back bright and early at six o'clock to finish off and pack everything into the van for delivery. During the past hour I've copped a few glances from Sally, but Ros and Joe seem to be too fully absorbed in their creations to even notice the time. Everyone is starting to yawn and stretch though, so when 11 o'clock comes around, I make the call. "Guys, you've been amazing. Everything is looking so brilliant and there's not much left to do in the morning, so do you reckon we call it a night?"

'Yeah, I'm starting to feel it," Ros admits, rubbing her neck and shoulders. "It all looks great though."

"All back on deck at six, ok?" I call out as Joe starts placing the prepared arrangements into the cold room and the girls do a quick tidy up and gather their bags and jackets. Sally is first out the door with a quick, "See you tomorrow."

As I head home, I check the temperature on my dash display. A bright green, luminous number 7 stares back me. I start to look forward to a hot cup of tea and a nice warm bed, maybe even a hot-water bottle. I suddenly wonder if the reason Sally seemed so keen to get away might be that she has a bigger, cuddlier heat source waiting for her at home.

I let myself in and flick on the lights as I walk up the hall. The reflection of the kitchen light bounces off my laptop on the breakfast bar right in front of me. *Is 11.30 too late to have a quick look?* I wonder. *And what was the name of that dating site?*

CHAPTER 3

Diving In

Good sense and an inability to keep my eyes open got the better of me last night as I began to wade through the myriad of online dating sites all vying for my attention. Today, I'm feeling a bit worn out after the late night and early start. I am also finding myself distracted from my work and quite eager to get back to my search on the dating site that I thought looked the most promising to my bleary eyes at 1.30 this morning–Wings Online.

When we delivered the bouquets to the bride she was over the moon and her bridesmaids gushed over them enthusiastically. Then a few last-minute adjustments with some wire and Blu-tack at the venue ensured that the church and reception flowers were spectacular as well.

Now comes the clean-up, which I've let Joe escape, leaving it up to me and the girls as he has an afternoon shift ahead of him at the nursing home. This part of floristry is the least fun, but the consequence of not doing it sooner rather than later is a foul-smelling florist shop–not what the customers expect when they walk into a room filled with beautiful flowers.

As we work through the sweeping, wiping and emptying of overflowing bins, Sally comes out with, "Maybe we'll all be working on my bouquets one of these days. Although I don't think I'll come in to help with the clean-up," she laughs.

Ros and I stop and exchange looks of surprise. "Just how long have you been seeing this Jim guy? Are you trying to tell us something?" I ask.

"Oh, no. Just a feeling. It's only been a couple of months so it's still early days, but he has mentioned the possibility of us moving in together."

Well, now I know how serious they are. Sally has been single for most of her life with just one serious relationship when she was in her late twenties. For her to be talking like this is really something.

Ros nudges her with her elbow and says, "It's so great that you've found someone you really like, and that you want to make plans with." Ros herself has been married for nineteen years and has two teenage kids still at home. I've always appreciated the fact that she doesn't try to match-make for us or presume that we aren't happy being single, like some married people tend to.

Now that the workroom is looking clean and tidy, I thank the girls again for their amazing work.

"Ok," says Sally, "I might head off. Jim is taking me to meet his son this arv and I'm a bit nervous."

"Just be yourself and he'll love you." I say as I give her a wink and shoo her out the door. Ros waits for me as I pause at the cold room to collect the dozen red roses, beautifully bunched and depressingly decorated in black ribbon, to drop off to Veronica Hart on my way home.

As I lock the front door to the store, Ros asks, "You ok with that lot?" and tilts of her head toward the bouquet in my hand.

"Yes, I'm fine with it. Thanks. I just hope she is as well."

* * *

I park outside the address given by *Jack Brown* for the delivery, slightly surprised by how up-market the neighbourhood is. I had imagined pulling up at a run-down house with the shades drawn and the garden in need of a good mowing. Instead, I make my way along a sandstone paved pathway toward a two-storey brick house with an immaculate garden. I ring the doorbell.

The woman who answers the door is all in black. Even her long straight hair–black. The pale skin of her face is a stark contrast and appears to float above the high round neckline of her pantsuit. I'm a little taken aback, but immediately feel better about the black ribbon on her bouquet. Maybe it does make some sense after all.

"Veronica Hart?"

"Yes. Oh are those for me?" she asks as she thrusts her thin, white arms toward me.

I hand the bouquet to her, watching her face closely for any signs of fear or distaste, but as she reads the card she smiles. "Cute," she says and reaches for the door with her free hand.

She casually thanks me and disappears behind the massive wooden door, leaving me somewhat stunned and incredibly relieved. I return to my van with the words of my therapist from years ago echoing through the cobwebs of my mind... *It's called hypervigilance... You need to learn to trust again...*

* * *

So many questions! What's my height, my body type (options are very tactful... Slim, average, athletic, a bit overweight), my hair colour, eye colour, religion, marital status? Do I have pets, kids, special food requirements? What am I looking for? On and on it goes.

Here's a challenging one... my age? I wonder how many people on these sites lie about their age and I also wonder whether I should lose a few years. I decide to be honest and type in 56 because that's what I will be on my birthday, in a few days' time. Now the bit that I left blank and have to go back to as it's a required field. *Profile name?*

That first night when I had a bit of a look at some dating sites, I couldn't believe some of the names that people (men) had called themselves! *Dateless and Desperate* (that's really going to get the ladies in); *Grumpy* (I couldn't see Sneezy or Happy but lots of *Happyman* and *Happytimes* although their photos seem to belie those names); *Skullman* (just plain scary); *Boxmaker* (even scarier); *Tallandhandsome* (says you); *Goodlooking* (again), and *Goodfun* (who looks like his idea of fun would be train spotting and he even lists War History as an interest).

I decide on *Fiori*. It's Italian for flowers and I can't think of anything else that sounds better, or that hasn't already been used by someone else. So the finished product reads…

***Fiori**, 56 years of age, divorced, 3 kids (grown-up), slim, 165cm, green eyes, brown/auburn hair, other spiritual, has pets, seeking male 54 to 64 with a good sense of humour and a nice smile, any colour everything, any number of kids and pets, at least 170cm, within 100km.*

Thinking I'm through the worst of it, I then realise I'm not. The site is requesting a photo. This is confronting for me because of my past. I've always kept a very low profile on social media and only finally agreed to even a minimal level of exposure so that I could promote my business. It is pretty much impossible to remain anonymous and run a successful business these days. I resisted online advertising for a year and tried handing out flyers, putting up posters and running some ads in the local paper, but business was still quite slow. As soon as I went onto a couple of social media sites, business picked up and I needed to hire Ros and then Sal. But still, there had been no photos of me–just the business and the flowers–and just the business name, not mine.

I shouldn't have to fear being recognised, but I still do. Twenty-nine years should be enough time. I'd thought that earlier, at the seventeen-year mark, until I got a phone call out of the blue on our home phone. "Is that ex-Constable Tess Merlin?" the voice asked. I couldn't breathe properly, and my heart was pounding in my chest as I recognised that voice. I somehow managed to alter the tone of my own voice and say, "No, sorry. You must have the wrong number."

I'd kept my surname when I got married and was careless enough to have our home phone registered in my name. Luckily there was no address listed in the phone directory, just the suburb, but after that call, I still needed to uproot my whole family and move. New house, new schools, new phone number–in my husband's name. I wasn't taking any chances and I certainly wasn't having another phone listed in my name.

These memories, and the thought of putting a photo of myself online suddenly feel too overwhelming and I break out in a sweat. I begin to question the wisdom of this whole idea.

Just then my phone buzzes and makes me jump. I see a call from my friend Marta on the screen. She's just the person I need to talk to right now.

"Marta, I think I just almost did something really stupid."

"What, again?" she asks in her usual upbeat way. Hearing her voice is already making me feel better and I laugh in response.

"What is it this time?"

"It might be better to explain in person. What are you up to today?"

"Nothing. Come on over. Or do you want me to come to yours?"

"I'll be there in half an hour. Just enough time for you to magic up some of those biscotti of yours."

"You're gonna make me fat," she mocks.

"Blame your Nonna. She shouldn't have given you that recipe. They're just too yum!"

* * *

Marta and Helen live in a gorgeous old Californian bungalow in the leafy village of Mapleton. They've spent every spare moment renovating over the past 12 months and the house is looking beautiful. The exterior has been rendered in a pale grey and as I pull up outside, I see that the newly painted, dark grey roof tiles shimmer with a slick from the light rain that has just begun to fall.

In reality, the renovations are mostly Helen's work, but that's basically been her job for around five years now. Buying, renovating and re-selling houses. Now they are at the point where they have to decide whether to sell and do it all again or stay put and enjoy the results. If they decide to stay, Helen will have to get a real job and she's not keen on that. Marta isn't keen on moving continuously, so this is proving a bit tricky for them to agree on. They knew when they decided to move in together that the time for this decision would come but it seemed a long way off in the future then, and they were in love and excited about living together.

As I scan the dark clouds overhead, I spare a thought for the bride who we just prepared the bouquets for. At least it was an indoor wedding and the weather this morning was a lot nicer for her. I park under the massive poinciana out the front. Running up the driveway to avoid the rain, my eye is caught by a newly dug-up garden bed with plants lined up in single file along its edge. The first two pots, with single white gerbera buds, lean in toward the rich soil, giving the impression of a synchronised swimming team about to dive in and commence their routine. They will look stunning once planted and will finish off the kerbside appeal of the property beautifully.

Marta has the door open waiting for me. We do our double-cheek kisses as is the tradition in her Italian family while she says, "Helen's at Bunnings, pretending to be a tradie again. She'll be home soon."

"How are those biscotti coming along?" I ask while patting their mini-dachshunds, Stubby and Carina who are jumping all over my legs.

"Just went into the oven, so won't be long."

We sit at the kitchen bench and Marta glances at my laptop bag which I am gently placing on the floor beside my stool.

"How come you brought that?" she nods in the direction of the bag.

"Marta, you are probably going to think I'm crazy..."

"Hmm? What's going on?"

"Well, when you rang me, I was just in the middle of setting up a profile on a dating site."

Marta's eyes widen and her mouth starts to form a little 'O' as I continue, "In fact, I've almost finished setting it up really, but then I got to the part where it wants me to upload a photo. That made me remember why I've never put my face online before. What if he's still angry? What if he's decided enough time has passed and is looking for me? I don't want to live in fear again, but this has made me realise that I *am* living in fear, still!" My voice has gone up a pitch, so I stop before I get too emotional.

Marta comes over and rubs my back, "I didn't realise that you wanted to find someone. You didn't tell me."

She stands back and looks me in the eye with her big, brown eyes. "What's happened? Tell me... Oh shit! No wait. I need to grab those biscotti out of the oven. Don't move a muscle."

As I watch Marta rescuing the biscuits, I think how lucky I am to have a friend like her, who knows me so well, and knows what I went through so long ago, and the effects it still has on me. She has always been there to support me. I don't think my ex-husband ever understood how intimidating it was to be stalked, to know someone was watching but not know where or when. For many years, that meant I was on edge all of the time. I didn't want to look attractive or invite attention when I left the house, and at one point I didn't even want to leave the house.

It had started seemingly innocently. I'd been in the force for a few years, mostly around the Gold Coast and I wanted to experience living and working in a smaller town, so I applied for a transfer. I was excited to be transferred to my first posting away from home–about 500 kilometres away. At Burmont.

Being a small town there were no barracks for women, so I had to find myself some accommodation. There wasn't much around so I booked into the caravan park for a few nights until I could take a good look at what was available. That very first day, when I'd only been in town for a few hours and just dragged my bags into the 18ft Viscount I was to call home for the next little while, I had a knock on the door.

Standing there was a tall, good-looking young guy with blonde hair and blue eyes and a big smile. He looked quite nervous as he said, "Hi, I'm Brian. I saw you booking in earlier. Are you the new policewoman?"

"Ah, yes, but how did you know that?" I was a bit taken aback by his appearance at the door and that question, but I wasn't too wary because he looked nice.

"You've got a Police Credit Union sticker on the back of your car," he said, nodding toward my old Holden Kingswood, "and everyone in town has been waiting for you to arrive. A policewoman in town is a bit of a novelty you know."

"So everyone knew I was coming and has been waiting to see what I look like? What are you, a reporter for the local newspaper?"

He laughed and leaned up against the bonnet of my car, "Aren't you going to invite me in?"

"Well, no. I have some unpacking to do," I answered, feeling like he was just a bit too forward with that suggestion.

"Well can I invite you for a meal at the pub tonight? Nothing fancy, just a welcome to town. I imagine you don't know many people."

I figured that sounded safe enough, and he *was* rather cute. Also swayed by the fact that I didn't have anything to cook on my miniature stove in the caravan, I accepted, agreeing to meet him there at 6.30pm.

I found out later that appearances can be deceptive.

CHAPTER 4

What's in a Name?

Marta clatters plates and cups in front of me and breaks me out of my thoughts. "Now, tell me everything," she says, sitting down on the stool next to me and giving me her full attention.

I tell her about Sally and how, out of nowhere, it's hit me that I am probably lonely. She gives me a bit of a soppy look and says, "You know you can come over here any time you feel like some company. Helen doesn't mind. She loves you."

"Yes, I know. And thanks, but you know what I mean? I don't *feel* lonely, but I sometimes think it would be nice to have someone to come home to, other than Lola."

Lola is my Golden Retriever. She's my constant companion and I've had her for nine years. Not only do I love her a ridiculous amount, but I also feel safe with her around, even though she's a big goofy thing and almost deaf.

"She hasn't once had dinner waiting for me when I get home and she never helps around the house!" We have a laugh, and both grab a biscuit in sync. Marta speaks first, "Surely Watts is over it by now, especially after that kind of warning? *It's thirty years.*"

I cringe at the mention of his name and note again how Marta only ever calls him by his surname. It somehow makes him seem less normal. More like a crim. "Twenty-nine." I correct her. "And you know I'd like to believe that. It's possible–but as soon as I'm confronted with a situation like this where I feel more exposed, it all comes back. I start to get scared."

Knowing that Marta has used her connections to keep track of where he's living, I ask, "Do you know if he's still over in WA?"

"Yes, I checked a couple of weeks ago. You know you would always be the first to know if there's any change."

"Yeah, I know. Thanks for doing that. I'd hate you to get into trouble for misuse of police resources."

Marta points to my laptop and says, "Come on, give us a look at what you've done so far. I reckon we can find a way to do this safely and I can do some magic with a photo or two so that even you won't recognise you!"

So, I log in, feeling more confident with Marta and her photographic skills at my side.

* * *

Like me, Marta found the names that people had chosen, hilarious. Her favourite was *Tropicalfunguy*. "After you go out with this one you'll need a topical anti-fungal cream," she giggled.

After an hour of just scrolling through pages and pages of headshots and unfortunate names, we've flagged and saved two that look promising.

"So, *Goldensands* or *Horseman*, what do you think?" Marta quizzes me.

"Ah, *Goldensands* I guess. Let's have another look at what they've written about themselves. I can't believe how many faces we've looked at, and only found two that look in any way appealing!"

"I know. What about the ones who are trying to put on a sexy face?" Marta says as she imitates one of the sultry looks.

"Gross!"

"And the ones with no shirt on?"

"Spew!"

"And that guy lying on his bed with the plush tiger?"

"Disturbing!"

"And all those selfies taken up their nostrils?"

"Please Marta, don't remind me."

"I mean, honestly, if they can't even take a half-decent photo of themselves how can they expect anyone to be interested? Maybe this site should have a look at some of these and do us all a favour by deleting them."

"Oh look. This *Goldensands* guy has dogs and likes reading and kayaking. That's good. Should I send him one of those waving hand things?"

"Yeah, you have to start somewhere. Who knows? He could be really nice."

As I click the send button, I wonder, out loud, "If he's nice, how come he has to resort to a site like this to meet someone?"

"Um, *you're* nice and you're on this site." She's right–about the fact that I'm on a dating site, and that's the last place I'd ever have imagined I'd be. Meeting people by just bumping into them at the supermarket only happens in romance novels, and bars and nightclubs are not my scene–and in my opinion shouldn't be anyone who's over the age of 35's scene either. So the options are very limited.

Last year, Sally talked me into going to one of those Over 50s Singles Trivia Nights with her and Jill. As soon as I sat down at the table, I knew it was a mistake. *What on earth came over me in agreeing to go?* I don't even like Trivia! The fact that they'd split us all up and put us in a girl, boy, girl, boy format so that we could meet new people made it even worse. I couldn't even enjoy some time with Sally and Jill. The stilted conversation before the start of the questions was the last straw. I said I was going to the Ladies' and went straight out the door. When I got to my van, I sent Sally a text and headed home before she could come out and try and talk me into going back in. *Never again!* I decided.

"Hey, according to his profile this 'Horseman' guy actually has horses. He doesn't look too bad, but he's only put up one photo so it's hard to tell. I might just wait and see whether *Goldensands* replies before I start contacting anyone else."

"Ok, but you'd better tell me every single thing that happens. This is exciting."

"It is, kinda. Of course I'll tell you. I need to bounce them off someone."

"I reckon it's you they'll want to be bouncing off. Plus Helen wouldn't be happy about that!" she joked.

* * *

I'd left Marta's in a better mood. I was feeling more confident and even optimistic about hearing back from this *Goldensands* guy, or even someone else finding my profile appealing and making the first contact with me. Now though, I start to wonder what my kids are going to think about this when I tell them. All of a sudden, I feel a bit embarrassed. I don't think I *want* to tell them. Maybe I'll just wait and see if anything happens first. Maybe one of them has even used a dating site and not told me. I wouldn't expect the boys to tell me that kind of thing, but Jacinta and I talk a lot and I think she would have said.

When I think about it, being on an online dating site has always seemed to me like a last resort–for desperate people who can't meet someone organically. But it seems younger people don't have the same view of it. They seem happy to admit that they met their partner, friend, lover, whatever, online. Even Sally admitted it.

I'm old enough to remember when people used to put personal ads in the newspaper. They always seemed very dodgy... Single man, 45, NS, SD, GSOH, seeking curvy lady for fun times. Well, they weren't *all* that dodgy, but they still creeped me out a bit. I always wondered what kind of person responded to those ads. It was almost another language and I'm sure there were subtle messages woven in amongst all of those abbreviations that only people who spoke the language understood. The online version is much less anonymous and at least most of them have a photo so you can get a bit of an idea of what they look like. I wonder if there is a secret language underlying what people write about themselves online too.

* * *

This morning, after having resisted the urge to log in again for a full 12 hours, I decide it's time to take another peek and see if I have any response from *Goldensands,* or if there's someone new that looks interesting. Settling in with my Sunday morning breakfast and Lola at my side, ready to gather any crumbs that fall her way, I open my laptop and login. And there it is–my first *kiss*!

But it's not from *Goldensands,* it's someone called *Financeyman.* I have to say, I don't mind the name–it kind of rolls off the tongue nicely and has a good ring to it, even though it sounds a bit similar to *Fancyman.* I hope for the best and can't wait to check out his profile. I don't remember noticing him when Marta and I were going through all of those pages yesterday, and now that I click on his profile, I see why I didn't have him flagged as a possibility. He looks a bit old in his main photo, but it says he's 59, which is within the range that I'd nominated. I take a look at some of the other photos, and he looks younger in them, but that could just mean they're older photos.

He's written a little paragraph about himself; the subtitle declaring that he's loyal, genuine and intelligent. He goes on to say that he's looking for a friendship first and then hoping for a committed relationship. Likes animals but doesn't have pets, drinks occasionally and doesn't smoke, loves the ocean and environment, has four grown-up children and family is important to him. Oh, and he's an accountant. Ok now I get the name–*Financeyman.* I also can't help but put him straight into a stereotype–*boring.*

I presume all of those jokes about accountants must have been made up for a reason, but I don't know any accountants, so I wouldn't really know. I decide to rescue him from the *boring* bin and judge for myself. I wonder if he can take a joke. If he can't then we'll have no hope of getting along.

What do I do now? I am such a novice at this whole new world. *Do I reply straight away, or does that look too keen? If I delay, will he lose interest and 'kiss' someone else?* I could really use some advice from someone who's done this before, but there's no way I'm asking Sally. I'd get no peace at work then, and everyone would know because keeping secrets is not one of Sally's strong points (although she had surprisingly managed to keep her relationship with Jim secret for a couple of months).

I decide to just send a *kiss* back and see what happens. During my cogitation, I've received another contact from someone called *Funtimepete.* I take a look at the summary of his details and feel a bit disturbed when I see his age is 35 and the first line of his profile is… *I like older women.*

I don't want to read any more, but sort of can't help myself. It's like the car crash thing, where you don't want to look but you can't look away. I can't help but wonder if people like this are even real. As I read on, I start to regret my curiosity. He continues… *Are you looking for someone with youthful stamina? I don't find young women attractive at all. I like a woman with experience. How about we create some experiences and memories…* Ok I've had enough!

As I move to close down his profile, I make the mistake of glancing at his photo. Again, I'm immediately sorry. He's bare-chested, his olive skin gleaming with so much oil that you almost need sunglasses for the shine bouncing off his body, plus he's got some poor innocent snake wrapped around his neck. His long dark hair is also an oil slick and almost outshines the thick gold chain dangling between his desperately flexed pecs.

The fact that someone like that has been looking at my profile and my photos sends a shiver up my spine. I'm glad that I read the information pages when I joined up with this site, so I know that I can block people if I feel uncomfortable about them, and even report them if they say something creepy, or send inappropriate photos. I quickly hit the 'Block' button on *Funtimepete* and sigh with relief as his image disappears.

I get the feeling this is not going to be all pleasant and fun.

CHAPTER 5

The Ball

I wake in a sweat fighting off a disturbing image of a half-man, half-snake creature trying to grab me but looking at itself in confusion when it realises it has no arms or hands to grip with and instead tries to lunge itself head-first at me as I dodge its attack and run for my life.

The unsettled feeling swirling and bubbling in my stomach like a mint dropped in a glass of Coke is all too familiar and reminds me of another time in my life when my sleep was constantly disrupted by disturbing images and nightmares. Only then the main creature in those dreams was fully human with many hands–all holding cameras.

* * *

The casual dinner at the Burmont pub on my first night in town seemed to go quite well, although I could see Brian constantly looking around to see if people had noticed him (with me–the latest attraction). He introduced me to a couple of his mates and was very interested in finding out every little detail about me. Looking back,

I should have seen that he was a bit odd. At the time I probably just thought he was nervous.

After the dinner he invited me to a B&S Ball that was on that Saturday night. I'd heard about the Bachelor & Spinster Balls and knew they could turn into wild nights in some small country towns where the social calendar was often quite sparce. I decided to go as I hadn't been to one before and I figured I'd rather go as a civilian than make my debut by attending one in uniform on a call out.

When I met Brian there at 6.30 that Saturday evening, there were people everywhere and most of them seemed to be already drunk–or stoned. There was even a distinct whiff in the air, and I wondered how people thought they were going to get away with that in a public place. Having met most of my colleagues, I couldn't imagine too many of them turning a blind eye.

The style of dress ranged from dressed-up casual (no thongs allowed) to full length elegant evening wear and dinner suits. Some of the long dresses had angry, clay-coloured clouds rising from the hemlines where they'd been walked through the red soil and the wearers had already danced their beautiful dresses into states of disrepair from the increasingly dirty dance floor.

Dancing was a crammed and sweaty experience with drunken, uncoordinated and over-enthusiastic moves going on all around me in a sea of people. Despite that, as the night went on, I found I was enjoying myself. Lots of other guys had asked me to dance and I basically danced all night. Dancing also cut down the number of questions I had to answer. If one more person followed up the question about what I did for a job by asking me if I ever had to use my gun, I just might have lost it with them.

I met a guy called Russell and he was a lot of fun, so we ended up dancing together quite a few times throughout the night. To his credit, he didn't ask me if I ever had to shoot anyone, so bonus points went to him for that. He chatted away and made me laugh while we danced. As he swung me around, I enjoyed the feel of his strong muscles under his strained white shirt and the way his wavy brown hair seemed to have a life of its own. What I didn't enjoy was the look I saw on Brian's face as I caught a glimpse of him standing at the side of the dance floor staring at us. His brow was furrowed, and he looked like he was biting his bottom lip. I felt his eyes drill into us, so I looked away quickly to avoid making eye contact with him.

It must have been close to 1am by that stage and I didn't feel like being around Brian at all after that. I decided it was time to leave. While Russell and I said goodbye, we made a plan to catch up the next day at one o'clock, for a lazy Sunday afternoon at Walan Lake, just north of town.

Back in the 80s there were no mobile phones, no emails, and my caravan certainly didn't have a landline. Russell had told me he lived in a share house, again no phone, so the best way for us to catch up was face to face. So, with our rendezvous organised, I went over and told Brian I felt a bit sick and just wanted to get a taxi home on my own rather than share one. I encouraged him to stay on and have fun, but he said he would probably leave soon as well.

The next morning, I slept in until around ten thirty before waking with my head pounding through a thick layer of fuzziness from the late night and too many drinks. I squinted into the bright sunlight as I wandered over to the shower block to start getting ready to go and meet up with Russell. Sunglasses now top of my list of things to take with me.

Stopping at the only café in town that was open on a Sunday, I just managed to make the breakfast menu cut-off. Since waking up I'd been craving bacon and eggs and a proper coffee. I swallowed a couple of Asprin as soon as I had some food in my stomach, then took my time enjoying the breakfast and reading the Sunday paper, knowing that the lake was only fifteen minutes from town, and I had plenty of time on my hands.

I arrived about twenty minutes early and scanned the area in the hope that Russell might be early as well, but the only people scattered around and swimming in the lake were families with kids.

At the far end I spotted an old and gnarled weeping willow with long, elegant branches sweeping the ground, creating a private sanctuary by the water. I made a beeline for this perfect little space and claimed it by spreading out my beach towel–the closest thing I had to a picnic blanket. I lay down to enjoy the dappled sun filtering through onto my face, congratulating myself on securing such a romantic setting.

I closed my eyes and tried to picture Russell's face, remembering that mop of unruly hair and the blue-green colour of his eyes. Several times the angry face of Brian pushed its way into the frame and I tried to block it out. His reaction to me dancing with Russell was so unattractive that it only served to make me want to spend less time with him.

For the first little while I couldn't relax, feeling excited to see Russell again and to discover whether the attraction from last night would be as strong when we were sober and in the light of day. I kept checking every few minutes to see if he'd arrived, but after a while, the late night and the peaceful surroundings got the better of me and I dozed off.

I woke with a start as a dog barked a short distance away, the hangover amplifying it in my fragile head and making it sound like it was barking right into my ear. I scanned the grassy expanses for a solitary figure that looked like Russell, but he was nowhere in sight. I raised my hand to wipe my chin where my dry mouth had somehow found enough moisture to deposit a line of drool. Quickly cleaning myself up I checked my watch. It was almost two o'clock. My heart sank as I faced the reality that Russell was probably just having a bit of fun last night and it was the booze talking when he said he was looking forward to meeting up with me today.

I drove back to my caravan feeling disappointed and confused. He'd given out a lot of signals that he liked me and wanted to get together, and I really hadn't thought he seemed that drunk. I put it down to poor judgement on my part.

Then I found out when I got to work on Monday that a young man called Russell Fulton had been assaulted outside the front door of his house in the early hours of Sunday morning, by someone who ran off before he could see who they were. He ended up in St. Patrick's Hospital for the next two days, having his head injuries monitored before getting the all-clear to be discharged and go home.

I thought this was just an unlucky coincidence, but in hindsight, perhaps I should have been more concerned about who his assailant was.

CHAPTER 6

Fudging the Figures

Financeyman wants to meet up. I shouldn't have worried about seeming too keen–he responded straight away to my return kiss. Since then, we've messaged each other back and forth a few times, covering the usual basic small talk, but also touching on some deep and meaningful topics as well. I found out his name is Perry. He's a vegan and is into meditating and yoga. Two days ago, he messaged asking if I'd like to meet up this morning at a vegan café in Minyama, a suburb about ten minutes away from mine.

As I grab my keys to head out the door to meet up with him for the first time, I re-read his last message, just to make sure of the time and place, and that he hasn't pulled out at the last minute. When I login, I notice a message has just come in from someone called *Blueeyes.* He's saying that he's keen to meet up with me when he gets back in town–that he had to go away unexpectedly for work.

I quickly click on his profile to find out a bit about him, and to see what line of work it is that's taken him out of town. His profile says he's a manager. *Hmm, that doesn't tell me much–managing what?* I wonder. I check his photos. His main photo is not very clear. Some of the other photos of him are a bit better, but for someone who's advertising themselves as *Blueeyes* I'd have thought he'd have a photo where you can actually see his eyes.

His message goes on to tell me he'd like to find out more about me and asks me about my work and what I like to do in my spare time. Do I have kids? He signs off as Marcus.

I decide I'll have to spend some time reading all of that again later and if I don't leave now, I'm going to be late for this coffee with Perry. On the drive into the city, I'm trying to remember Perry's details and not get them mixed up with this Marcus guy's.

* * *

When I arrive, three minutes late, he's sitting in the beautiful outdoor area of Green Nature vegan café. The florist in me admires the hanging white star jasmine and climbing yellow rose, intertwined with two varieties of ivy, a solid and a variegated, on the overhead pergola. He immediately recognises me and bounces out of his chair and walks quickly over to greet me, smiling.

As we do a bit of an awkward handshake that turns into a half-hug, we introduce ourselves and head over to the counter together to order. He insists on paying, even though I offer to get my own. I order a long black with sugar and milk on the side and lemon drizzle cake, and he goes for a healthy-looking slice and a lemongrass and ginger tea, making me feel a bit like I should have ordered something healthier. *What's he going to think of me and my food choices?* I decide I should just be able to eat what I like and not feel judged by someone I don't even know.

He's wearing grey jeans and a dark blue button-up shirt–and wearing them quite well on a slim but muscular body, with no sign of a beer gut. *No wonder,* I think, *if he eats like this all the time.* In a strange co-incidence, I'm wearing my pale grey denim skirt and a navy jumper with three-quarter sleeves. I draw attention to our similar outfits by saying, "We look like our mums shop together." To my relief, he gets it and laughs.

As we sit down, I'm encouraged by an apparent sense of humour. "I'm glad to see you can have a laugh," I say. "How do you feel about the stereotype some people put accountants into?"

"Ha. Were you worried that I'd be serious and boring? I hope I don't fit into that mould. I don't believe in stereotyping people, especially by their career choice. And I have been known to laugh at accountant jokes, and even tell the odd one or two myself now and then. Although we accountants prefer to tell lawyer jokes."

"Ok, so you tell me one and I'll tell you one."

"So," he says, "what do you call a lawyer who speaks to *one* person a day?"

Before I can even have a go a guessing, he says, "Popular!"

"Ha," I chuckle and add, "I think I've heard that one told about accountants rather than lawyers."

"Ok, what's yours?" he quizzes me.

"Why was the accountant so excited about taking 10 weeks to finish his jigsaw puzzle?"

Perry looks me in the eye, and I notice that his eyes are a very deep blue, darker than any blue eyes that I've seen before. It gives me a bit of a jolt and I look away. "I give up. Why?" he asks.

"Because it said 8 to 10 *years* on the box!" I look back to catch his reaction, noticing how crinkles form in the well-worn tracks around those laughing, bluer than blue eyes.

He chuckles and says, "That's a good one. I thought I'd heard every accountant joke out there, but I haven't heard that one before." I wonder if he is just being gallant in saying that, but his reaction, and those eyes, seem genuine.

The coffee and cake are delicious, and I feel quite relaxed with Perry. He's intelligent and interesting and I'm enjoying our conversation. We bounce from politics to sport and eventually to talking about family and kids. At this point I feel like he's a bit uncomfortable and he's started fidgeting with his serviette and pushing his plate around in front of him. Then he looks up and says, "Look, I don't want to lie to you. You seem really nice and that would be a bad way to start out."

Oh no. Here we go. I'm dreading what's going to follow this statement and imagining something like *I'm married, or I'm bi-sexual,* but what comes out is, "I didn't put my real age on that site because I don't feel that old, and I don't want to hang around with older people."

A vision of *Funtimepete* pops into my head with his declaration about only liking older women. So now I'm thinking I've got the opposite on my hands with this guy. *He only likes younger women!*

"So how old are you then?"

"69".

"69?" I say this a little louder than I meant to and receive some quizzical looks from the people at the next table. I lower my voice, "But didn't you say you're 59 on your profile?" His cheeks have reddened slightly and he's holding up his hands in front of him, apologising, "I'm really sorry, but telling the truth about my age just hasn't worked for me."

"But dropping ten years? That's massive!"

"This is why I wanted to get it out in the open now. I don't feel comfortable lying to you."

"Yeah, I don't feel comfortable about that either. And fudging the figures is not a good look for an accountant," I add with an awkward half-smile. Until this point, I felt like we'd been having a really good conversation. Now I'm feeling a little bit–well, *lied to.*

CHAPTER 7

Birthday Girl

"69? That's nearly 70!" Marta informs me.

"Yes. I thought 59 was ok because he was 3 years older than me. But being 69 means that he's 13 years older. He could nearly be my father. Well, not quite but you know..."

"Wow. So does he look 69?"

"To be honest–ha, honest... But to be honest, he probably looks about 63 or so. You know, if he wasn't so nice otherwise, I'd just walk away and forget about him, but he's intelligent and I enjoyed his company. He's just confused me totally. Can I go out with someone who's that much older?"

"Did he ask you to go out with him again?" Helen's voice wafts through from the kitchen along with some amazing smells from the dinner she's preparing for us all. Helen and Marta offered to have me and the kids over for dinner to celebrate my birthday. I call them kids, but they're all in their twenties now.

Nick is currently spending a year in Canada with some mates, skiing and boarding and travelling around. Canada seems to be the new Europe–we all wanted to do the backpacker thing in Europe when I was young.

Cinta and Dan will be arriving any minute though, so I'm keen to get this topic of conversation out of the way before they turn up. I can't imagine trying to explain things to them when I don't even know how I feel about this whole situation myself. I've been tossing up taking down my profile and ditching this whole online dating thing. Just go back to my quiet, routine life. That sounds so much easier to me right now.

"Yes," I answer, "after he'd apologised about six times, he asked if I'd like to go and see a movie on Tuesday night. There's a Spanish film on at Caloundra and he's a member of the Foreign Film Society."

"Did you say yes?" Marta takes over the interrogation again.

"I did. But now I just don't know. Why did he have to lie about his age and make this so difficult for me?"

"Why *did* he lie? Surely you asked him that?" Marta adds.

"Of course. He reckons he originally put down his real age and the only people who *kissed* or messaged him, or responded to his efforts at contact, were all in the blue-rinse set. He met up with a few but said that every one of them looked nothing like their photo and had lied about *their* age."

Marta considered this and then asked, "So, what is your major concern with him? That he lied, that he's too old, or that you'd be concerned that other people would think that he's too old? That they'd think you were out with your dad?"

Marta's question makes me stop and think. Deep down I know that I *am* probably concerned about what other people would think. Aside from the fact that I'd done some calculations and been daunted by the proposition that when I was 67, he'd be 80.

"Well, I can understand his reasons for doing it, so I can't really say I'm put out too much because he lied about his age. Plus, he's apologised so many times that I believe he felt really bad about it."

"What about a spark?" This question comes from the kitchen and initially I wonder if Helen can't get the cooktop working, but then I realise what she means.

"Oh. Was there a spark between us?" I take a minute and realise that if I have to think about this, then the answer is no.

"You know what? I didn't feel it. I enjoyed his company, but I didn't feel any butterflies or fireworks."

Just then the doorbell rings and Marta and I follow the excited dachshunds down the hallway to greet the kids. They arrived together in Jacinta's car and Dan has a bottle of red wine in one hand and a bottle of white in the other. "I wasn't sure what you and Helen drink Marta, but I know Mum will make a dent in the Shiraz." We all hug and Marta relieves him of the bottles before leading the way inside for us all to chat to Helen and help with plates and drinks.

Marta's Italian influences have rubbed off on Helen. She's prepared a feast of hand-made gnocchi in a pesto sauce with pancetta and Parmigiano, accompanied by a fresh garden salad with garlic, lemon and olive oil dressing.

Jacinta's partner Brad is a chef, so he hasn't been able to join us tonight because of work, but Cinta put in a request for him to make one of his signature tiramisu desserts that I love so much. After we demolish the gnocchi, everyone insists that I stay put while they clear away the plates. Minutes later Cinta emerges from the kitchen with the irresistible, creamy, chocolatey, coffee tiramisu, topped by six candles–she and her entourage singing 'Happy Birthday' to me.

"I appreciate you leaving the other fifty candles off!" I laugh and blow out the six.

Cake eaten and coffees almost finished, we all share any snippets of news from Nick and his Canadian adventures. He's a lad of few words, our Nick, and the only way to get an idea of what he's been up to is to piece together the little bits of his news that he's provided us with or shared on social media.

"He said it was minus 21 degrees Celsius a couple of days ago, and only got to about minus 10 all day," says Jacinta.

"Thank goodness he found that bar job and isn't still shovelling snow off roads and driveways during that kind of weather. Has he mentioned meeting any new people, or whether Sarah has decided to go over and join him?" I ask Jacinta. She and his girlfriend Sarah talk occasionally, so she usually has the most news to share. As she catches us all up on the details of Sarah's upcoming trip to Canada to join Nick, I glance over at Dan.

I make a real effort not to keep asking him about whether he's met anyone because I know he gets sick of people asking him that. He's the oldest–still only 27, but he's the only one who's not in a relationship. Not since Rebecca, his high-school sweetheart broke his heart three years ago and started seeing one of his 'mates'.

He catches me looking at him and says with a half-smirk on his face. "Ok Mum, I know you're busting to ask so I'll put you out of your misery. Yes, I've met someone, and we've been seeing each other a bit for a few weeks now."

Everyone is delighted with his news, and we all begin throwing questions at him left, right and centre.

"Ok guys, it's no big deal. Just had to mention it sooner or later. Thought I'd get that over and done with in one go while you're all here."

After we've pumped the important details out of him, like her name, where she lives, how old she is and what kind of work she does, the next obvious question from me is, "How did you meet?"

"We go to the same gym. I'd seen her there quite a few times and was working up the courage to talk to her. In the end, she said she'd felt the same. Wanted to talk to me but wasn't quite game to make the first move. I kind of came to her rescue one day when the weights fell off one end of her squat bar."

"Aw, that's so romantic Dan. *Her hero.* How could she not fall for you after that?" I say, shooting him a smile and a wink.

"Yes, she was the one who suggested that we get together afterwards so she could buy me a drink as a thank you. We just got along straight away. She's been single for a couple of years as well. She reckons she's had time to have a good look around, date a lot of losers and work out what she really wants... and of course that's me."

"How does a young girl, like her, or even a young guy for that matter, look around? Where do you meet people these days?" Helen asks.

Good on you Helen, I think, catching the conspiratorial look she sends me.

Dan lists off a few of the more popular bars and pubs in town, but says he still thinks a lot of people meet through friends or at parties. Then he says, "Recently, Bec tried meeting someone online for a while, but she didn't have much luck with that. She said she met up with a few guys just the once–mostly losers. I tried it too at one stage, but same."

I'm tempted to admit to dipping my toe into the online ocean but decide there really isn't much to tell at this stage. I decide to wait and see how things go.

CHAPTER 8

A Gift

I had the perfect excuse to visit Russell before he left St. Patrick's Hospital. I was following up on the investigation into his assault. It's often the case that people remember things a day or so after a traumatic event like his, so a follow up interview was recommended. It's also often the case that victims and witnesses think about the event so much and try so hard to remember that they start inventing details–filling in the blank spaces with something from a show they've watched, or something someone else says. It all gets swirled around in their head and they become convinced that it's true.

Russell didn't have any startling new details to provide but he seemed pleased to see me. He gave me a big smile and shuffled himself up to a sitting position on the hospital bed. He patted the space he'd created on the mattress so I could sit. I claimed the very edge, sitting a little gingerly–ready to spring up quickly if needed. I had convinced my partner Noel to go and find out about our *victim's* injuries and condition while I interviewed him. I made sure to keep an eye on the door because I really didn't want Noel to come back and catch me cosying up with a person that I was supposed to be questioning.

As I glanced around the stark room, I wondered if he'd had anyone else come and visit him while he'd been in hospital. I realised that I didn't even know if he had any family–or friends for that matter nearby. I was suddenly aware that I really didn't know much about him at all.

Russell spoke first. "I was wondering how I was going to apologise to you. Thought I'd feel a bit weird rocking up at the Police Station and asking for you."

"Don't be silly–you've got nothing to apologise for. I should maybe apologise for all the names I called you on Sunday." We shared a laugh.

"How long did you wait around for me at the lake?"

"Oh, maybe 5 minutes–I'm a stickler for punctuality you know," I joked. "No, it was so lovely there that I lay down and snoozed for a while. It was two o'clock when I woke up and I was a bit confused that you hadn't turned up because you'd seemed so genuine at the ball."

"You were the first thing I thought of when I came to. I didn't even know what day it was and when the nurse told me it was Sunday and told me what had happened to me, I remembered you and pictured you waiting for me up at Walan. Felt really bad," he said looking down at his hands. "I asked if I could check out–or whatever you call it, but she wouldn't let me."

"Ah, be discharged," I offered.

"Yeah that. She's a bit of a dragon," he whispered while checking the door, "said I'd be in for at least another 24 hours."

"So can you really not remember what happened when you got home from the B&S Ball on Saturday night?" I asked, partly because I wanted to know but also because I felt like I should be doing some official questioning.

"Not after the part where I got to my door and was fishing around in my pocket for my keys. Everything after that is gone–just blank.

The next thing I saw was the dragon lady's face yesterday morning. That was a bit scary to wake up to," he joked.

"Do you feel ok though?"

"Yeah, apart from not remembering, and a bit of a headache, I feel normal. I really want to catch up with you though. Can we try again, on Friday night?" he offered a crooked smile.

"Yeah, that sounds nice." I smiled back at him.

"Do you want to meet at mine around seven? We're having a house party."

Just then I heard voices in the corridor and jumped up as my fellow officer Noel walked in. I was confident that I'd been quick enough to avoid unnecessary questions about the seating arrangements.

"So Mr Fulton," I finished up my 'questioning' in a more official voice, "Can I just confirm the address where the assault took place?"

"57 Butler Street, officer," he smirked, knowing exactly why I asked that question.

I found it hard not to laugh, especially at being called *officer* by him. I was very glad that I had my back to my partner.

* * *

The novelty of living in a caravan had worn very thin. It only took a week, but then I'd never been a willing camper. Camping holidays were like torture for me. I didn't understand the appeal of leaving a warm, spacious home with a comfortable bed, a private toilet, a clean bathroom with hot water and a floor that you can be confident is not going to provide a raft of fungal foot diseases, to go and sleep (if you're lucky) in a hard, lumpy sleeping bag with the dread of having to get up in the middle of the night and hike to a scary, stinky loo and back. Not to mention the sand in the tent, the mosquitoes in the tent and the proximity of other people in the tent. Give me a nice apartment or even a cabin and it's happy holidays.

I'd checked out the few available long-term rentals around town and found a cute little cottage that I felt excited about moving into. It had two bedrooms, a cosy living room, a small but clean bathroom, and a kitchen with the old-fashioned range cooker that doubled as a heater. The only negative was that the toilet was a bit like an addition on the back of the house. The little dwelling must have had a backyard dunny and later had the flushing toilet annexed on. The location of the loo meant that I would have to go down two stairs and through the original back door, which didn't really appeal for midnight visits, but there was a second, newer back door past that, so I didn't imagine I'd feel worried or unsafe going down there in the middle of the night.

When I picked up the key from the real estate agent on Thursday afternoon, he said, "Let's hope you stay longer than the last one." I wasn't sure what he meant so I assumed that the last tenant broke their lease or something.

"Oh, did the last person have to leave early?" I asked.

"I thought you'd have known. That last policewoman rented it on a six-month lease and left after three weeks."

That was news to me. Brian had given me the impression that I was the first policewoman they'd had in town and no one at work had mentioned anything about another policewoman. I asked him what her name was, but he mumbled something about confidentiality and how I should know that anyway.

Moving into the cottage was an exciting step for me. This was the first time I'd lived anywhere other than at home, with my family and an array of pets. All my possessions could fit into the back seat and boot of the Kingswood. Clothes, records and record player, speakers, sheets, blankets and towels, tennis racquet and my sparkling new saucepan set which was my leaving home present from Mum. I couldn't imagine that I would need much else, apart from a few plates, cutlery and cups, but I was yet to discover how quickly a person gathers *stuff* when they have their own place.

Friday was my rostered day off, so I used the day to move in and get settled. I'd set up the record player and was singing along to my favourite Talking Heads' album, *Remain in Light* as I hung up my clothes and spread my few possessions around the house. I felt like I was finally doing my own thing, feeling very independent and grown up. I was also feeling a bit nervous about going out with Russell that night.

On the rare occasions when someone I'd liked had asked me out, I'd get enormous butterflies in my tummy. Richmond Birdwings, or at least Ulysses. I'd feel so sick I wouldn't be able to eat, which was quite distressing because the date usually involved going out to dinner somewhere really nice and I'd end up eating about a teaspoonful of dinner and then wondering what we'd talked about because I'd been concentrating on not throwing up on the guy half the night. I was quite relieved that Russell had asked me to a party rather than out to dinner. At least I might be able to eat something before I went.

A flash of light caught the corner of my eye and made me glance out the bedroom window. I just caught a glimpse of the back of a silver car slowly driving off. I didn't think it could have been anyone coming to visit me as I hadn't heard any car doors or anyone knocking, but that wasn't surprising considering how loud I liked my music.

I decided to take a bit of a break from unpacking my clothes and go out and investigate the garden. I hadn't taken much notice of the yard when I'd looked at the cottage and decided to rent it, but this time as I walked outside, I noticed lots of shrubs and weeds, some neglected rose bushes and the remnants of what might have once been a pretty garden. I vowed to get out there and tidy up and plant a few flowers on my next day off.

I also noticed the rusty old letterbox, precariously hanging onto a wooden post by the front gate. I remembered that the rustic look of this place was part of the appeal, but I also thought that letterbox was probably going to fall off in the poor postman's hand when he tried to put a letter in it. Carefully, I held it by the base as I opened the lid and peered inside–expecting to find a pile of left-over mail from the previous occupants. Instead, I saw a beautiful little pink box with a perfectly tied pink bow!

I looked up and down the street, half checking to see if any neighbours were looking but also to see if there was any sign of the silver car. I didn't spot either, so I carefully closed the dilapidated letterbox and headed inside with my unexpected present. It then hit me that it might not be for me–maybe it was meant for my predecessor or even the person who'd lived here before her, seeing as her stay was so brief. *Well, how was I supposed to know that? There was no name or address on it. I just wanted to open it.*

I loosened the bow and opened the lid. Nestled inside on a bed of pink tissue paper was a thin gold chain with a white opal heart attached. It was delicate and very pretty. I held it up to my neck in front of the mirror and admired how it looked against my olive skin. I presumed that it was from Russell–probably his way of saying sorry for standing me up on Sunday. I still hadn't come across a note or card, so I had a good dig around in the tissue paper–nothing. I lifted the box up and looked underneath, and under the lid–still nothing. I even looked on the back of the heart thinking it might have a sticker or engraving there, but there was nothing written anywhere to confirm who it was from, or even that it was meant for me. I decided to claim it though, figuring it *must* have been Russell slipping it into the letterbox and driving off in that silver car. *But then I remembered that hadn't told him where I lived, so how had he managed to find me?* I decided it was probably because it was such a small town and word got around.

I felt I should wear it to the party because I didn't want to appear ungrateful or rude if it was from Russell. Deciding what else to wear took way too long and a pile of discards began to build into a mountain on my bed. I finally decided on a sleeveless white cotton blouse with my favourite blue jeans–the ones that really hugged in the right places. I knew my legs and butt were my best body parts and as I surveyed the overall effect in the mirror, I unbuttoned the top button of my blouse, so the pendant was more visible. As I did this, I heard my mother's voice in my head telling me to do it up. *They all know you've got breasts; you don't have to flaunt them.* While living at home I always got this or a similar comment whenever I'd tried to leave the house looking even the slightest bit sexy. I blocked out the voice and nodded at my reflection. I wanted to feel sexy and look good for Russell, so I decided that button was staying open.

I managed to eat a bird-sized meal in between deep breathing and sipping a ginger and lemon tea–my granny swore by ginger to settle tummy upsets. Then I headed off with my butterfly collection to Russell's place.

57 Butler Street was a big old Queenslander style home with a massive verandah wrapped around the front and one side. There were only a few people on the verandah, chatting and watching over the rail as I parked and walked up the drive. Even with my nerves in a tangled mess, I took a second to check out the cars parked close by. I didn't find a silver one. The two cars squished into the garage space under the deck were a white Ford Falcon and a yellow Holden Gemini, making me a little uncertain of my presumptions about the unofficial postman. I touched the heart with my fingertips as I approached the driveway, wondering if maybe I should have left it at home.

Russell descended the stairs two at a time and reached the bottom before I got halfway up the drive.

"So glad you could make it," he said, giving me a hug. "I wanted to introduce you to the flatmates before everyone else arrived." He took my arm and led me up the stairs to where three guys were standing in a rough semi-circle waiting to say hello. There was also a girl looking very relaxed in a squatter's chair near the top of the stairs. She grabbed her drink and stood up to come over and join us.

I met Brooksie, Tama, Daz and finally Letitia. Remembering names should have been a given for someone in my line of work, but I was hopeless at it. I'd probably remember Letitia, but that was about it. She was a tall, striking girl with long blonde hair and when she spoke, I caught a hint of an accent that sounded German to me. I bet that most people would remember Letitia–she was a stunner. I was relieved when Russell told me that she was Tama's girlfriend rather than a 'flatmate'.

Russell took me inside and gave me the grand tour of the house. Its beautiful high ceilings and intricate fretwork panels over each doorway still grand but definitely in need of a coat of paint. I decided from the wear and tear throughout, that it looked like it had been a rental for a good number of years.

"Let's get you a drink." Russell offered as he led me into the kitchen. "I was trying to remember what you were drinking at the ball. I'm hoping it was Canadian Club and dry because that's what I bought for you."

"Well, I was just going to have a soft drink but that sounds really good, thanks." I told myself that the ginger in the ginger ale would be good to settle my tummy, and I reasoned that the whiskey might help me to relax a bit too. "That was very thoughtful of you to try and get my favourite drink in for me."

"Hey, I'm just that kinda guy." He gave me a cheesy grin and handed me the drink, in a proper whiskey glass with ice and a lemon wedge.

"Are you also the kinda guy who gives his heart away to almost-strangers?" I asked as I grabbed hold of the heart around my neck.

Russell's brow furrowed and he gave me a strange look. "What do you mean?"

I pulled the heart forward and looked down at it–he followed my gaze. "I'm going to feel pretty awkward if this isn't from you." I could already tell just from looking at him that I'd put my foot in it. He looked totally bewildered.

"Hang on, so are you saying that somebody gave you that and you don't know who it was? And you thought it was me? How can you not know who gave it to you?"

"Someone dropped it off in my letterbox. I did wonder how you knew where my new place was, but I figured it was you apologising for Sunday."

"Hey sweetheart," he said with a very convincing Humphrey Bogart impersonation, "I think you're gorgeous, but I play a little more hard-to-get than that." He tapped ash off an imaginary Bogart cigarette and switched back to his normal voice. "And I *don't* know where you live, but I do hope to find out when you invite me back there one of these days."

"Ok, now I feel bad. Not only for assuming that it was you, but I reckon I must be wearing someone else's jewellery. This obviously wasn't meant for me." I started to fiddle with the clasp to take it off, but my fingers couldn't seem to work it open, so Russell stepped around behind me to help. He easily undid the clasp and lowered the pendant down into my cleavage from his position behind my back. As he did so, he gave me a little kiss on the top of my head and said, "Don't feel bad. I'm cool. I'm sure you'll figure out who's it is. Then I'll know who to tell to back off my girl." His words made me blush. *His girl.* I felt excited that he seemed so keen on us becoming boyfriend and girlfriend. He grabbed my hand to lead me to the music. "Let's go. We need to dance."

The party was still in full flight well past midnight, and I was having such a great time that I didn't want to leave, but I had an 8 o'clock start the next day so one o'clock was my self-imposed curfew. Most people at the party would have had the weekend off so they could party on and sleep-in. As reluctant as I was to go, I knew I'd be sorry if I stayed late, so I told Russell that I needed to leave.

He came out with me to see me off. When we reached my car, in the semi-darkness, I turned to say goodbye. Without any warning, he pulled me in for a kiss. I didn't resist. I'd been hoping that he might do just that. I looked up into his sea-green eyes before closing mine in anticipation. It was a short kiss, but it was on the mouth, and it left me looking forward to more. As he released me and moved back toward the house, he put on his Bogey accent again and delivered that classic line, "Here's looking at you kid."

I giggled.

On the drive home, I smirked as I thought about Russell, on a cloud of happiness. The kiss, and his silly impersonations. I couldn't believe that I'd giggled. I'd never been the giggly type–so something was definitely up.

When I arrived home and unlocked the front door, I almost stepped on an envelope that seemed to have been slipped under my door. I picked it up and took it into the kitchen where I sat at the little melamine table and examined it. There was no name on the front, so I opened the envelope and took out the note inside, reading in the stark glow of the bare bulb above me.

I hope you like your necklace... You looked beautiful wearing it... I'll be seeing you...

I immediately dropped the note like it was on fire and looked around me–suddenly feeling very alone and vulnerable–but at the same time feeling like I may not have been alone.

The kitchen window had no curtains and I felt like someone was watching me from the darkness outside. I told myself I was over-reacting, but I had goose bumps all over and a hot tingling up the back of my neck. I could hear crickets and all the normal night sounds, but they seemed amplified in my ears, as was my heartbeat, thumping loudly and much more quickly than normal. *Someone must have been watching me to know that I wore that chain tonight.*

I quickly flicked off the kitchen light and used the muted glow spilling from the living room to guide me to my bedroom. I felt my way to my navy work handbag in the bottom of the wardrobe and opened it quickly, my fingers grasping with relief around the cool, hard rubber of my baton. I tucked it into the waist of my jeans, wondering if the person who wrote that note had any idea that the recipient would have a weapon. I was thankful that once issued with a baton, it became an officer's responsibility to look after–on and off duty.

I reached up and grabbed my suitcase from on top of the wardrobe, then made my way back to the kitchen feeling less vulnerable but still exposed. I used the suitcase to block the view through the kitchen window. Once that was in place, I felt safe enough to turn the light back on.

The other rooms all had curtains, but some of them were a bit flimsy and I didn't feel like they were enough to effectively block the view of someone looking in, especially with the lights on inside. I systematically went through each room and checked the cupboards, the shower, under the bed and double-checked the front and back doors.

Despite feeling sure that no one had gained entry to the house, and that it was secure, I still felt rattled and uncertain about whether someone could be just outside. I turned off most of the lights and sat at the kitchen table to catch my breath and try to work out how I was going to get any sleep.

I re-read the note over and over. There was no name–no signature, and it had been typed so there was no chance of identifying anyone's handwriting (not that I knew what anyone in the town's handwriting looked like anyway, but it indicated to me that they'd thought ahead and didn't want me to know who they were). 'I'll be seeing you…' *Did that mean I'll be watching you? Should I make a run for my car and go and stay at Russell's? But I hardly knew him.* I didn't have a phone connected to the cottage, so I couldn't ring anyone.

After sitting for half an hour or so and listening to every tiny sound, I could feel my heartbeat was almost back to normal and I had talked myself into trying to get some sleep. I checked my bedroom one more time and propped a chair under the door handle just to be sure.

Another hour later, I finally nodded off–my baton still tightly grasped in my right hand.

CHAPTER 9

So Many Options

"So this dear little old lady,–let's call her Doris–has got her daughter and three grandchildren all sitting there in her room, visiting, when I walk in to bring her medication. She looks at me and says to her daughter, 'Don't trust him', pointing at me," says Joe while tapping his chest with the fingertips of both hands, 'he's just after my fucking money!'"

We all gasp and laugh at Joe's rendition of yesterday's shift at the nursing home.

"I don't imagine the old darling swore once in her life before getting dementia," he says, finishing off his story.

Joe, who's just popped in to say hi, continues to entertain us with more stories for the next half hour, always careful to not use anyone's real name or other personal details.

I have a few stories of my own but I'm not quite ready to share them with my workmates. Since my first meeting with Perry, I've had the movie date with him, a phone chat with another guy using the profile name *Goodtimes*; agreed to meet up with someone called

Oceanrider this afternoon after work, and also arranged to have a coffee with *Blueeyes* tomorrow morning.

Thinking about it now, I wonder if maybe I've slightly over-booked. I can feel my strong competitive streak starting to push me to win at this. I probably need to slow things down and think about what I'm really doing–and why. Remind myself that this is not a competition and stop comparing myself to Sally and how it only took her two weeks to meet Jim. If it were a competition, she'd have won anyway. I've been at this for over three weeks now and I don't feel like I've gotten very far. I've even felt a bit rejected when a couple of times I sent a *kiss* to some new guys that popped up, and they said *thanks but no thanks.* I wouldn't have thought this would feel like a rejection, considering these are people I haven't even met or spoken to–they don't even know me–but it still does.

I think about how the whole format of online dating has taken a lot of the personal aspects out of being attracted to someone. I know there's so much more to finding 'the one' than looks and the ability to write a good profile, but online that's about all there is to go on–initially. In such a limited environment that intangible spark can't happen naturally, and even though we go through and tick the boxes on our *partner shopping list,* the sparks and hormones just don't fly. For that to happen you really need to interact with someone in person. I feel like there's going to be a lot of anticipation and disappointment while I wade my way through this sea of lonely strangers. I can see a lot of situations where, similar to my current experience with Perry, I meet someone, and we get along but are never going to be more than friends.

Of course, it's great to make friends, but I feel like I've got enough of those and that's not the aim of this exercise. Plus, I do have a tendency to be impatient, so that is not helping at all.

The movie date with Perry was ok, but I found myself looking for things about him that I might be attracted to rather than just enjoying the night out. The movie was very slow-moving and because it was in Spanish, we had to read the subtitles and concentrate the whole time.

When the film was about a quarter of the way through, Perry reached over and took my hand. I got a real shock because it's been so long since someone held my hand at the movies–*or anywhere*–and because it was an unfamiliar hand. You know how you just get used to the feel of a long-term partner's hand and their skin, and how their hands and bodies shape with your own? That's all I'd been used to for twenty-two years, those same hands and skin, and here was a totally different feel and shape that I struggled to mould into.

I felt a bit concerned that there was still about seventy minutes of screen time to go and wondered what the etiquette was regarding letting go at some point. I was relieved to find that at least his hand wasn't too sweaty, but I couldn't honestly say that the whole hand-holding experience was enjoyable. It didn't give me butterflies or a warm and fuzzy feeling–it just felt awkward. I tactfully (in my opinion) extracted my hand after about half an hour as I needed it to assist my other hand to dig around in my bag for a mint.

Helen's question about whether or not there was a spark with Perry had been swirling around in my head for days and this *date* had helped to clarify that I liked the guy as a person, but I didn't see any potential for anything other than friendship.

After the movie, when we were saying goodnight to each other in the car park, I thanked Perry and gave him a quick hug and stepped back so I could avoid any confusion about goodnight kisses or longer embraces. He asked if I'd like to go out to dinner the following Friday night. I don't believe in leading people on, and I am usually quite direct and honest, so I said, "Ok, dinner would be nice, but only as long as we split the bill. I enjoy your company Perry, but I reckon we'll just be friends. What do you think?"

His face was hard to read, and his gaze dropped as if he was examining my new tyres as he said, "I had hoped there might be something more, but of course we can be friends."

When I got home that night, I ended up sending a message back to Marcus (alias Blueeyes), after re-reading his message and his profile again. I decided I needed to see what some of these other people putting themselves out there were like. He said he's keen to meet up rather than message each other repeatedly. Apparently, he's spent a lot of time in the past chatting to people only to find that whilst everything sounds really good on paper, in person it is a totally different thing.

I get that. Everyone is busy with no time to waste. Not that I'd call the time I'd spent talking to Perry a waste of time. I would, however, call the time on the phone with *Goodtimes* a huge waste of ninety precious minutes of my life that I will never see again.

This guy, who told me his name was Ian, also reckoned that he'd prefer not to send messages, but would much rather chat on the phone. I let him know that I'm not known as a big phone chatter but said ok to a quick call just to see if we should look at meeting up. Thank goodness I didn't end up stuck in some café or restaurant with him. From the moment I said hello when he rang, to the moment he finally wound down his monologue enough to allow me to end the call, he talked about himself.

Occasionally he'd ask a question, but as soon as I'd answered he'd swing the conversation around to his favourite topic again–Ian. I heard about where he'd travelled, how good he was at his job, how he and his ex-wife met, why they'd divorced, how great he was with the kids, how he'd written a book, run a successful business and can still run 5km in 25 minutes. When I mentioned that we'd been on the phone for an hour and a half, trying to use that as a way to finish the call, he told me I must have been fibbing when I said I didn't like talking on the phone!

"So, what do you think?" he finally said. "You sound quite nice. Would you like to meet for a coffee?"

I couldn't believe it. I am constantly astounded by people like him. They seem so totally self-absorbed that they don't pick up on anything. "I don't think we'd be very well suited, but thanks for the call," I said.

"Oh, I thought we got along really well. Ok then. I'll leave it at that, if that's what you want."

I let out an audible sigh of relief as I hung up and felt grateful for the anonymity of the phone.

I gave myself a few days to recover from that experience and agreed to meet up with someone who calls himself *Oceanrider*. He contacted me initially, and we've already exchanged a few messages. He looks a bit like an old surfer in his photos, with unruly blonde hair and leathery looking skin, but seems to have a kind face and a nice smile. His messages are witty, and he can spell, but his grammar is hit and miss. I always find it hard to overlook bad spelling, especially now that there's spellcheck. I think the only valid excuse might be if English isn't their first language, otherwise it just seems lazy to me.

I decide to give *Oceanrider* the benefit of the doubt. Mr *Goodtimes* had deplorable spelling and grammar–I should have known better than to let that slip through–could have saved myself the pain of that phone call.

Oceanrider (alias Guy), wants to meet up at the lookout at Moffat Beach and have fish and chips and sit and watch the sunset tonight. I thought that was an excellent first date option, cute and enticing, and much more original than the coffee shop meet-up that most people seemed to opt for. So, we're locked in for 6pm. He says I'll recognise him by his Hawaiian shirt! I'm not sure whether to cringe or laugh.

Then tomorrow I'm meeting Marcus (of the alleged *Blueeyes*) for the first time. He wants to try the new café that's just opened on the outskirts of Noosa. It's about 30km away from my place, but I've also heard good things about it so I'm happy to drive that far because I'm keen to try it too. Apparently, the people who run it are French and the pastries are extraordinarily good.

Sometime today I need to ask the girls if they will look after the shop for me tomorrow. Tuesdays are usually slow days in the floristry trade so this shouldn't be a problem.

As the last customer from our Monday morning rush leaves, I decide there's no time like the present. "Sal and Ros, would you guys mind if I took tomorrow off?" I ask. "I need to go to the dentist and have a few other errands to run." I'm running with the well-worn dentist excuse, but I convince myself that I'm not lying because I didn't actually say I had an appointment–and I *do* need to go to the dentist–just not tomorrow.

"Oh, hot date is it?" Joe pipes up.

I laugh, hoping it sounds convincing and mentally cursing Joe for jokingly calling me out. I answer flippantly, "Anyone thinking my dentist is hot needs to make an appointment at the optometrist's as well!" This is quite the opposite really–my dentist could well be described as 'hot'.

Before Joe finally makes a move to leave after his extended half-hour pop-in, he heads over to read Sally's latest words of wisdom. I read them this morning when I arrived and was again struck by how pertinent and thought-provoking her messages have become. This one is short and comes from a surprising source. It reads, *May you attract someone who speaks your language, so you don't have to spend a lifetime translating your soul.* She has cited it as coming from Jim Carrey's Instagram posts.

"This one is so poignant Sal. You and your Jim have found each other and seem to be speaking the same language," says Joe after reading the quote.

"Yes, Jim said that quote has been used a lot by other people as well, but I hadn't seen it before and I imagined you all wouldn't have either. I just thought it was beautiful. If only everyone could find someone who gets where they're coming from–and heading to, for that matter. Someone who just gets *you*," she adds, looking in my direction.

I don't have a chance to respond before Joe says, "I know, right? All the guys I meet just want me for my body!" He strikes a pose and an impressive pout. "To be honest, I would like to meet someone who wants to have a deeper connection, where we get past the egos and the physical attractions to what Jim's talking about there," he says, pointing at the quote on the wall.

"Ah, you will," says Sally encouragingly. We all add our positive opinions on this and then Ros asks, "Did anyone listen to that podcast where Russell Brand was talking about ego and Trump? It was brilliant."

Our conversations in the workshop lately seem to have that ability to go from crazy stories and silly banter, to detailed floristry discussions, to deep and meaningful conversations and back again in no time. All thanks to Sally… and her Jim. Jim has really had a positive influence on Sally. She's happier and healthier, bringing her own salads and other healthy lunches instead of making trips to grab take-aways, and he's indirectly had an influence on all of us, even though we haven't even met him yet.

Could I please find one who speaks my language, I silently wish. Maybe my *Oceanrider* this evening, or maybe Marcus– tomorrow.

CHAPTER 10

It's Curtains for Me

As I stood outside The Drapery, armed with my list of window measurements, my eyes could not rest, constantly scanning the street for other eyes focused in my direction. The words of the typewritten note were still forefront in my mind.

I'll be seeing you…

I imagined it was not very often that the Burmont Drapery had someone waiting on the doorstep at 9am on a Monday morning to buy fabric, but I wanted to get the job done as soon as possible so I could stop feeling so exposed, especially at night. I waited impatiently until the doors finally creaked open and I made straight for the heavy fabric section.

Being forced to do Home Economics at school had ensured that I knew how to sew, and in fact I quite enjoyed it, having made some dresses and skirts that I was proud to wear. I didn't, however, have a sewing machine so that was a slight setback to my plan of making nice thick curtains to go over all of the windows. I figured I might just have to buy one, so I asked the hovering shop assistant about what they had available. "Well, do you want brand new, or second hand?" she asked.

Second hand was an option I hadn't considered, but as I hadn't planned on spending a lot of money on this kind of thing, I jumped at the suggestion. "Oh yeah, second hand would be better. What do you have?"

She took me past rows and rows of fabric rolls, down to the back of the shop where there was a little line of tables with sewing machines set up on them. "We run classes here for people who want to learn how to sew," she informed me, "but we have way too many machines for the amount of people who come. The boss wants to sell those two," she pointed to the two least impressive of the collection.

"Which one's the cheapest?" I asked.

After some negotiation, I bundled my new, second-hand Janome into the boot of my car, along with a pile of the heaviest curtain material available in the shop. A dark brown damask with smatterings of rust and light brown autumn leaves. It wasn't unattractive, but it was not something I would normally go for. This time, however, my main priority was privacy, so brown on brown it was.

Having taken some action to make myself feel safer, the next decision I needed to make was who to confide in. I had thought of little else since Friday night. My first instinct was to talk to Russell, but then I made myself stop and think about whether it could even have been he who wrote the note. I kept reminding myself that, even though he was cute and funny, and I felt butterflies when I thought about him calling me *his girl,* the fact was that I hardly knew him.

The timeline suggested that he couldn't possibly have gone to my house at any time on Friday night, because he was with me the whole time. Plus, he didn't know where I lived (although I'd told him about half-way through the evening when we were organising our next date), but he didn't leave my side after that. Plus, I totally believed him when he said he knew nothing about the pendant. He couldn't have faked the surprised look he gave me when I suggested it was him trying to apologise for standing me up.

My first suspect had always been Brian. I was reminded of that look that he gave me and Russell at the ball. The memory of it gave me a small shiver. Also, I was still feeling a little uneasy about the way that he basically pounced on me as soon as I got to town–like he wanted to lay a claim on me before anyone else had a chance to meet me. And how he took me to the pub that first night to show me off–he was certainly looking around to make sure people noticed. But I didn't really understand why he (or anyone) would want to give me a gift and not take credit for it. *Should I just confront him?* I wondered. *How embarrassing if it wasn't him though.* I decided to wait.

In getting to know the guys I worked with at the Station, I had found that one of them knew Brian and was friends with him. They played footy together for the local rugby league team–The Vikings. Geoff was on duty the night of the B & S and he said he saw us arrive together. I remembered seeing him and Noel, his partner that night, walking around outside the venue. If they all knew each other there was no way I could talk to any of them about suspecting Brian of being behind this weird behaviour.

I often find men are worse than women at gossiping (although they would assure me that men don't *gossip*–they just talk), so I feared this would find its way back to Brian via Geoff in no time.

On the Monday after the ball, Geoff even asked me if I liked Brian and wanted to go out with him again. I thought that was a bit personal, so I just said, "I hardly know the guy. He just took me to the pub when I first arrived last week."

"And then he asked you to the ball?"

"Yeah."

"But he said you didn't leave with him. How come?"

This question really got my back up. "Ah, that's probably none of your business," I said, feeling that he was being way too nosey, and probably on a fishing expedition for his friend.

"Hey, don't get your knickers in a knot. Just asking. Brian's my mate."

"I'm just here to do my job, have some fun and meet a few people. I'd also like to keep my private life private," I said in a tone that hopefully indicated the end of that particular topic of conversation.

I was already starting to learn some of the negatives about living in a small town. Everyone knew the local cops and it was pretty much impossible to go out in public and not be noticed. I imagined that what I was feeling must be about a fraction of a percentage of the way actors and people with high profiles felt when they tried to find some privacy. I didn't envy them that.

I felt like I couldn't talk to anyone else at work about my concerns because I'd only been there just over a week and hadn't formed any friendships. I'd found the civilian roster clerk, Don to be really nice and easy to talk to, but I'd already noticed that he liked a bit of a gossip on the side. Adding to my dilemma was the fact that when I'd imagined verbalising my situation to someone, I worried that it could sound quite innocent and harmless. *Someone gave me an anonymous gift and left me an anonymous note.* It was the feeling that note gave me when I read it, and the feeling that someone was even watching me read it. I couldn't convey *that* in words.

I rubbed my upper arms with my hands to try and shake off the uneasy feeling that thinking about it always gave me. I decided to talk to Russell when I saw him the following night. We were going to get a Chinese take-away and he was taking me to the Drive-in to see The Terminator. A new movie with Arnold Schwarzenegger that everyone was talking about. We were both keen to see it. Anticipating sitting in the car with Russell and having a bit of a cuddle and kiss made me feel excited and helped to move my thoughts away from the note–to more pleasant things.

* * *

Russell pulled up outside my place in the yellow Gemini. I had been secretly hoping when I'd seen it parked under the deck at his house, that it belonged to one of his flatmates. It seemed not. I was ashamed to say I felt a little embarrassed about being seen in a yellow Gemini and even tossed around the thought of offering to take my car–because it was bigger (being my excuse).

I opened the door and invited him in, taking a sideways look at the car as I closed the door. As if he'd sensed my lack of enthusiasm for his car he said, "Sorry, I've got Dazzer's car tonight. My passenger window doesn't close properly and I figured you might get cold. Although I did also consider still bringing it because that would give me an excuse to cuddle you a bit more." He moved in closer and gave me a kiss hello.

"Mmm, hello to you too," I said as I turned and led him into the kitchen. I didn't want to break the mood, but I did want to show him the note and see what he thought.

"Welcome to my little cottage. Do you want the grand tour?"

"Yes, of course," he said as he grabbed my hand. "Lead on," he added with a flourish of his free hand.

We only had to turn on the spot to see the lounge/dining room and I pointed down toward the back annex area, "That's the loo if you need it and the bathroom is just here next to the kitchen."

"Hmm, and that must be the bedroom?" He pointed at the doorway opposite the bathroom. "Can I see?"

"Of course," I answered, trying to sound casual whilst a small somersault went on in my tummy. At the door we both stood and looked in, as though the room had some invisible barrier preventing us from entering. Feeling a little awkward, I pulled him toward the door to the other tiny bedroom and waved a hand into that room saying, "The spare room. So now you've seen the full extent of this palatial home."

"Wouldn't want to try swinging a cat in that one," he commented as we turned away from the second bedroom and moved back to the kitchen. I collected the note off the kitchen table where I'd placed it before he arrived. "Before we go, I wanted to run something past you if that's ok?"

"Sure, what is it?"

"You know how the night of your party I was wearing that necklace and I told you I didn't know who it was from, and even thought it might have been you?"

"Yeah. Did you find out who put it in your letterbox then?"

"No, but when I got home that night, I found this," I said as I handed the note to him.

I watched his face as he read it, hoping to gather something from his expression. He frowned and looked up at me from under his puckered eyebrows. "This is a bit creepy. No name–and typed rather than hand-written. The only thing creepier would be if the words were all made up out of glued together letters cut out of some magazine."

I was so relieved that he'd taken it seriously and not just passed it off as a prank, but his words also made me feel unsettled.

"Yeah, they obviously want to be anonymous. I can only hope their aim was for mysterious and they've inadvertently come off as just plain creepy." This was my latest way of down-playing it in my own mind.

"Well, I don't like it. I'm glad you probably know self-defence and could most likely throw some weirdo like this on their arse if they stepped out of line."

"Ha, yes. And I've got my baton. And I sleep with it."

"Geez, I'm gonna have to behave myself," he laughed.

He read the note again and asked, "Have you reported this to the police? No, I'm not joking–I know you *are* the police, but shouldn't you report it all the same?"

"Well, I wanted to get your opinion on it because I haven't felt comfortable telling anyone else, and on the face of it, it could appear quite innocent. It's a tricky situation being the only woman at the Station. I don't want to look like a sooky la-la, you know? I have to work with this bunch of blokes, and I need to prove that we women are as tough as the guys. Something like this could change how they view me as a colleague–as partner on shifts."

"Yeah, I get it. Ok, but if you feel unsafe or scared ever, you can come over to our place".

"That's sweet," I said and placed a kiss on his cheek. "Thanks."

"You don't reckon it could have been that Brian guy, do you?" he asked while taking one last look at the note.

"That possibility has crossed my mind and I even thought about fronting him, but I don't want to embarrass myself if I'm wrong, especially since I found out that he and Geoff from work are friends. Geoff loves a chat and I also feel he's quite the chauvinist. Can you imagine once he'd spread it around? I'd have everyone thinking I'm paranoid."

"Well, if you do decide you want to have a chat to Brian, I'm happy to go with you."

"My back-up? That's cute. Thanks."

"Ok, let's hit the road. We don't want to miss any of Arnie!" he said, "And I'm starved."

'Um, one more thing," I ventured.

"Yeah?"

"How about we take my car? It's bigger."

"Ha, you're embarrassed to be seen in the *Yellow Caramello* aren't you?"

"Maaybee," I said as I grabbed my keys and double checked the door behind us.

CHAPTER 11

Noises in the Night

Arnie's muscles were spectacular, and we got to see all of them. I hadn't seen a nude male scene in a movie before and it shocked me a bit. In fact, I hadn't seen many naked male bodies in general. Only the second one I ever saw was a body on a slab at the Morgue, which my fellow Probationary officers and I watched being cut open and all the bits weighed and examined as part of our Police Academy training.

One of the girls and a couple of the guys in my squad couldn't handle it and had to go outside. The other two girls and I toughed it out. The squeamish ones copped a bit of a razzing, but I think every one of us there (except for Parksey, who I fear to this day has serious mental issues and wonder how he managed to pass the psych test at the interview), showed respect for the person that was the sum of those parts–and more. It highlighted our own mortality. Reminding us that we would be just that one day–a body on a slab–and could possibly end up under the knife of a forensic pathologist ourselves.

Little did any of us know then that we'd been spared the full sensory experience. We were in a sealed off viewing room with glass walls, so it wasn't until I was required to attend my first real death and post-mortem that I experienced the smell of it–up close–in a very small morgue. There's nothing like it–the smell of death and all its stages. Then, when you think it can't get any worse, there's the *saw.* In the small autopsy room of that little morgue, the sound bounced off the brick walls and bombarded my ears and pounded my temples. Once that saw blade started to hit the bone of the cadaver's skull, the tone of the sound changed, reverberating through every part of my body. I had to go outside until the sawing stopped. As soon as it stopped, I was fine. Of course, I'd attended several more autopsies after that–it was an unavoidable part of the job.

* * *

The concept of a weapon like the Terminator scared the hell out of me and the special effects in the movie were making it seem all too real. I found myself gripping Russell's arm so tightly that I felt I must have been leaving bruises. I was also constantly looking around the Drive-in parking lot as though Arnie might pop up out of nowhere at any moment. Russell did a great job of providing safe, warm cuddles and we managed to find some less gory and terrifying moments to have some long, enthusiastic kisses.

When we got home to my place, I asked if Russell would like to come in for a coffee. "I actually mean a coffee too, by the way," I added.

He came in with me and as I closed the door, he leaned in for a kiss. "Coffee too?" he asked. "Does that mean there's cake as well?" I appreciated his sense of humour and felt it eased a potentially awkward moment.

Still in an embrace, we shuffled our way over to the couch and bounced down with him taking the weight of the fall and me on top. Our bodies meshed together perfectly, and I felt a strong attraction building between us. He was a great kisser. His hands were strong but gentle as they traced the curve of my neck and back. As his hand moved lower, I felt a tingle of excitement but gathered my resolve and altered my position slightly to send a signal that it was a little too far too fast. "I might pass on the coffee," he said some time later when our lips unlocked, "just wanted to see you safe home–and kiss you some more."

I waved him off at the door, after numerous 'one last kisses' and enjoyed the warm glow I was feeling, along with the slight sting and tingle around my lips where his stubble had irritated the skin. I performed my new nightly ritual of checking all the doors, windows, cupboards and under the bed, and then settled into bed with my trusty baton. The warm feeling around my lips was a lovely reminder of those kisses we'd shared and soothed me to sleep in no time.

Something woke me, and as I opened my eyes, I tried to identify the shadow of the sound that had roused me from my sleep. In that confused moment, when transitioning from sleep to wakefulness it was difficult to know if I'd heard something, or if I had dreamed it. Then I heard it again. It was coming from the front of the house and had a squeaky quality that I'd heard before. A second later I identified it–the lid of the letterbox opening–or closing. I still hadn't replaced it, and perhaps that was a good thing because a nice new one wouldn't have made a sound.

I bounded out of bed, baton in hand and picked my way through the furniture in the dark, arms held out in front of me like a fictional un-dead. I reached the front window and pulled my new curtain aside a fraction, hoping that wouldn't make me visible if someone was still there. What I saw made me drop the curtain edge and crouch to the floor–there was a person standing at the gate–just standing there and looking at the house.

I desperately wanted to take another look, so I crab-crawled to the other side of the loungeroom window and ever so slightly pushed the curtain aside. He was still standing there–looking and not moving. The night was dark with only a sliver of a new moon so I couldn't make out much more than an outline of what looked like a man, in a dark windcheater with the hood pulled up over his head. His face was bathed in dark shadows from the hood, but I could tell he was facing toward the house rather than the street.

What reason would someone have for standing in the street at this hour? If they were waiting for a lift, they would be facing the street. As I watched him, scarcely daring to breathe, I wondered if he might have seen me moving behind the curtain. *Otherwise, why was he still staring in this direction?*

I had no idea what time it might be, but I couldn't go and check my watch. My eyes could not leave this person. Keeping as still as possible, I watched him watching my house for another couple of minutes before he turned and walked away. A few seconds later, I heard a car door closing and a motor starting up but couldn't see anything at all, not even a glow from headlights. My curiosity was almost on par with my alarm–I really wanted to know what he had put in my letterbox but there was no way I was going outside the house until I had the clear light of day and a safe and warm cloak of sunshine surrounding me.

Sleep eluded me. The hours dragged by like time had gone into a twisted warp. The silence felt like a palpable weight on my chest, only lifted every now and then by a bird call or other harmless night sound that sent a start through my body. At first light, I dressed and cautiously walked out to check the letterbox, hoping my neighbours weren't awake yet, especially Mrs Vescovi on the right–she seemed very interested in my comings and goings.

My hand hovered over the letterbox for a second as I considered whether there could be any danger in opening the lid. Before being transferred to Burmont, I had been at a busy city station where we had on several occasions, been called out to attend bomb threats. There'd been recent talk of a 'bomb squad' being set up, but last reports were that it consisted of two people and was notoriously hard to contact and slow to respond, so it was still a case of whoever got called to the job having to get in there and do the searching for bombs. It always scared me, and one time we even had to search a big shopping centre. It was next to impossible to look through every single shelf in every single store with a crew of four officers. I had to evacuate a Stefan hair salon full of ladies having perms and colours. By the time we'd finished our searching, I think there may have been some ladies having a very bad hair day.

I took a breath and flipped the lid. Inside was a single sheet of paper–another note. I tucked it into my hand, unread, and walked back up the path with as casual a gait as I could muster. Once inside, I leaned my back against the closed door and unfolded the flimsy sheet of paper with unsteady hands.

Slut... Heavy curtains don't hide everything... I saw you on the couch with lover boy... I'm watching you.

I felt like I'd been slapped in the face by that word–*slut.* If anything, I believed I was the opposite–*whatever you called that.* Not quite a prude but definitely not one to sleep around. And the comment about the curtains and being able to see us on the couch had me rattled. I had been confident that nobody would be able to see in through the new, heavy drapes. I felt embarrassed and angry to think that someone was watching Russell and me kissing, and I was confused about how they could even see us. Yes, the light was on but still... I looked at the curtains and noticed there was a slight crack where the two curtains just didn't quite meet in the middle. I hurried over and pulled them together. Too little too late.

Just then, I jumped as there was a knock on the door. I called out, asking who was there.

"It's Mrs Vescovi dear," she said, so I opened the door.

"You're probably lucky I get up at the crack o'dawn," she began, setting me to wonder what on earth she could be talking about. As I started to form the question she said, "Best I just show you love. I don't like to use such language."

Confused, I followed her out the gate, onto the footpath. She stopped and silently pointed to my front fence. I gasped in horror as I read the word written there, in big black letters on the faded beige paint covering the Besser block fence. *SLUT.*

I looked up and down the street, mortified to think that people had quite possibly already seen the word, even though it was only a quarter to six on a Wednesday morning. There was always someone up and about early. I felt panic rising, frantic to remove or cover the offending words as soon as I possibly could.

"Oh Mrs Vescovi this is horrible. I'm not, you know… that." I said, pointing at the offending word.

"I know dear," she replied kindly, "just some silly prank I suppose. I saw you come out just now to your letterbox but you didn't get as far as seeing this so I thought I should show you."

"Oh thank you," I said as I touched her arm and gave her the best smile I could muster, whilst also registering the fact that she was watching me so closely that she knew my movements. "I'm so grateful to you for letting me know straight away."

The heavy black letters drew my eyes back immediately. "I need to cover this up somehow. Have you seen many people going past this morning?" Mrs Vescovi noticed the quaver in my voice and put a comforting arm around my shoulders.

"That's alright love, I don't think too many people are up at this hour. I have some old cans of paint under the house if you want to see if they're any good still. Not the right colour, of course, but might do until the hardware opens and you can get down there and find your colour. Or will you get the landlord to fix that?"

"No, I'll attend to it myself. The less people who know about this, the happier I'll feel." As I said this, I hoped I was sending a clear hint to Mrs Vescovi to not spread this story around the neighbourhood.

"Of course, of course," she said, "it's all very unpleasant. Young people these days–I don't know–no respect," she continued, shaking her head. "Now, come with me and I'll get you that paint. I think there's some white and maybe some mission brown. Take what you like, they're no good to me."

"That's very kind. Thank you," I said as we headed off to the little hidey hole under the front part of her house. Mrs Vescovi told me she was going to find me a paintbrush and left me to brave the spiders alone. After a quick scratch around in the dark little storage area, a spot which under normal circumstances I would never willingly enter for fear of snakes, spiders and whatever else could lurk there, I emerged with the only three cans that I could find. They all felt as though they could be empty but on prising them open with the screwdriver that Mrs Vescovi lent me along with the paintbrush, I found that there was a dribble of mission brown in one, a congealed yellow disc in another and about an inch of reasonable looking white paint in the third.

I set to work immediately and mixed the brown into the white paint tin to give it better coverage potential over the dark letters. I started painting quickly and after a few minutes of slapping on a thick coat of the paint, I stood back and surveyed my patchwork. It had been effective, but I knew I'd still need to go to the local hardware store as soon as it opened to get another coat on before I would feel comfortable that it fully covered the insulting graffiti.

Before that though, I wanted to see Russell. I needed to talk to someone and what I needed most of all was a hug. As I drove to Russell's place, I checked the time. It was twenty to seven so I hoped I might still catch him at home. His work as a boilermaker had him starting work early most days but if he'd already left, I could catch him at the engineering workshop. He'd told me it was just him and his uncle working there so I felt sure he wouldn't mind me dropping in.

"Russ didn't come home last night," Tama informed me when he answered the door, rubbing his eyes and looking very much like I'd just woken him. I hadn't stopped to think that the rest of the household might not need to get up early for work.

"Well, at least I don't think he did. Didn't hear him come in." He leaned over the balcony and shook his head, "No Yellow Caramello either, so Dazzer's gonna be pissed off. Didn't you two have a date last night? I thought he must've stayed at your place."

I was a bit taken aback that he would presume that, but I tried not to show it. I even fleetingly wondered if he could have written the nasty message. I pushed the thought aside and answered, "Yes, we did, but he left around 11.30. Maybe I'll just head down to the engineering works and see if he's there."

"You could try that, but he would've swapped cars again because he knows Darrell needs his to get to work. Take a look. Russ's Falcon is still here so that doesn't make sense."

"Well can we just check his room to make sure? I'm starting to get a bit worried." As I said this Letitia wandered out looking like a movie star in a sheer silky nightie. "What's up Tess?" she asked.

I explained on the way down the corridor to Russell's room. We stopped outside his closed door. There was obviously movement behind the door with drawers banging and footsteps audible from outside. "Hey mate, Tess's here looking for you," Tama called through the door. For the first time I was struck by the thought that he might not be alone in there. *Was I about to be very embarrassed?* There seemed to be enough noise coming out of there for an army of people.

The door opened and Russell gave me a quizzical half-smile before asking, "Are you OK? You look frazzled." With relief I scanned his little room and saw that he was alone.

Tama and Letitia had started to head back toward their room. I called after them, "Sorry if I woke you guys. I hope you can get back to sleep."

Tama waved, "No worries." "See you soon," said Letitia.

When they were gone, I launched myself into Russell's arms and clung on until he prised my hands loose. "Hey, what's going on? Why are you here? Not that it's not nice to see you again so soon, but something tells me this isn't just a *miss you already* kind of visit," he said as he guided me further into his room and we sat on the bed.

I didn't really know where to start, with what happened at my place in the early hours or why no one heard him come home and where the (normally very visible but not visible at the moment) yellow Gemini had ended up. I launched into my story first.

"Well, a noise woke me in the middle of the night, so I looked out the front window and saw this guy just standing there outside my place looking in, and I found another note in my letterbox this morning. But worst of all, he's written horrible things about me on my fence." My voice faltered a bit and Russell put his arm around me and pulled me in closer.

"So you actually saw this guy? Could you tell who he was?"

"No, it was so dark last night. Remember at the drive-in how spooky it was when the lights went out and I kept thinking Arnie was going to pop up out of nowhere and attack us?"

He chuckled, "Yeah, not much moon last night."

I looked up at him and could see the concern in his eyes. I felt so much better just talking to him and having him beside me. Then I remembered to ask what had happened to Darrell's car.

"Yeah, that was really strange. You know how I left yours at around 11.30? Well, I got about half-way home and the old Gem starts to splutter and jerk. I looked at the petrol gauge and it was on empty–below empty. I'd checked it when I got in it to come over to your place and there was just under half a tank, otherwise I would've filled it up for Daz. I have to say, I smelt a petrol smell when I got in to drive home from yours but didn't think much of it. In the end I had to just leave it on the side of the road and hoof it home."

"What's the story there then? Has it got a leak, or a faulty gauge?"

"Well, it didn't have. You know Daz is a mechanic, right? Mechanics always look after their cars and Daz loves that ol' girl, so he wouldn't put up with leaks or faulty parts."

He stood and fished around in his chest of draws, producing a pair of socks, then sat back down beside me to put them on. "I was just rushing around trying to get dressed so I can take Darrell down to look at it before work."

"Oh, sorry, yeah, you'd better get going then," I said without much conviction. I didn't want to go home. I just wanted to sit there a bit longer and feel his warm body next to mine–and feel safe.

"But hang on, you didn't tell me what that nutcase wrote on your fence–or in the note."

I pulled the note out of my pocket and handed it to him. I pointed to the first word *Slut*, not wanting to say it out loud even. "He repeated that little gem in black paint on my front fence."

CHAPTER 12

Juggling Dates

Having managed to finish all of our orders for today, we clean up and complete the nightly ferrying of flowers and buckets into the cold room, followed by the never-ending cycle of bucket cleaning and refilling to avoid slime build-up. I often feel that I've gone from crime prevention to slime prevention.

I say goodnight to Sally and Ros, adding, "Don't forget I won't be in tomorrow. The shop will be yours to decorate however you like, and order whatever you like from the market van."

"Oh yeah, orange and yellow day it is," grins Ros while doing a little dance with her hands. Of course, they know that these are my least favourite flower colours and whether consciously or not, I tend to neglect ordering them on our twice-weekly market order. On the rare occasions that I do take time off, I always come back to bright displays of orange and yellow.

I close the door after Ros and Sally leave and take a moment to sit and gather my thoughts. It's five thirty and I have half an hour before I'm due to meet Guy (*Oceanrider*) at the beachfront at Moffat for fish and chips.

Here to there is twenty minutes, so I don't have time to go home. I have a quick sniff of my armpits and give them the nod of approval. A light spray of coconut perfume in the air around me is as close as I'll get to wearing perfume, but some of it obviously sticks because I can smell it on me, and other people sometimes tell me I smell like the beach. I'm presuming they mean that in a nice way, and not that I remind them of rotting seaweed.

I open my laptop to take one last quick look at Guy's profile and photos before I head off. His smile makes me smile, (which I only realise after I've been sitting there for a couple of minutes with a silly smirk on my face). I take this as a good sign though and leave for our first meeting feeling optimistic.

Leaving my van in the carpark at our agreed meeting spot, I take the walkway through to the beachfront lookout. I can feel the last tendrils of warmth on my back from the setting sun and admire the light and shadow patterns of the pandanus trees and other bushes lining the pathway. As I emerge, I spot (can't miss) a bright yellow and pink Hawaiian shirt with a guy inside, who looks a lot like the *Guy* I'm expecting to meet.

He's leaning way back on a pandanus like he's posing for a poster for an old Elvis movie, and when he sees me approach, he pushes himself off and walks toward me.

"Hey, you made it," he calls from a few metres away, his words revealing a slight accent that I can't quite place immediately. "At least I hope you're Tess. Are you?"

"Hi, yes that's me. And there's no doubt with that shirt that you must be Guy."

"Ha, yeah. Didn't want any awkward mistakes, although I suppose I could have been making one when I presumed that you were you," he laughs.

He points over to a spot right on the edge of the grassy hill that overlooks the beach and I see a blanket laid out with a blue esky and a package wrapped in butchers' paper sitting on top. He starts walking in that direction as he talks, "I thought I'd claim this spot because it can get a bit popular up here at sunset. I hope you don't mind that I already grabbed the fish and chips, but I thought we might lose the spot if we had to go and order and wait." We can see the Fish & Chip shop from the hill and there are a lot of people waiting around outside, so I admire his initiative in getting in and beating the crowd.

"Good thinking by the look of that line-up. What did you get for us?" I ask while rolling his accent around in my head in an effort to identify it. *French maybe?*

"I have (sounds like *av*) a good range, so if you like fish and chips, there's bound to be something in here that you'll like." He starts to unwrap the package as I kneel on the blanket and take a peek at what's inside. Once open, he spreads the paper out and rips off a piece for each of us to use as a plate. The array of seafood looks fantastic. There's crumbed whiting, cod and a couple of slightly smaller, indeterminate looking fillets, along with a big serving of chips and four potato scallops.

"This looks amazing!" I say as I move in close to the seafood buffet. "Whiting is my second favourite fish, so well done there."

"What's your favourite then?" he asks as he grabs a piece of the mystery fish and a handful of chips.

"Flathead, but it's not often available."

He holds up the crumbed piece of fish that he'd just selected, "You're joking? You know what this is don't you?"

"That is not?"

"It is so. *My* favourite too. I always order flathead if it's available. Now if you tell me that you love chicken salt, I think we should just close the gate and call this a match made in heaven."

I do love chicken salt but I'm reluctant to admit it in case it sounds phony–like I'm just saying it to go along with the rest of this string of little coincidences.

"Ok, I'll admit I am partial to a little chicken salt now and then, but I wouldn't go as far as to say I *love* it. Did you get it on the chips?" I grab one and taste it in answer to my own question.

"Always," he says as he bites into an enormously long chip with a good coating of chicken salt.

"You like to fish?" he asks, and before I can answer, "and you like to surf?"

"Well, I do like fishing, but I've never learned how to surf."

"Ah, I'll teach you. I keep many boards and one especially good one for learning. Of course, only if you want to learn?"

Listening to the choice and placement of his words, I'm really curious now about where he is originally from, but I don't want to come right out and ask, I also don't want to guess French because that seems too obvious a choice, but the way he structures a sentence and the dropped 'h' makes me think that's where he's from. It's difficult to tell because the accent is slight and sometimes not even noticeable. I try a different approach, "Ha, Guy's Surf School. Sounds like it's no women allowed though–*guys only.* Or should I pronounce it *Ghee's* Surf School?" I add.

"Ah, very perceptive. I have given up on hoping for people to pronounce my name as it was in Belgium and I've been here since I was twenty-six, so I'm used to the Aussie way of it. Now, you didn't answer my question. *Would* you like to learn how to surf?" He looks at me, waiting for an answer, and I notice that his hazel eyes have golden flecks around the edges and the laughter lines around his eyes are nestling into their well-worn creases. As I return his gaze, I feel something that I haven't felt for a very long time. The slight flutter of a butterfly wing brushing the sides of my tummy and the sense that my face is about to betray me by changing colour to a bright shade of red.

"Let me think about that one," I say as I break the eye contact and look out over the ocean. There are still a couple of surfers out on the small waves, and I watch them briefly before asking, "Is it more dangerous to be out surfing at this time of day?"

"So they say, but it doesn't stop us."

"Do you go out there on sunset too?" I ask, hoping to hear him assure me that he doesn't.

"Not usually. Only if the surf is really good. I never go alone though–better odds if there's a few of us out there." He looks at me with a grin, waiting for my reaction.

"Bloody crazy. There's no way you would catch me out there at dawn or dusk. I will think about your offer of a lesson though–at a *sensible* hour. Are you a good teacher?"

"Well, this is my job, so I should be good at it."

"What? You're a surf instructor?" I say incredulously.

"No, no, not surfing. I'm a lecturer at the Uni." You'd think he'd told me he was an astronaut and I consciously have to close my mouth because I feel it has dropped open. He looks as much like a lecturer as I do a WWE wrestler.

Trying not to sound as surprised as I feel, I say, "Oh great. What do you lecture in?"

"Psychology and Counselling."

Again, my jaw seems to lose its ability to hold my mouth closed but I quickly make the necessary adjustments.

"You're surprised?"

I know my slack jaw must have betrayed me so there's no use denying my surprise, but I hesitate before admitting it.

"It's ok–most people are. I look like an old surfer, which of course I am, but I spent my early years with my head continuously in a book, and I have a life-long wish to learn and to study people. Alongside of that is my love of the ocean. I had to toss up the decision when starting to study–whether to take Psychology or Marine Biology."

"Sorry, yes. It wouldn't have been my first guess if you'd asked me what I thought you did for a living. Do you find that people change after you tell them that? That they try to choose their words more carefully in case you're psychoanalysing them?"

"Very often. Yes. This happens a lot and it is a shame. But I can't do that unless someone allows me to. Right now though, I just want to get to know you and what you like to do. There is so much to learn when you just meet someone." He's making me feel very comfortable and relaxed now and I agree with his comments about having so much to learn. I also feel like I *want* to learn more about him and that makes me feel hopeful.

I turn my head to look at the sky behind us and immediately grab for my phone. The colours of the sunset are spectacular. If an artist portrayed the sky as it is, with its dazzling pinks and oranges, it would be seen as exaggeration or artistic licence, but here it is, this every-day event in nature, with no fanfare or herald–a silent and majestic display that had I not met up with Guy today in this spot, I would have been blissfully unaware of.

"Wow, thank you!" I say as I snap a photo of the quickly disappearing colours. "If you hadn't chosen this spot–if you'd organised to meet up at a café or restaurant, we'd have missed this."

"I am so lucky to be able to see that most days from my house," he says as he points up along the coastline towards Battery Hill. "I live just up there and because it's high, I have the view of the ocean as well as the view of the sunset in the west."

I follow the direction of his finger and notice some spectacular houses along the ridge.

"I would invite you to come to my home, but you might feel that is too forward for a first encounter?" He says this with an inflection that could leave it open to a rebuttal.

I am tempted, partly out of curiosity to see what his house is like, but partly because I'm genuinely enjoying his company. Instead, I answer, "Maybe next time."

"Ooh 'next time' sounds very good. Perhaps we could meet at a 'sensible hour' and try the surfing and then you could come back for some lunch? I still don't know what *you* do though. Do you work full time?"

"Yes, I have my own business, so I work full-time plus, plus. But I also have a bit of flexibility some days, so if there would be less people around on a weekday, then I think that's what I'd prefer–if that suits you?"

"Yes, my schedule gives me two days each week with just evening classes, so how about next Tuesday?"

"Roger that," I say.

"Roger? Who is Roger?" he asks with a concerned furrow settling in between his eyebrows.

"Oh, it just means great. So… great! How about 8.30?" I feel a bit silly and want to move on quickly.

"8.30 is a good time, before the sun gets too hot. But also, I would love to know before we part, what is your business?"

At this point, I think about how much I value my privacy, and how hard I have worked over the years to ensure that I feel safe, after experiencing what it feels like to be afraid to even open a window or the front door. My automatic response would be to give a general answer, like *I work in retail,* or *interior design,* but I feel like I can trust my instincts in relation to Guy and push myself to answer more openly.

"I'm a florist."

"Beautiful. This suits you to perfection."

I feel flattered by his compliment and as we sit and watch the sky darken, we chat about our jobs and about general topics–nothing too personal. I'm relieved that he hasn't asked any awkward questions and get the feeling that we may both be quite private people. I know for my part that I can't open up straight away to someone I have only just met. It will take time.

After an hour or so of chatting and shooing the increasing number of mozzies now surrounding and feasting on us, I suggest that we make a move. He agrees and we both get to our feet, momentarily standing close in the dim light. He places a hand on my arm.

"It has been so wonderful to meet you," he says and leans in to gently kiss both my cheeks.

"Yes, it has been lovely to meet you too."

Guy begins gathering up our rubbish and his blanket and bundling it all into his esky.

"Ok, bye," I say as I turn to start carefully picking my way back down the path to my car.

"Oh, wait, I'll see you down," he says and hurries to my side to escort me safely to the carpark. I can't help thinking that this is really thoughtful, and although I wouldn't admit it, it makes me feel safer now that the light has faded and the trees on the sides of the path appear to crowd in closer. Each shadow they cast becoming a hiding place for one with evil intent.

CHAPTER 13
Sabotage

I'd told Russell and Darrell that I would follow them to where the Gemini had finally come to rest, out of petrol on the side of the road.

When we arrived, Daz immediately opened the bonnet and began investigating what had happened to his precious little car. I moved to Russell's side, and he put a comforting arm around me. "Did you manage to get any sleep last night?" he asked, then in an attempt to lighten the mood added with a cheeky smirk, "Maybe I should've stayed."

I smiled back at him, "Hm, yeah, well we've been accused of all sorts, so it wouldn't have made much difference to my reputation if you had. You know I'm starting night shift next week and this is going to make me feel a bit creeped out–coming home to an empty house just after midnight every night for a week."

I had only started to think about it in the middle of the night while I was watching the dark, menacing shape of that person outside my house. Sure, I'd learned self-defence at the Academy and I had a lot of techniques to use on someone if they tried to attack me, but I never underestimated the element of surprise. And with the bushes and gardens running up close to my little rental cottage, there were numerous places for someone to hide.

The knowledge that Russell had been the victim of such an attack only recently was also very much on my mind. I imagined that his experience was something that occupied his thoughts too.

I reached up and gently touched the back of his head, "How's your head? I'm sorry, I forgot to ask you last night."

"It's been fine, but I'm still none the wiser as to what that was even about. They didn't steal anything from me so what was the point? Unless it was just plain jealousy?" He rubbed the back of his head and added, "I think about it a lot, as you can imagine, and that's the only explanation that I can come up with. No one I know hates me enough to do something like that. Should we do something about that Brian?"

Before I could answer, Darrell popped out from underneath his car and wiped his hands on his already grubby looking pants. "Some bastard has cut the fuel line."

"Are you sure?" I asked this and then immediately remembered that he was a mechanic. "Sorry, of course you would be."

"Yeah, did a job on it. I'm gonna have to tow this down to work and see if I can get a new line on it today. Russ, can you give me a tow? I've got a strap in the boot."

"Sure mate, 'course." Russell started to head toward his car and turned back to me, "Can I pop around this arv after work? I think we've got a lot to talk about."

That always sounded ominous to me when someone said, *we've got a lot to talk about,* but I figured he might just be concerned for me and want to talk about that.

"Yeah that would be great, and I'll cook dinner if you like?"

He gave me a thumbs up and hopped into his car. "See you around five-thirty," he said and turned his focus to starting up his car and positioning it in front of the Gemini to hook it up for the tow.

I drove home feeling alone and suddenly very tired. I had the day off and it was still not even eight o'clock, so I decided to try and catch up on some sleep and then head out to the hardware for the paint. I also needed to go to the BCC supermarket to grab some groceries so I could cook my first dinner for Russell. I didn't even know what he liked to eat. The only meal we'd had together was the Chinese takeaway we'd shared at the drive-in. He seemed to really enjoy that, but I wasn't going to attempt cooking Chinese food.

Having lived at home with Mum until being transferred to Burmont, I had hardly done any cooking. I'd bought myself the Women's Weekly Dinner Party cookbook when I found out that I was getting the transfer, but I'd only experimented with one recipe out of that–steak with green peppercorns, lemon beans and roast potatoes. It turned out ok so I guessed that would be what Russell was getting for dinner. I planned to play it safe and cook him something edible. I wanted his first impression of my cooking to be a good one.

As I approached my cottage, I scanned the fence to see if I could make out the letters that lay beneath the fresh coat of paint, but to my relief it just looked like a dark shadow underneath the beige. Another thing that I noticed was a faintly darker patch on the roadway outside my house–right about where Russell had the Gemini parked last night.

I pulled into the carport and walked out to the roadside to take a better look. There was a large area where the bitumen looked darker and a little shiny. I looked around to make sure no one was watching and that the road was clear of traffic before getting down on my hands and knees and sniffing the area. I pulled back, coughing and wishing I hadn't sniffed quite so deeply. The petrol fumes were still there–no doubt from the half a tank of petrol that had leaked from the little Yellow Caramello.

I turned to walk up the path to my front door but hesitated at the letter box and half raised my hand. *Should I check it again?* Thinking that would be extreme and resisting the urge, I dropped my hand and pushed myself forward. At the front door as I was about to put the key into the lock, I tried to imagine that it was midnight, and I was coming home from a night shift. I turned and looked around me, noticing how close the bushes were to the tiny front porch–perfect hiding places in the dark of the night. There was a light on the wall to the right of the door and I knew that it worked because I had turned it on last night when Russell was leaving.

I'm always in two minds when members of the public ask for advice about using porch lights. They're great for lighting the door and part of the pathway, and for making it easier to find the right key and position it into the lock, and they provide a feeling of safety and visibility. On the other hand, leaving the porch light on is a clear message to people that you're out and that this would be a good time to break in or whatever other mischief someone might want to do while no one is around. And that visibility can also bring a feeling of vulnerability–highlighting a target. *If only there was a light that would come on automatically when someone approached.*

I made a mental note to ensure that I had my torch with me in the car throughout the next week. I also decided I should buy some hedge clippers at the hardware store and get to work on the shrubbery before my first shift on Monday night.

* * *

Russell arrived right on half past and tapped on the door with an upbeat rhythm. He looked all shiny and clean–like he'd just stepped out of the shower, and he was carrying a bottle of wine which he switched to his other hand so he could bring me in for a hug and a kiss hello.

"Hey before it gets dark, come and have a look at the fence and tell me if you think I've covered it well enough. And I found a patch on the road that smelled pretty strongly of petrol this morning."

He deposited the wine on the kitchen table and we headed outside. Standing together on the footpath he gave my painting the nod of approval and then turned toward the street saying, "Yeah, I could still see that patch on the bitumen when I pulled up just now."

As we moved back inside and I closed the door behind us, Russell sniffed the air. He seemed a little disappointed with the result. "I can't smell any amazing aromas coming out of the kitchen. What's cookin?"

"Well nothing yet, except some roast potatoes in the oven. Everything else won't take long to cook, so I haven't started any of that."

"What's the everything else going to be?"

"Nothing too flash, just fillet steak with peppercorns and lemon beans," I say, hoping it sounds fancy enough.

"Sounds good. Where are your glasses?" he asked, holding the bottle up and giving it a little wiggle.

I located a couple of wine glasses that I'd hurriedly unpacked just before Russell arrived, giving them a quick rinse before handing them to him.

He poured a generous amount into our glasses and held his up formally, like he was going to make a toast but simply said, "Cheers big ears."

I feigned insult and covered one ear with my free hand, saying, "I was hoping you hadn't noticed."

He stuttered a little and back-peddled as though he believed he'd offended me.

I put my hand on his arm and laughed, "It's fine, I'm just winding you up. I happen to think that my ears are one of my strong points."

He took hold of my face and gently turned my head from one side to the other saying, "I'd say they're two of your strong points, but there's a few others I prefer." He leaned in and brushed my lips with his, "These are pretty high on my list," he whispered and then pressed his mouth against mine in a long and sensual kiss that sent tingles up my spine.

I eventually pulled myself away and reminded him that I had potatoes in the oven and the rest of dinner to get on with.

"Ok, while you're doing that, let's talk about what's going on with you and these notes and all of that. Plus, later I want to check your locks and see how secure your windows are. I don't want to scare you, but if this person is the same one who snuck up and whacked me from behind, then they're capable of being violent and I don't like to think of you in danger. It's got to be beyond coincidence–what happened to me on the night that I met you. Like I said earlier, I really think we need to do something about that Brian guy."

I stopped cutting up the beans and went to sit at the table where Russell had just settled himself. I took a sip of the wine and said, "I agree. It seems too coincidental that on the night that we meet you end up in hospital with concussion. And I can't forget that look that Brian was giving me and the way he was staring at us on the dancefloor. But we need to look at this logically and not jump to conclusions."

He covered my hand with his and asked, "Is it possible to check for fingerprints–on your letterbox?"

"That's a bit extreme when you look at what this person has actually done. The only offence they've really committed here is wilful damage to property by painting on my fence, unless we can prove it was the same person that assaulted you. My letterbox has loose bits of rust all over it so it would be too hard to dust for prints anyway. And how would I get Brian's prints to compare them with. I suppose I could try find out what his surname is and see if he's got a record. Do you know his name, or anyone that would?"

"Well, he plays A Grade for The Vikings so maybe they have a programme with the players' names in it, or maybe you could make official enquiries with the Club? Oh wait on, Brooksie knows a guy who plays reserve grade, maybe he could find out."

"Yeah, I don't want it getting back to him that I'm asking about him at the Club, and I especially don't want it getting back to Geoff that I'm checking up on his friend. If you think Brooksie can be trusted to be discreet, maybe, but otherwise I'll find out somehow this week."

"Isn't there someone–one of the other coppers–that you could talk to about all of this? Someone who can keep their mouth shut?"

"Like I said, I need to be very careful with how I come across at work. I have everyone's eyes on me because I'm new and I'm a woman. I haven't been in the job that long, but I've found out pretty quickly that it's a boys' club. Of course, I can't say that goes for every single one of them, but I need to get to know the guys here a bit better before I would trust one of them with something like this."

"Yeah, I suppose it must be tough breaking new ground."

"You know, there was another policewoman here before me, but she was only here for three weeks. I only found that out when the agent mentioned it when I was signing up to rent this place. I'm presuming she must have had a temporary placement. I had a couple of those when I first graduated from the Academy. The strange thing is, when I asked about her at work everybody seemed to clam up and then change the subject. Nobody would talk about her, not even Don, and he loves a good chat."

"So, do you think something might have happened with her?"

"Again, I don't know, and it will take a bit of time and careful investigation to find out. I asked Mrs Vescovi next door because she would surely have met her when she was living here briefly, but she said she just kept to herself, and she really didn't know anything about her. For now, I need to play it cool and gather as much information as I can–we can," I said with a smile and a squeeze of his hand. "I'm so glad to have you to talk to, and I haven't said this before, but if it is my fault that you got cracked on the head and ended up with concussion, I'm really sorry."

Russell scooted his chair back and put his arms out, leaving his lap open for me to go and sit. "You've got nothing to apologise for. Come here you." He enveloped me in a big hug and we stayed like that until I heard my tummy grumble loudly, reminding me to get on with dinner.

CHAPTER 14

Night Vision

Dinner turned out better than the first time I'd cooked it for my family, even though the potatoes were bordering on burnt, but tactfully called crispy, thanks to our prolonged cuddling during cooking time.

After dinner Russell turned serious, saying, "Right, let's check those windows and doors."

After he'd shaken and rattled all of the lounge windows, which were the timber sash type, he gave his seal of approval and we moved onto the bedrooms. I hadn't realised that in my room there was a sliding window with a catch that only held very loosely and when he applied some pressure it released and opened. This scared me a bit as there was no screen or other barrier to hinder someone climbing through. They'd be able to get in very easily. There were also sliding windows in the other bedroom and bathroom.

"These aren't good enough," he said, "I'll measure all of these sliders and get you some metal rods from work to put in the window tracks so you can open the window a little bit, but not far enough for a person to fit through."

I followed him down to the little annex where the toilet was located as he checked the louvres in there, as well as the lock on the back door. This door had a bolt as well as the normal door lock, so I felt confident that it would be safe.

"Do you keep this internal back door locked as well?" he asked, pointing up the two stairs to the original back door.

"Yes, at night I lock it. But I do feel a little scared when I have to get up to go to the loo in the middle of the night, so I usually try not to. Just hold on as long as I can."

"Yeah, well it's pretty secure but old louvres like those in the dunny can be removed pretty easily and being down the back here you might not hear it as much."

"Hmm. What was it they used to use before we had toilets? Oh yeah, chamber pots. Looks like I need one of those." We laughed, but despite my attempt at humour, the whole process was making me feel quite unsettled.

We went up to the front of the house and he examined and tested the lock on the front door. "This is a good lock, fairly new, and a solid timber door, so no worries there. Let's find some makeshift rods to put in those dodgy sliders for now."

He went back into the kitchen and started banging around until, armed with a wooden spoon, a spatula and a ruler, he made his way to the bedrooms and bathroom and dropped them into the tracks of the offending windows. He opened each of the windows until they hit the obstruction and he seemed happy that his props were effective in stopping them from opening further.

We settled onto the couch and I leaned up against him, enjoying his closeness and appreciating the effort he was making to try and keep me safe. I felt like it showed that he cared about me. I couldn't help but glance at the curtains on the front window to make sure they were closed properly. The thought that last time we were sitting (or lying) on the couch, someone was peering through and watching us gave me a shiver.

"Thanks for this, hey," I said, "I appreciate your concern."

"Well, I'm not finished yet. I wanted to talk to you about when you're on night shift next week. I've been thinking about that since you mentioned it this morning. With what's been happening, even *I* would feel a bit creeped out coming home to an empty house in the dark at midnight. So why don't you just come and stay at our place while you're on those shifts?"

"Oh that's sweet, but no, I'll be fine. I'm going to cut back the bushes around the path and open all of that area up, and I've got a good torch–and my trusty baton."

"Hmm, maybe just think about it. The guys would be cool with having you there. So would I of course."

I shot him a look and a raised eyebrow. He quickly added, "There's a fold-out bed in the sunroom at the end of the verandah if you're worried about appearances. You could use it... or not?" He gave me a cheeky smile before continuing, "Ok, the other option is a dog."

"A dog?"

"Yeah, a watchdog. Letitia volunteers at the pet rescue and they're always looking for people to foster dogs. You could borrow one, or even adopt one if you really liked it. She's always trying to bring them home, but the landlord is onto her. He said he'll kick us out if we try to sneak in any more pets. The last one she brought home was a mastiff that drooled all over the place. Of course, they have ones that don't drool..." He stopped and bit his lip before continuing, "I'm not doing a very good job of selling you on this option am I? Letitia would have you signing up for one in no time."

"I love dogs. I just don't know if my landlord would allow it either. I suppose I could find out. Don't know how I'd feel about giving it back though. I'd probably fall in love with it and then I'd be stuck with a dog when I get transferred out of here, or go home–God, Mum would hit the roof!"

We discussed the options a bit more without making any decisions, finally deciding that it was easier and much more fun to snuggle and watch TV. In the end not much TV was watched either. A lot of kissing happened instead. I was finding it more and more difficult to peel myself away from him as the night went on, but at around eleven o'clock, we both jolted upright on hearing a loud thud on the roof at the back of the house.

* * *

Feeling frustrated that he couldn't see her and cursing her for closing the gap in the curtains that had been his channel to watch her, the man moved to the side of the house looking for another vantage point. The added darkness afforded by the trees enveloped him as he stealthily moved from window to window, increasingly disturbed that he could find no way of seeing what she was doing. He knew who she was doing it with, but he needed to see.

Upon reaching the back of the house where there was only the one set of louvres, his frustration grew and along with it he felt a wave of panic–so unlike him that he was momentarily confused by the recognition of it. His anger at his own weakness along with the fact that someone like her could be able to thwart his efforts caused him to lash out. *She'll be sorry,* he thought. *I'm the one who calls the shots.* He grabbed a half-brick from the border of the garden and hurled it blindly at the house. He immediately heard thudding from inside the house, like someone running toward the back door. He realised that his normal escape route via the front fence was out of reach. Needing to get out quickly, his only escape now behind him, he turned and ran, jumping the back fence to avoid being seen. No sooner had his feet hit the ground than two dogs came running toward him, barking loudly.

Damn these dogs, he thought as he kicked out at the bigger one. He smiled as he heard it yelp and retreat momentarily. He would make sure they didn't bother him again. *My plan will see to that,* he thought as he ran toward the street. *But next time I need to be patient and more careful.* He began to formulate his plan as he slowed his pace and sought out the shadows.

* * *

Russell quickly jumped up and ran down to the back door, while I ran to the front and drew the curtain aside to look out at the front yard and the street beyond. I couldn't see anything there, so I ran down the back to see if Russell had caught sight of anything. As I got there, he was opening the door to take a look around outside.

"Wait, there's a torch near the washing machine there, take that and I'll grab my other one," I said as I rushed back up the two little steps to get my spare from the kitchen, I also detoured to the bedroom and grabbed my baton for good measure. Outside, the dogs belonging to the neighbour over the back were barking and I wondered if it was from Russell crashing around in the garden, or from someone making a getaway through their yard.

We shone our lights down into their yard as far as possible but saw nothing, then checked around my back yard and up the sides of the house as well. There was no space under the house, so at least we could be sure no one could hide under there and tackle or trip us as we walked past.

"Did you see or hear anything out here–apart from the dogs?" I asked.

"I heard a creaking noise that I think came from that old fence down the back there," he said, directing his torch beam onto the dilapidated timber paling fence between the properties. "I reckon someone has jumped it and then set the dogs off as they went through that yard."

"I wonder what that thump on the roof was though."

"Well, we can check it out in the morning. By the way–*I'm staying the night.*"

Before I could form an objection, he added, "No arguments. There's no way I'm leaving you here on your own."

We made our way back inside and locked the door again. Russell took me by the shoulders and turned me to face him. "This is beyond a joke now–you need to report it–tomorrow."

"Yeah, I'll talk to the Senior. He said at work yesterday that he wanted to see me tomorrow. I think he wants to check on how I've settled into the team."

"Ok, that's settled. Now, let's go to bed. I'm buggered."

He casually strolled off in the direction of my bedroom, while I just stood and watched, bemused that he obviously thought he was going to sleep in my bed–with me. He turned and said, "Are you coming?"

"Ah, not sure." I answered, stalling. "You don't even have a toothbrush–or pyjamas."

"Will I need them?" he asked, in a suggestive tone, then added in his normal voice "Hey, I'm only stirring you. I can be a gentleman and just cuddle you if that's what you want? If I'm forcing my way into your bed, the least I can do is behave–unless of course you want me to misbehave?"

I walked up and put a hand on his arm, "This is a big enough step, just having you stay. I think we need to take it slow. Some cuddles would be nice though."

I brushed my teeth and Russell swirled some toothpaste and water around and then helped me check the doors and windows again before we hopped into bed. I felt awkward and nervous as we lay down together and pulled up the blankets. We hadn't discussed it, but I felt like he would know that having a man in my bed was not a regular occurrence for me. Just to be sure I said, "I don't make a habit of this you know."

He rolled over to snuggle in and said, "Might be a good time to start."

"Hmm, we'll see." I gave him a deliberately short kiss goodnight and turned over so he could spoon me. Still feeling a little uncomfortable about the surprise ending to the evening, I had trouble trying to get to sleep. But Russell was true to his word and didn't try any moves on me. Before long, he was snoring gently in my ear. I was still thinking about what it could have been that landed on my roof, and who launched it there. I also couldn't help wondering if I snored when I slept. I was so unused to sleeping with someone that I was almost afraid to go to sleep in case I embarrassed myself somehow.

My brain finally stopped whirring around in circles and the gentle, rhythmic sound of Russell's breathing lulled me to sleep.

CHAPTER 15

It's a Dog's Life

At work the following day, I found it really hard to concentrate as my mind kept going to back to the night before, reminding me that I needed to talk to the Senior Sergeant in a couple of hours, but also reminding me of the wonderful feeling of Russell wrapped around me as we slept. Waking up to find him next to me had made my stomach flip, and the fact that he was staring at me when I woke embarrassed the hell out of me at the time. Thinking about it later, it just made me feel warm and happy. I could feel a smile playing at the sides of my mouth, but I caught it in time and brought myself back to the job at hand.

I needed to work out how to word what I was going to say to the Officer in Charge. I imagined he would be hoping for me to just confirm that everything was fine and that the guys had given me a good orientation. Well, they had–mostly, and work was going ok, but everything was not fine once I left work. Trying to put this into words in my mind and thinking about how it would be received by the boss, left it all sounding a bit over-dramatic.

So, I got a necklace with an anonymous note – really quite harmless. *Then I got another note saying someone saw me making out with my boyfriend* – only slightly remarkable. *And someone painted an insulting word on my fence.* That part I knew was an offence–Wilful Damage.

'Just report it to one of the guys–don't bother me with it,' I imagined him saying.

The elusive person in my yard and the cut fuel line all sounded speculative. I was half-way into convincing myself that it could be a mistake to bother my Officer in Charge with it at all. I hadn't had a lot of contact with him and the times I'd heard him talking to other officers, I'd noticed that he seemed quite gruff and serious. I supposed he had an image he wanted to portray, but it didn't make him feel very approachable, or likely to be empathetic about what had been happening to me.

Most of the older brigade that I'd met in various stations so far, seemed to be tough nuts who didn't generate a welcoming atmosphere to younger officers, especially female ones. I had a Sergeant at my last station though, Bill Jackson, who was one of the loveliest men I'd ever met. I wished he were my boss here, instead of Senior Sergeant Bollington.

Just then the phone rang and Don answered before placing the caller on hold and looking over at me. "I've got a woman on the phone who says her dogs have been poisoned. One of them died and the other one is at the vet looking really sick. She wants someone to come out."

"Yeah, I'll go. Get her name and address and phone number and tell her I'll be there shortly."

Don handed me the note with her details and I glanced at it as I grabbed the keys to one of the patrol cars. *Joyce Gordon, 16 Clancy St…* "Shit," I let slip out and then tried to cover it as Don gave me an enquiring look. "I just jabbed my hand on the key hook," I lied. In reality, I had just recognised the address of the neighbour at the back of my house–the one whose dogs were barking at around eleven o'clock last night while Russell and I were searching my back yard.

Noel looked around and said, "Do you want me to come on that job with you?"

"Ah, yeah, if you're not busy, sure." I figured it might be better to have someone else go to the complaint with me so I could focus on the job rather than my own concerns.

Mrs Gordon was obviously watching out for us because the door opened even before we'd knocked. She was a plump little woman in her sixties, and she looked like she'd been crying. Her eyes were red-rimmed behind her glasses, and she clutched a handkerchief in her hand as she held the door open for us. "Come in," she said softly, "or do you want to look around outside first?"

"We'll come in and take some details from you first Mrs Gordon," I said. We followed her to her lounge room and then all sat on her dark floral genoa lounge chairs. I introduced myself properly and also Noel. The whole room was quite dark with the furniture mostly in mahogany and the heavy curtains closed.

I took out my notebook and pen and started to question her for details on what had happened. "When did you notice that your dogs were unwell?" I began.

"It was about half past eight this morning. I heard our Boz making these gagging noises in the side yard. I went to have a look and there was little Roxy, just lying still in the garden and not moving. She had foam around her mouth, so I ran over to her and tried to help her. But she didn't move. I could see she was gone." Mrs Rogers broke down then and dropped her head into her hands. Her whole body heaving with sobs. I looked at Noel, feeling helpless. He just shrugged his shoulders like he didn't care too much, but surprised me by saying, "Would you like me to get you a drink of water or something, Mrs Gordon?"

She lifted her head and wiped her eyes and nose with her hankie. She looked at Noel like she was seeing him for the first time. "Oh no, I'll be fine. Thank you. It's just hard talking about it. We've had Roxy for 14 years." Her voice was shaky, and she dabbed at her eyes again as she said, "She was Richard's dog really, and now she's gone to be with him." The sobbing took over again.

"Yes, I'm so sorry, I know this is very upsetting. We won't keep you too long. Just a couple more questions," I assured her. "What about your other dog–um, Boz was it?"

"Yes, he's at the vet's now. He was frothing at the mouth too but at least he was breathing. He's a staffy and quite heavy. Mr Greaves next door came to help. He drove us down to Barker's–so lovely of him. I'm sure he put little Roxy in his car too, but I don't know where she is now." She seemed distressed by this and looked from me to Noel for some kind of assurance about where Roxy might have ended up. "Do I get to bury her? Someone's poisoned them you know. Do they have to do a post-mortem or something?" She looked to me again, as if I should have an answer. I didn't.

"Ah, I think you might have to talk to the vet about that," I suggested. "Do you know how Boz is now?"

"I rang the vet just after I rang the Police station. They said when I left him there that they'd let me know if there was any change, but I couldn't just sit by the phone and wait. Apparently, he's hanging in there but no great improvement yet."

"Do you have any ideas about what happened to them? Did they eat something that you know of?"

"I don't give them food in the mornings. Richard didn't believe in dogs having breakfast, so they only get their dinner in the evening. Someone must have thrown some kind of bait over the fence, but why would anyone do that to my dogs? They don't bark a lot and they're always kept locked in the yard so there's no reason."

At the mention of barking, I decided to follow up on last night, "Have they been barking more lately, or have you seen anyone unusual around?"

"Something set them off late last night and I got up to have a look out, but I couldn't see anything. They were both fine at six this morning on our little walk to the park and back and they didn't eat anything while we were out. Do you think that's when someone put the baits out for them? While we were out walking?"

"Well, we will look into it Mrs Gordon and we'll talk to the vet and see whether they can confirm that it was a bait of some kind. Did you find anything lying around, like some meat or anything?"

"No, I've looked all around but you should take a look too. You might see something I didn't. My eyes aren't what they used to be." She stood and asked, "Do you want to go out there now, or do you have more questions?"

Outside, she showed us the two spots where the dogs were when she found them, sobbing and sniffling softly as she moved around the area. After we had all searched around the front and sides, I moved toward the back yard to check it as well. The others eventually joined me.

I looked up and took in the view of my place from a totally different perspective. The cottage looked tiny from the back, and I could see that the trees around the back of the house would provide easy cover for someone if they were trying to skulk around without being seen. I mentally added another tree pruning job to my list.

Mrs Gordon's yard was slightly elevated in comparison to mine and I could clearly see an object that looked like part of a brick on the roof of my back annex. I was both glad to have been able to identify what caused the thud and disturbed to think that someone had intentionally thrown it up there. *But why–to scare me?*

I assumed that Mrs Gordon didn't realise that it was me who'd moved into the cottage that backed onto her house and I didn't think it would be a good idea to let her know. The last thing I needed was people coming directly to me to report things rather than going via the station.

I brought my attention back to searching her yard and after finding nothing of interest, we thanked her and took our leave.

When we got back into the car, Noel said, "Poor old chook. She obviously loved those dogs. Man, I hate it when people do things to animals. People–fair enough, well you know, *some* people, but dogs. Nah. If someone tried something like that on mine, they'd live to regret it. That's if it *was* some grub throwing them a bait."

I felt like I was seeing a different side to Noel. He was kind to Mrs Gordon and he obviously cared about animals. I began to wonder if I shouldn't just let him in on the strange things that had been happening to me, especially as one of them was most likely connected to the job that we were currently working on together.

"What kind of dog have you got?" I asked as I started up the car.

"We've got two. Labs. One yellow and one black."

"Aw gorgeous! Love labs," I responded, steering onto the road toward the Veterinary Surgery.

"Actually, my missus keeps on at me about asking you over for dinner, to welcome you to town. You could get to meet them then. That's if you want to?" He sounded tentative and seemed a bit embarrassed asking me.

"Oh, that's so nice of her. Of course, I'd love to meet her–and the dogs."

"Great. I'll find out when Nicki wants to have you over and let you know."

As I parked outside Barker's, I decided to bite the bullet. Noel had opened up a little bit about his private life to me and I felt like I could do the same. I unclipped my seatbelt and half-turned toward him. He seemed to get the message that I wanted to talk. His hand paused on door handle.

"Before we go in, I think I should tell you that I believe that Mrs Gordon's dogs *were* intentionally baited. I live just over the back of her place and at around eleven last night, someone threw something on my roof. Straight after, her dogs were going off."

"Gees mate, what's going on there?" he asked, half-turning in his seat and showing interest. "Did you see anyone?"

"No. I think they hoofed it over the fence and through her yard, setting the dogs off. Look, there have been a few other incidents that

I haven't told anyone about, except for one friend." I didn't want to bring Russell's name into it straight up. "The first couple of things seemed quite innocent so I just thought it was a prank or something, then it got a bit nasty."

"Yeah...," he said, sounding either disbelieving or like he was trying to remember something. I wasn't sure which, but I continued with my story. I told him about the strange gift on my very first day in my house and the anonymous note later that night.

"This sounds a bit familiar–but keep going. What else has happened?" he asked. I wanted to ask why–and how it was familiar, but I went on and told him about the man standing outside my house and the nasty note and graffiti, the cut fuel line on my friend's car–everything. Once I'd started, I just let it all come out–all the time trying to gauge his reaction. When I'd finished, I felt a wave of relief from getting it all off my chest.

"So you haven't reported any of this?" he asked. "Not even the wilful damage to the fence?"

"No. I was thinking of talking to the boss about it in our interview today, but I'm a bit hesitant. He seems pretty stiff and unapproachable."

Noel agreed and asked if I'd like him to prepare a report about the fence. When I shook my head he pressed me for a reason.

"So many reasons–a big one being that word itself–*slut*," I answered honestly. "I was mortified. And I don't want other people knowing and then having them wonder if I deserve the title somehow. I don't!"

"Well, people around here don't know you well enough to call you anything yet. Any idea who's doing this stuff?" His tone was reassuring. I still didn't know whether to tell him about Brian though, or Russell, and my suspicions about what happened to him. Brian's friendship with Geoff and the fact that Noel and Geoff worked a lot of shifts together made me hesitant to say too much in that regard. I knew how long an eight-hour shift could seem when there was not much happening. If you got on well with your partner, you tended to talk a lot, to pass the time.

I didn't answer his question but gave a shrug. He continued, "I think we're all grown-up enough to not be shocked by the word *slut*, and to realise that the kind of people who do stuff like deface someone's property don't have very reliable judgement anyway. But, yeah, I can see how it might upset you. What about the other reasons why you haven't reported it?"

"Well, just that. I don't want to be the *upset*, defenceless female in the eyes of my colleagues, including you. I can't have an image of being soft or sooky. How would that look? How I act and handle myself is under extra scrutiny–because I'm a policewoman and people around here aren't used females in the job. I'm talking about you guys as well as the public. There'll be assumptions and generalisations about all policewomen if I look like a delicate little flower, getting upset about stuff that could in the end just be a nasty prank." I looked over at him to try and gauge what he might be thinking, but I couldn't read him.

"It's a boys' club you know," I said, holding his gaze, "it's been that way for so long that it's really no surprise. I can even understand in some ways. This is a tough job. We see and deal with some really unpleasant stuff and we all want to know that our partner has our back when we need them. Some guys with old-fashioned views on women, probably wouldn't trust us to be the kind of backup they need. But hey, I could beat a couple of the guys in my squad in an arm wrestle and I was the second-best shot in the squad, so I reckon I'd rather have me than some blokes if things turned pear-shaped." I stopped myself because I felt a bit like I was having a rant and I didn't want him to feel like I was having a go at *him* in some way.

"Hey, I've worked with women before and I don't have a problem," he sounded defensive. I started to regret bringing up the whole gender issue. Then he added, "But I know some guys do, so there's no doubt you're going to have your work cut out for you trying to change their minds–especially here. You're not the first you know."

Especially here. I needed to find out what he meant by that. And *you're not the first*...no one else had wanted to talk about my predecessor, maybe he would.

"Who should I be expecting to have the most trouble with in changing his mind here, or should I say their minds?"

"You'll have to figure that out for yourself. They're my mates so I'm not going to name names. I know some of their attitudes are a bit off, but they've always treated me well."

"Well can you tell me what happened to the last policewoman? Nobody seems to want to talk about her. Was she really only here for three weeks?"

"Again, I can't talk about that. Except to confirm that, yes, she was only here for three weeks." He seemed uncomfortable as he looked out the window and reached for the door handle, like he wanted to end the conversation. "We'd better get on with this job. If you want me to put in a formal report on your fence damage though, I can do that."

"I'll just get you to hold off for the moment and I'll let you know. Can I ask you to keep this all to yourself for now as well–just until I decide what's the best way to go?"

"Sure, I won't say anything," he hesitated a moment with the door open and one foot on the kerb. "Look, I *can* tell you that policewoman's name was Sue Ryan, you'd be able to look that up in the logs anyway. I *can't* tell you any more about her but that doesn't mean someone else couldn't. She and Nicki seemed to hit it off and they'd chat a bit–but I didn't tell you that."

He exited the car fully and put his hat on as he strode up the stairs of the Veterinary Surgery without a look back in my direction. I hurried to catch up and was right behind him as he entered the reception area. We asked to speak to the person who treated Mrs Gordon's dog that morning and took a seat while the receptionist disappeared through a 'Staff Only' door behind her desk.

As we waited, in silence, amid the smells of dog, disinfectant and some other unidentifiable aromas, I replayed in my mind the last part of the conversation that we'd just had in the car. I felt like we had formed some kind of mutual trust there, reinforced by his hinting that his wife might be able to tell me more about the big mystery surrounding the previous policewoman. I couldn't help feeling like everyone at the Station had been sworn to secrecy on that topic. I supposed that proved he could keep a secret. I felt like I could trust him not to gossip with the other guys about my problems.

After a few minutes, the vet came out to talk to us. He told us that Boz was improving and they were confident that he would recover. When I asked whether he could tell if the dogs were baited, he responded, "It's a definite case of baiting in my opinion. I've run some tests on the saliva around their mouths, and a partially chewed fragment of meat from Roxy's mouth. The results are consistent with deliberate poisoning."

"Thank you doctor," I said. "Were your tests able to identify the type of poison used?"

"I'm still working on that, but I'll let you know any further results."

We thanked him again and departed.

As we hopped back into the car, I asked, "Am I supposed to call them 'doctor'? I never know with vets."

"Well if you're not supposed to, I bet they love it when you do," he laughed as he pulled the door closed.

Back at the Station, I started to type up the report on the baiting but couldn't concentrate on that as I was only too aware that my appointment with the Senior was in just a few minutes' time. After verbalising everything to Noel, I had decided not to mention anything to the boss. I even felt silly to think that I was considering doing just that earlier in the day. Noel would definitely be the one I'd ask to report on this–as soon as I'd done my own checking up on Brian.

CHAPTER 16
Nice Guy

It's still quite early when I arrive home from my meet-up with Guy, although from the welcome Lola gives me you'd swear I'd been gone for weeks. Admittedly, I did go to Moffat Beach straight from work so she would be starving by now. Once I have her fed and happy, I decide to watch a bit of TV and take some time to relax.

Knowing that I've got the day off tomorrow and Sal and Ros will be the ones getting up early to open up, I pour myself a glass of shiraz, grab my mobile and plump up the cushions to make myself comfortable on the couch. Lola takes this as a signal to join me and plonks herself on my legs and nudges my elbow for a pat.

I close my eyes and absentmindedly stroke her head. The action is so relaxing and therapeutic that I can feel my shoulders untense and drop almost immediately–I could drift off to sleep quite easily, but it's only nine o'clock and I want to make the most of this quiet time. I need some space to think about this evening as it unfolded with Guy and how I feel after spending that time with him. Obviously, there was tension in my shoulders, but there is also a warm and exciting feeling that I may have met someone genuinely nice.

He really wasn't what I was expecting after reading his profile and looking at his photos. I know that I shouldn't be judging people by their appearance, but in the online dating world that I now find myself, it is almost impossible not to. I suspect that the tension that was creeping into my shoulders is to do with the fact that he's a psychology lecturer, and therefore most likely an experienced psychologist. I've only ever met psychologists in a professional setting. I remind myself that they just people–*he's just a person–like me.*

I have to say, he's not like any therapist I've been to–and I've worked my way through a few. After my experiences in Burmont, I became a twenty-five-year-old recluse. I did not want to socialise with people, I cut my hair short and stopped wearing make-up or trying to look attractive. I lived at home with my mum and only left the house to go to work. Even that became difficult, as it involved speaking to people and working closely with other officers.

Mum would sometimes try to talk to me about what had happened and why I came back home, but I just couldn't tell her. "It just didn't work out there–I wasn't happy," was my standard response.

We didn't have a close relationship, even though I was an only child and Dad had died when I was twelve. Sometimes I felt like she didn't really want kids at all, and I must have been an accident. Anyway, I didn't feel like I could share my intimate personal experiences with her. Plus, they would shock her. She'd been such a strict Catholic all of her life. I could see no good reason to burden her with the knowledge of what I'd been through. She would have so many questions, and her imaginings of the events–maybe even worse than the actual events… No, I'd pondered it many times and decided she would never know.

After almost a year of living my hermitic lifestyle back at home, and Mum hoping that I'd snap out of it, she made an appointment with the GP and forced me to go. She liked to say 'encouraged' but I felt like I didn't have a choice. When she told me she'd made the appointment, she broke down and started crying, saying, "I feel like my daughter is gone. You're my only family now and I need you. Please Tess–please at least try!"

The GP was nice enough, but not someone that I felt I could open up to. After giving him a sketchy outline of my experiences and how I was feeling, all he could do was to refer me to a psychiatrist. I doubt he even knew that *psychologists* existed. The thought of seeing a psychiatrist just filled me with dread. It seemed to carry such stigma in those days–that you'd only be going to a psychiatrist if you're crazy. It took me another two months to get up the courage to make an appointment. The first of many.

* * *

So now I wonder, *as a psychologist, is Guy going to be a little too interested in my past?* Of course, I would eventually have to tell him, but I would only want to do that in my own time. I do feel my guard going up in that I fear he could see me as a project or a patient when he knows what I've been through. If we are to become more than just friends, I can't feel that way when I'm with him.

Just then a message pops up on my phone. It's from Perry, wanting to know if I'd be available tomorrow night for that dinner we still haven't been on. The thought makes me feel a bit crowded and a little bit like it would be an obligation rather than a fun thing to do.

A month ago, I had no men in my life–now I have three jostling for my time. *Should I have just left well-enough alone? Was I really lonely or was I just wanting to prove to myself that I could do this?* I try to fathom my motivation, deciding that it is probably a combination of reasons, and my competitive nature would be right up there, along with trying to prove to myself that I'm not scarred by the past, and not scared of opening up and trusting someone again. As well as reassuring myself that I'm still attractive.

I give up trying to analyse myself and type out a response to Perry. *How about next week? I'm having a very busy one...* Before I finish,

I have a call coming in–my quiet time is well and truly shattered. Looking at the screen I see that it's Jacinta, so I abandon the text and answer her call.

"Hello baby–you OK?" I say. I'm always glad to hear from my kids but somehow always on edge that there might be something wrong when they call rather than text.

"Hey Mum. I'm fine, how are you? You're not trying to sleep are you?"

"No, I'm on the couch with Lola, just winding down."

"You sound tired. Are you feeling ok? Winding down from what?" As she shoots her questions at me, I can hear the concern in her voice. Lately, I've been considering telling her about my foray into online dating and had already decided that I would talk to her the next time that I saw her on her own, but now seems like as good a time as any, and I'd like to hear what she thinks.

"Oh, just a big day at work," I'm stalling, trying to formulate the right words, "and after work I met up with someone down at Moffat Beach for fish 'n chips. Just got home really." I know I'm sounding a bit mysterious and Cinta can't resist a mystery.

She takes the bait and jumps in with more questions, "Who's this someone? Is it a male someone?" She has asked me before if I'd like to meet someone since her dad and I split up. She wanted to assure me that she'd be fine with it, that she and the boys didn't expect me to stay on my own forever. I appreciated that but it hadn't even been an obscure thought on the horizon, until now.

"Yes, it was a male someone and he seemed quite nice."

"Was it a blind date?" she asks, excitement in her voice.

"Well, are you sitting down? This might shock or surprise you, but I met him online."

"Oh my god Mum! You? On a dating site? I don't believe it." She's now sounding amused and shocked. "But good on you," she recovers and adds. "I'm really glad. Now I want to hear all about it–and him."

"Well, I knew you would. So do you want to drop in on your way home from work tomorrow so I can fill you in, in person?"

"You bet. Wow, I knew it must have been a guy. If it was just one of your friends, you'd have said their name."

"Ha, you were right–more so than you realise. That's his name–Guy!"

She laughs, "Well, let's hope he's Mr Nice *Guy*. I suppose he's heard that one a few times."

"No doubt. But on first impressions, he does seem nice."

"Ok, I won't pump you for answers tonight but when are you seeing him again?"

"Tuesday. He's going to teach me to surf."

"Good grief Mum. What next? Online dating, surfing, are you going skydiving next week as well?"

"Hmm," I tease, "I'm not sure yet–maybe."

When I hang up from our chat, I take another sip of my wine and just as I settle back in with Lola, I realise I haven't finished my text to Perry. I go ahead with the suggestion of next week and send the message on its way. Almost immediately he responds with, *No problem, can we try for Tuesday night?*

Aargh, here we go again, I think. I reply, *Thursday is better for me, if that suits?* Without even thinking, I've avoided booking myself out for Friday night because deep down I'm hoping that Guy might want to get together then. And Tuesday? Well, I don't want to feel rushed on our surfing date. Who knows? He might want to spend rest of the day together.

I allow my mind to slip back into my earlier musings about Guy, and I find myself smiling as the image of his pose up against the pandanus comes to mind.

CHAPTER 17

F Off

On the dot of 1400 hours, I knocked on the closed door, bearing the title: 'OFFICER IN CHARGE'.

"Enter," reverberated through, or under the door.

I obeyed and presented myself at the large pine desk, concealing the substantial bulk of Senior Sergeant Bollington.

"Sit." His economy of words did nothing to relieve my unease at being summonsed to his office for the first time. He signed a paper in front of him and pushed it to the side. He then selected another foolscap sheet and held it up for me to see. I couldn't read it from where I was sitting.

"Constable Merlin, this is your report and gun licence application for Tom Wiley out on Twin Peaks Farm. I need to talk to you about that–and any future reports that you'll be submitting."

I briefly wondered if I hadn't provided the required information, or gone into enough detail, but I prided myself on writing a comprehensive and well-structured report, and I'd done other gun licence applications before, so I couldn't help feeling surprised.

"Yes sir?" I said, deciding to adopt his word economy, but also at a loss to know what else to say.

"You need to put an 'F' after your name and number on your reports," he said, in a matter-of-fact tone as he leaned forward and handed me the report, presumably to make the amendment. My arm responded and my hand automatically reached out to take the offending piece of paper, but my mind was cyclonic. Responses whirled around, possible reasons for his request whirled amongst them–none of them plausible–all screaming *discrimination.*

My mouth opened and I must have looked like a fish out of water–I was struggling to find words that would not be detrimental to my position–to my career. I was a Constable with a five years' service, and he was a Senior Sergeant. Directions given must be followed, but this? I was incredulous. I grasped at the possibility that perhaps I'd misheard him. *Yes, that seemed to be the only possible explanation.*

"I'm sorry, could I just clarify that?"

"It's not that difficult. You need to put an 'F' in brackets next to your name when you sign a report." His repeating of it and telling me *it's not difficult* only made it more confronting.

Aware of my rank, and his, I tried for a respectful tone. "Could I ask why, Sir? I have never been asked to do that before."

"Well, isn't it obvious? So that I, and anyone else reading the report know that it was written by a female officer."

His response felt like a kick in the guts, *physically.* I couldn't believe what I was hearing. Feeling like I'd been thrown into some bizarre dream, I was suddenly transported to another office and another Senior Sergeant telling me something equally fantastical–that seemed at the time that *it* must be a bad dream also, but it wasn't. I couldn't disobey then, and I felt like I couldn't again.

'Kiss a Cop' seemed like a good idea to the powers that be who introduced it for the New Year's period that year, which was coincidentally only weeks after I was sworn in. In reality it was a misguided effort to improve the public image of police officers. Quite possibly it was welcomed by many male officers, especially the older ones who had pretty, young ladies coming up and wanting to kiss them. But no one stopped to think about how it might be for a freshly sworn-in, innocent and never been kissed young lady of nineteen, to have sleezy, drunk and smelly older men coming up and claiming the right to grab them and kiss them–all with the blessing of the Commissioner of Police.

My head reeling from those memories, I brought my focus back to my current predicament. *How could I have been so naïve as to think that I'd been called in so that he could check on how I was settling in? How could I have been considering confiding in this man?* My anger began to burn–my face turned red as a result of it. I found I couldn't just take this one on the chin.

"I'm sorry, Sir, but I can't do that." I heard myself speak, but I was still shocked to hear the words as they came out of my mouth.

"And why not? This is a direction, not a request." His voice was slightly raised, and his tone more severe.

"I can't imagine what difference it would make if someone knew a gun licence application report, or any other report for that matter, had been written by a male or a female officer, Sir."

"It's not up to you to imagine, and it's not your place to question. Just do it. That will be all." He waved his hand toward the door. I hesitated, but decided discretion was the better part of valour in that moment. I turned and walked to the door, clutching my report in a tightly balled fist, and clamping my mouth shut to avoid further protestations.

I stormed back to my desk and launched the report onto the desk and myself into my chair. I could feel the eyes of Noel, Derek and Don, all on me. I didn't trust myself to speak, so I made a trip to the toilets to take some much-needed deep breaths. At least, being the only female in the station meant that I had the ladies' room to myself. I thought that a small compensation for how insulted I was feeling, but I took advantage of the quiet space and the opportunity to gather my thoughts.

I emerged from my fortress, forcing myself to smile and act naturally. I'd used my time out to make a decision, and I proceeded to my desk to complete my mission. I only had an hour before the end of my shift, so I set to work. Thankfully, no one came near me or questioned me about my earlier demeanour. I really didn't want to talk about.

Grateful of my touch-typing skills–as I was every time I watched one of the guys tap away with two fingers, struggling to type a few words–let alone a full report, I completed my report on the alleged baiting of Mrs Gordon's dogs. I signed my name. I added my rank and number. I did not put an 'F' in brackets next to it.

I ripped the paper from the typewriter rather dramatically and carefully reviewed what I'd written. My plan was to make a statement by presenting the report in the normal way, so I didn't want to be embarrassed by any spelling or typing errors. Satisfied with my work, I lay it, and the unchanged firearm licence application report on top of the tray marked 'Snr Sgt In Tray'. I then gathered my hat and bag to sign-off on my shift. Noel was also finishing up and came to sign-off at the same time.

"You ok?" he asked quietly.

"Yeah, I'll tell you about it later. I need to go for a run and then I need a big glass of wine–and maybe a dart board with Bollington's face on it," I said in a hushed voice.

"Yikes mate. Can't wait to hear this one." He scratched his head as he put his hat on and we both left the station. Outside, he said, "Hey, I rang Nicki and she said tomorrow night, if you're not busy?"

"Oh, that would be great Noel. Cheers. I'll bring wine." I silently wished I could bring Russell, but it was still early days with him and our relationship, so I wasn't quite ready to introduce him around as my boyfriend. Besides, I thought that maybe Nicki would be more inclined to talk freely if it was just me there.

* * *

After enjoying a lazy rostered day off, I parked outside the address Noel had given me. I'd come bearing wine–red and white because I'd forgotten to ask him what Nicki liked to drink. This was the first time I'd gone to a colleague's place for dinner. I felt a little strange being on my own and them being a couple, but I knew I could hold a conversation and being new to town, there were a million questions I could ask to break any awkward silences.

As I walked down the short driveway to their small double-brick home, I heard the dogs barking inside the house. The door opened and Noel greeted me, holding one dog's collar in each hand. "They're friendly but I'll hold them so they don't jump all over you." He pulled them to one side to make a gap for me to enter.

I stopped and popped one of the bottles under my arm so I could give each dog a pat in turn, while saying, "I don't mind if they jump."

He released them and they vied for position, both trying to get my attention. They were big dogs, so when they jumped their paws landed on my stomach. I could feel a scratch from one already. Nicki came over then to rescue me as well, admonishing Noel for not keeping the dogs off me and gushing into a warm welcome. She was not at all what I imagined. She was petite with long brown hair and dark, smiling eyes.

"Hi Tess, I'm Nicki. It's so great that you could come. And this is Dolly," she said patting the yellow lab, "and this is Duke," turning her attention to the black.

Noel took the wine from me and headed toward what I presumed was the kitchen, while Nicki steered me through a quick tour of the house. The dogs trailed behind us. The house was compact, but still considerably bigger than my cottage. It had been decorated in bright colours and as we moved from room to room with Nicki chatting the whole time, I felt like the decor was a reflection of her personality. Bright and cheerful.

The tour concluded in the kitchen, where we found Noel with three glasses ready to be filled. He'd opened both wines and invited us to help ourselves.

I poured myself a red. As the others filled their glasses, I thanked Nicki for inviting me round.

"That's easy, I know how hard it is moving to a place where you don't know anyone. It must be even harder when you're a bit of a novelty as a policewoman. Small towns can be full of gossips, and we have our fair share of those. I even copped enough attention as the wife of a policeman when we first arrived."

"Yeah, I do feel that I have extra eyes on me at times." As I said this I thought of the notes and the feeling I often had of being watched. I shot a quick look at Noel and wondered if I should ask the question that I really want to ask of Nicki straight up, but he changed the subject and suggested we move into the lounge where it would be more comfortable.

As the evening went on, I relaxed and enjoyed their company. Nicki was a much better cook than me. She seamlessly presented three courses of delicious food and didn't seem rushed or frazzled at all. During dinner, I found out that Noel and Nicki had only been in town for a year. I asked them to give me a bit of background information on the other guys at the station and how long they'd been in Burmont.

I learned that Derek (Constable) was single and had just started dating a kindy teacher; he'd been in town for three years and didn't want to leave. Mark (Constable–who Nicki and I agreed was very cute) was a fairly new arrival. He was single but just started going out with a friend of Nicki's. Geoff (Const 1st Class) was married, and his wife was a bit stand-offish. No kids. She worked at the Chemist, and they'd been in town just over a year. Ray (Senior Constable) was also married, and they had a little boy. My hosts didn't know much about them because Ray was so quiet. Jim (Sergeant) was married with two kids and seemed to be a permanent fixture. Then there was Senior

Sergeant Bollington. I found out he'd been Officer in Charge of the station for six years and no one liked him much, although he and Geoff had worked together before at the Traffic Branch in Nixon.

The mention of the name Bollington prompted me to tell them about what happened at work yesterday. I knew Noel was bursting to know the details.

As I recounted what I had been requested and then directed to do, I saw the looks of disbelief cross their faces. "And now I might be in a lot of trouble because I purposely didn't put an 'F' on the report I submitted about the baiting that we went to yesterday. I'm just glad I have a couple of RDOs and then night shift before I have to face him again."

Nicki looked at Noel and asked, "Have you heard of this before–a policewoman having to do that?"

"No. It sounds ludicrous to me. I don't think he asked Sue to do that. Can he even make that kind of request, or direction?" he directed this question toward me.

"Well, I'm about to find out. I'm going to try and ring my old Sarge from my last station and ask him. He was a nice guy and I'd imagine he'd know if this is legitimate."

Noel stood up and asked, "How about a glass of port?"

Nicki declined, but I accepted his offer. He moved to the bar and poured a glass for me and one for himself. After he'd handed me mine, he placed his on the coffee table saying, "Give me a few minutes, hey? I might just take the dogs out for a quick stretch and give you girls a little bit of time together. I know you have things you probably want to talk about." He nodded in my direction. I took this as his not-so-subtle way of saying that it would be a good time to ask Nicki about Sue Ryan.

As he slipped from the room, Nicki asked, "Do you know what he meant by that?"

"Yeah, that was him clearing the way for me to ask you about the girl who was here before me, and to maybe tell you about a few things that have been happening to me."

Nicki leaned forward in her seat, looking concerned. "Don't tell me the same things are happening to you as happened to Sue," she said incredulously. "Are you ok?"

"I'm ok, but I'm confused about why this stuff is happening. I hadn't told anyone at work about it until yesterday when I told Noel. He seemed like the most approachable out of all the guys and I'm glad I told him."

"Yeah, he's a nice guy," she smiled. "I know–I'm biased because he's my husband, but I think you made the right decision."

"I can't believe I was actually thinking about telling the Senior before that little episode today."

"Well, it's probably best that you didn't, not if you want to stay here anyway. Sue told him and straight after that she was transferred out."

I couldn't believe what I was hearing. "Do you know exactly *what* she told him?'

"No, she wouldn't say exactly. I think she just told him that someone was harassing her–leaving creepy notes and stuff. Is that what's happening to you?"

"*Yes.* So this is not just about me. I thought it was but now that I know it happened to Sue... but who would want to do this, and why?"

"I really don't know. Noel didn't say anything to me about it happening to you though. He's so scared to mention Sue or the whole whirlwind transfer situation. None of them will. They were instructed not to discuss it you know."

"Well, I appreciate him going out on a limb for me by letting me talk to you about it. I don't want to get him into any kind of trouble. Can you tell me any more about what kind of things were happening to Sue?"

Nicki's description of what Sue had told her was almost as disturbing as what had been happening to me, and similar in a lot of ways. Although she didn't receive an anonymous present–she got similar notes in the letterbox and heard disturbing noises at night. She also couldn't shake the feeling of being watched.

"Did Sue happen to go out with anyone when she first arrived in town?" I asked, half-expecting her to mention that someone called Brian was hanging around as soon as she arrived.

"No. She had a boyfriend already. He lives at Agnes Water, a couple of hours away. He came and stayed on the first weekend she was here though. It was after that that she got the nasty note calling her a slut."

Damn, I thought. *That puts a big dent in my theory about Brian. If she didn't go out with him then maybe it's someone else altogether. Unless he asked, and she refused him.*

"Do you know if any guys asked her out at all?"

"None that she told me about."

"Was it just the note calling her… that name?" I still had trouble getting that word to come out of my mouth. "He wrote it all over my front fence–in big painted letters!"

"That's disgusting. Who does he think he is? *You poor thing.*" Nicki placed a hand on my arm.

Being able to tell another woman was such a relief for me and hearing the concern in her voice, and perhaps a couple of glasses of wine, had the effect of making me feel very fragile. I couldn't stop the tears as they welled up in my eyes and began to trickle over onto my cheeks.

"I'm sorry. I've just had to put on a brave face and keep all of this to myself."

She put her arm around my shoulders and said, "You can talk to me anytime. Sometimes guys just don't quite understand."

I pulled myself together and told Nicki about the incident the other night with the brick and about the dogs over the back being baited.

"Yes, Noel told me about the dogs, but not the connection to you. I'm so angry that someone would do that to that poor old lady's dogs. And what does that mean for you? That he wants to come back and doesn't want dogs barking and letting everyone know he's there?"

The front door opened then, and Noel called out, "Just us." He disappeared into the kitchen while the dogs clambered in to greet us as enthusiastically as when I'd first arrived.

"I'm being very careful about leaving these two out in the yard now. Even though from what you've said it sounds like that wasn't just a random act, I would be devastated if anything happened to my babies," Nicki said.

"Yeah, that's a good idea. It can't hurt to be careful. So, Nicki, have you and Sue still been in touch since she left?"

"No, I tried to get a number for her, but haven't been able to. All I know is that she went back to the station that she'd just come from."

"Oh that's a shame. That would probably have been embarrassing for her–going back. Did she say anything else before she left? Did she ever say if she suspected anyone?"

Nicki thought for a moment and then raised a finger, "I think there was more she wanted to tell me when she called in just as she was leaving town. She was a bit flustered and didn't make a lot of sense. She started to say something about boots, something like 'I could smell the shit on them', but when I asked what she meant, she just said, *I don't want to be seen as a victim Nicki. I'm sorry, I've got to go.*"

Noel either had very good timing or had strategically been listening for the right moment to re-join us. He emerged from the kitchen just as Nicki finished speaking. I looked at my watch and saw that it was getting late, so I stood up to prepare to leave. I thanked them again for dinner and we walked together to the front door. Nicki pulled me in for a hug, saying, "Don't forget, you can come for a chat anytime."

Leaving their house, I felt slightly less alone, but my head was spinning with all of the new information that I'd learned over dinner. Especially those strange words of Sue's, about the 'shitty boots'.

I knew my next step. I needed to find her.

CHAPTER 18

Meeting Blueeyes

On the drive up to Noosa, I have twice resisted the urge to turn around and abandon the meet-up with Marcus–alias Blueeyes. I had such a good feeling after meeting Guy yesterday that I can't imagine I'd be lucky enough to meet two people in two days, who are both lovely. However, I really don't like people saying that they're going to do something and then not doing it, and I feel it would be very bad form to pull out of this meeting at the last minute, so I eventually arrive and park in the street, a few doors down from our rendezvous.

Les Beaux Rêves Pâtisserie et Café is in a beautiful old cottage, which has been newly painted in a gleaming white, with a bright pink Bougainvillea being trained to grow up the front and side walls. As the café has only newly been renovated and opened, the plants are still quite small, but the little sprays of pink give a preview of the dazzling display they will eventually create as they creep their way up the trestles and contrast their beautiful pinks and greens onto the stark white background.

As I walk briskly along the footpath I glance at my watch before crossing to the other side of the road. I'm two minutes early, but I imagine he would also be here by now. As I enter, the aromas of coffee, vanilla and freshly baked pastries caress my nostrils. I take a deep breath and enjoy the delectable smells as I look around for a middle-aged man on his own. All of the tables are taken, and I spot him sitting at a table in the corner, looking down at his phone.

He glances up and sees me approaching and gives me a wave. It's tricky to convert the online photo image to a real-life person, but the fact that he seems to be the only guy of the right age and general description in the café alone, makes it a lot easier. Walking up to some innocent guy sitting there trying to have a quiet coffee and read his emails would be embarrassing.

"Hi," he says, standing and motioning to the other chair at the table for me to sit. He doesn't move to shake hands or hug me. "I'm Marcus. You must be Tess."

"Hi Marcus. Great to meet you," I say as I sit opposite him and take a close up look at his face. He seems to be wearing those glasses that have transitional lenses. The café is brightly lit so the lenses are quite tinted and I'm finding it difficult to see his eyes. He did advertise their blueness, so I really want to check them out.

I believe people's eyes tell so much about them. I like to look people in the eye when I'm talking to them, to be able to get an idea of what they're really like. And not least of all, to see if their smile carries through to their eyes–and if they crinkle at the corners when they laugh or smile. *Guy's did,* I can't help but think, as a memory of his face flashes through my mind's eye.

"Should we go up and order first and then have a chat?" he asks.

"Yes, it seems really busy," I reply. "I'm bursting to see what amazing pastries and cakes they have."

We line up behind another couple and check out the display cabinet in front of us. He doesn't talk while we're waiting, and I feel a little awkward, but soon it's our turn to order. Everything in the cabinet looks so enticing–so picture perfect–so *French.* There are little squares and triangles that are an ideal size for someone who can't decide which one to choose, or for a child, and then the massive profiteroles and mille feuille with glistening icing and dustings of bright white icing sugar.

I can't decide, so I order two of the smaller cakes and my usual coffee. Marcus quietly inspects the range and finally decides on a mille feuille (although he calls it a vanilla slice even though it has a little sign with its name on it). He obviously doesn't speak French, or even want to have a shot at pronouncing it. It should be interesting watching him eat this though. There is potential for him to end up with icing sugar from ear to ear. I certainly wouldn't choose something like that at a first meeting with someone. He also orders a hot chocolate. His choices lead me to think that he's definitely not a health freak and not watching his weight.

He looks quite trim for a guy of 55. (If he really is 55 that is. My experience with Perry has made me suspicious of the validity of the information people put up about themselves now.) He's got light brown hair that is about half grey, but there's plenty of it, with no signs of balding. He's generally attractive but I just wish I could see his eyes properly. I have a vague sense of having seen him before somewhere, but I have no idea where.

As we sit back down at the table, he jumps straight in without any chit-chat–like he has a prepared list of questions. "So what do you want to get out of this online dating business?"

I look him in the eye (well, the glasses really), and say, "Wow Marcus, you're straight in with the hard questions. I can't really answer that because I don't even know. Sometimes I question being on there at all and feel quite happy on my own, but other times I feel like I'd like to share things with someone–to have someone caring and close enough to really talk to, on a deeper level than just small talk. How about you? Seems like you're not one for small talk after that question."

"Yeah, I'm not a hundred percent sure but she needs to be attractive and open-minded and not hung up on her ex." This comment is making me feel a bit uncomfortable. It's sounding very egotistical and demanding. "What's your situation with your ex–presuming that you have one?" he adds.

"Sure I have one," I answer, noting a slightly defensive tone in my voice, "and we get on fine." There's no way I'm going to go into details with this guy after just meeting him 10 minutes ago and feeling a sense of futility in sharing information with him because his questions and attitude are pretty much telling me that we're not going to get along. I also can't help comparing him to Guy and finding him lacking in so many ways already. I figure he wants me to ask him about his ex, but I really don't want to oblige, and I'm not interested, so I try changing the subject to something more general.

"You mentioned that you have kids in your message. Do you see them much?"

"No. My bitch of an ex has turned all the kids against me. They won't let me near the grandkids either."

I'm shocked that he's just launched into bad-mouthing his ex, but then I find that he's only just started as he continues, "She's the one who's got problems. She's on so many prescription drugs that she shouldn't be allowed near them. She's paranoid."

I'm not sure how to handle this. Marcus is getting a little agitated and I can see he's jiggling his leg up and down like he's nervous or something. As I'm looking down at his jumpy leg, I notice that his pant leg has risen up slightly and I can clearly see a bulky, grey band around his ankle.

Alarm bells start ringing in my head as I try to look anywhere but down in that direction–hoping that he didn't notice that I'd noticed. That band screams electronic monitoring for an offender on parole or probation. All I want to do is leave but I don't want to cause a scene or alert him. *Is this why he seems familiar to me? Have I arrested this guy sometime in the past?*

Just then the waitress arrives with our food and I'm incredibly glad of the distraction. I sip my coffee and regret ordering two cakes. I have no appetite now and looking at them makes me feel nauseous. For appearances sake I nibble on a couple of bites and grab the serviette to wrap up the rest, saying, "Wow, I think my eyes were bigger than my stomach. These are very rich. I might just take the rest home for later."

"Yes, I noticed you weren't eating much." Marcus sprays icing sugar over the table as he speaks.

I'm calculating in my head how long I need to sit here to be polite, or what kind of excuse I can make to get out of here quickly. I figure I can't walk out while he's in the middle of spreading his mille feuille all over his face and the table (flakes and crumbs have now joined the icing sugar in both positions), so I decide to make a trip to the ladies to give myself some space to think, and to pass some time so that hopefully he has finished his demolition work by the time I get back.

In the peace and refuge of the sterile environment of the newly tiled toilet I can finally take a breath–albeit a strong, lemon disinfectant filled one. I dread going back out there and sitting down, only to have to pretend to want to make conversation, whilst counting down the minutes until I can depart in an unspectacular fashion.

I take a moment to consider whether there could be a reasonable (and acceptable) explanation for why he would be wearing an electronic tracker, but I'm finding it difficult. My mind is ticking off all types of crimes that would be considered suitable for an ankle monitor–nothing on my mental list is a minor offence. Most of them involve aggression or assault and that is the last thing I need in my life. I have been there and done that and do not want to re-visit. But there's something about his face and his demeanour that I can't put my finger on.

Strangely, the thought hits me that I might never want to come back here to this wonderful new French café after this experience and I feel a bit cheated. He's tainted my only chance at a first impression, and I don't even remember tasting the half a mini-pastry that I ate just now.

I remind myself that this guy doesn't know that I used to be a police officer, so I'm at least thankful that we haven't had a lot of small talk, or talked about what kind of work we do, although he did ask in one of his initial messages, but my answer was vague. I assure myself that he really doesn't know much about me at all–and I plan to keep it that way. If I can just hang in there for another fifteen or twenty minutes... Then I have an idea. My friend Marta could be my excuse to get away. I quickly send her a text and ask her to ring me in ten minutes. She replies *Ok. You alright? xx*

Yes, I'll explain later. Thanks xx

When I head back to the table, I notice Marcus is looking down at his ankle and pulling down his pant leg to cover the bulky attachment. I feel like turning around and retreating back to my lemon-scented sanctuary, but before I can even attempt that, he looks up and sees me seeing him pulling his trouser leg down. I force myself to smile and walk toward our table and sit.

"Ah, look..." he says glancing down to his ankle, "this is coming off in a couple of days. It was all a big mistake, and it wasn't my fault. I didn't do anything wrong. My wife lied to the police and got her crazy friends to back her up and I ended up being charged with something I didn't do."

I am curious to know what the charge was but feel the need to ask in a light-hearted kind of way. "Oh that's rough," I say. "What did they reckon you did?"

"Had me charged with break and enter but I still had a key, and it used to be my place anyway, so it can't be break and enter. I only went there to look for something that was mine that I knew she'd hidden from me when I moved out a couple of years ago." Then he looks directly at me and says in an awkwardly upbeat tone, "Hey, you're not a copper or something are you? You never did tell me what your job is."

This strange attempt at a joke and the interest in my work is making me very uncomfortable. I can't help wondering if there is a reason that he's mentioned being a copper, but I'm not going to give him any more information about myself. Plus, I wasn't buying this story–that wasn't a serious enough offence to deserve an ankle monitor, unless he did something else during the break and enter, like assault someone. Of course, there's no way I'm going to let him know that I'm not convinced, so I say, "Well, hopefully that's all behind you now."

I pick up my cup to take another sip of my coffee and am suddenly in two minds as to whether I should even drink it as it had been sitting on the table while I'd been in the loo. *Could he have done something to it? Would a person do something like that in a coffee shop– in broad daylight? Doesn't that only happen in bars?*

The path of the coffee cup from the table to my mouth seems like a marathon and the questions in my mind are relentless – *should I, should I not?* Just as the cup reaches my lips, my phone rings. *Thank you Marta!* I silently shout.

I quickly lower the cup back to its saucer and grab my phone. "Sorry, I'll have to take this. I'm on call," I say, sounding like an emergency doctor or something else indispensable. "Oh, no… ok, yes I'll get back as soon as I can. Don't worry… ok, yeah… thanks." God knows what Marta thought about that string of nonsense, but I plan to ring her back as soon as I get out to the van.

"I'm really sorry but work has gone crazy and I'm going to have to get back," I say, hoping he doesn't ask me again what 'work' is. I grab my bag and start digging around for my wallet, saying, "Hey, let me get this on my way out, seeing as I'm running off. Take your time and enjoy the rest of your hot chocolate." He still has a stray crumb and a dusting of white icing sugar shadowed by a line of dark brown from the chocolate, on his top lip.

Surprisingly, he says, "No, I'll pay for this. Maybe I'll let you get the next one."

Mate, there ain't going to be a next one, I think, but instead say, "Thanks, see you later."

"I'll message you," he says as I'm half-way to the door.

I turn and wave, avoiding an actual answer and trying to hurry but not look like I am, as I head out onto the street. I breathe a sigh of relief and hurry down and across the road to my van. Once inside I lower the window to let the warm air escape. I turn to grab the seat belt and glance out the window as I pull the strap across my body, ready to clip it into place. What I see makes me freeze mid-movement. Marcus is standing outside the café, with his phone held up in both hands and angled toward me, as though taking a photo of my van–the one with the beautifully crafted logo and motif telling everyone my business name and location.

I am hit by waves of disturbing memories and *that sound,* rolling relentlessly through my mind. *Click, click, click.* My heart pounds and I realise that I've not only stopped moving–I've also stopped breathing. After a moment, my lungs struggle for a breath and I break the trance and snap into action, taking off so quickly that I almost collect a cyclist as I pull out onto the road. *Maybe it's nothing. Maybe he was taking a photo of something else. Maybe he just thought the artwork was really good.* The alternative does not bear thinking about… not for a second time.

CHAPTER 19
Offline

'Marta, oh God, Marta, I need to talk to you.' This is the third time I've rung her now and I've left a voice message each time. I've also texted asking her to call me. I pocket my phone, put the van back into gear and pull out onto the road again. I want to drive straight to her place, but I know she'll be at work. All I can do is wait. I decide that I need to just get myself home and try to calm down.

After I left the café and each time I pulled over to use my phone, I had enough of my wits about me to check the rear-view mirror to see if anyone (Marcus) was following me. I'm pretty sure the coast was clear in that regard, and I presume that if he's so inclined, he probably figures he knows where to find me. I don't feel much relief at not being followed, just bewilderment and concern about what the hell he was doing and why.

For the rest of the drive home I try my best to concentrate on the road, but I can't help mentally cursing the fact that I couldn't afford to have a car for private use, as well as the work van. I've always wanted to–always felt too exposed driving around in a van with my business name and the suburb on it, but I'm also businesswoman enough to know that the advertising power of a sign like that is too valuable to ignore.

Somehow, I see my way through the cobwebs of past images mixed with the new image of Marcus standing with his phone directed at me. An image which has now been branded into my brain along with the horrors of the past. I hear the shutter click, over and over in my mind. I make it home without injuring myself–or anyone else.

* * *

I shakily drop my keys onto the hall table and head straight for my laptop on the kitchen bench. I sit on one of the stools and force myself to take a deep breath, talking myself through the techniques I've learned over the years to cope with rising fear and anxiety.

My breathing settles into a strong and steady rhythm and my mind begins to function somewhat rationally again. I allow myself to consider the possibility that I may have over-reacted. Perhaps I've jumped to conclusions that are totally wrong. His reasons for taking that photo could be innocent. His interest in my work could be normal. His obscure familiarity could be coincidental. But then I think again of the tracker on his ankle. He's been guilty of *something*–or at least he's been convicted of something. Something of a nature that warrants that kind of monitoring. I feel my face start to heat up and my heart rate speed up again.

I try Marta again, with no success. I open my laptop and sign into Wings Online. There are things I can do to block *Blueeyes* and I need to do something *right now*–something proactive, to protect myself.

In the few weeks that I've been on this dating site I've learned that when someone looks at my profile, their action will show up on an activity list for me to see. I also realise that when I look at someone else's profile, I'll show up on *their* list. I've found that a bit off-putting on the occasions where I've thought someone looked ok and then when I clicked on them and read their profile it was obvious that they were totally unsuitable. I didn't want people like that thinking I was interested in them because I'd clicked on them.

To avoid that, I've started blocking any that I look at that seem unsavoury. Like *TeddyB* whose profile when I clicked into it, just went on about how tactile he was, and what a good kisser, and how a relationship needed to be physical. And *Smarties* who simply wrote *I want pretty and intelligent, if that's you then apply now!* I didn't imagine he would be receiving many 'applications'.

Last week I discovered that I could copy and paste profile photos and information and save them in a file offline. I did this with Guy's information so that I could go back and read bits I might have forgotten, without him getting notified every time I clicked on his profile (and thinking that I was fixated, or a person with a very bad memory). The knowledge that I could do this alleviated my poor memory problem, but then raised new concerns for me that other people might do this with my profile–even saving photos of me. It made me feel uncomfortable and I vowed to get off this platform as soon as I met someone decent.

Since it was only yesterday that I'd met Guy and felt good about him, I'd been thinking I should wait a bit longer to be sure, but now I can't bear the thought of Marcus, or who knows what other kind of weirdos, looking at my photos and profile. *I feel exposed and unsafe– I want to crawl into my old familiar shell–back into anonymity.*

My mind feels foggy and my limbs suddenly heavy. The blood pounding in my temples makes it hard to think. *Slow down,* I tell myself and my mind clears enough to prompt me to save a photo of this person (just in case my worst fears are justified, and I need it to show the police). Trying to select a photo where his face is distinguishable is difficult as the glasses hide his eyes in all of them. Feeling a palpable urgency to get this over and done with quickly, I select the best two and copy them to my laptop. I block him and take down my profile entirely.

With *Fiori* no longer online, I let go of a breath that I hadn't even realised I'd been holding–and shut down the computer.

Finally, Marta rings about an hour later. She's concerned and apologetic, explaining that she couldn't ring or text me back because she was called out on an urgent job. She knows that I'd never ring her at work unless it was really important, and the fact that I'd rung her four times has her on high alert.

"What's going on Tess? Your messages sounded frantic."

"*Oh Marta.* I've just met up with that *Blueeyes* bloke and he's some kind of *crim.* I should have just cancelled. I was tempted to but thought it would be rude. Rude? Bloody hell, he's wearing an ankle monitor and I'm worried about being *rude*?"

"Slow down. What do you mean? You're kidding, right? Someone wearing an ankle monitor to a first date and expecting that to go well?"

"I think he was trying to hide it. He had long pants… anyway besides all that he was dodgy. He seemed strangely familiar, and he kept asking about my work. The way he talked about his ex was nasty and then I spotted the monitor and went to the loo and texted you. When I got back, he knew that I'd clocked the tracker, so he tried to lie about it. Jokingly asked if I was a *copper*. Thank goodness you rang when you did–I really needed to get out of there." I take a breath and continue before Marta has a chance to speak, "But that's not the worst of it. I got back to the van and saw him standing outside the café taking a photo of me on his phone!"

"Wait, wait. Are you sure that's what he was doing?"

"Had to be. He was holding it up in both hands and looking in my direction."

"Looking for reception, maybe?"

"Nup. It's freaked me out. I knew this online dating shit was a mistake."

"Ok, I know this must seem threatening, especially to you, and with good reason, but it could still be totally innocent. Let's think of some things we can do to make you feel safer." She doesn't need to mention my past. I know that she understands why this has set off alarm bells for me.

"I've already blocked him online and taken down my profile. I haven't given him my mobile number, but he could easily find the shop number if he wanted. The name and suburb are all over the van."

"Yeah, but if he sees you're not online any more that might be the end of it. Did he say he'd be in touch or anything?"

"Said he'd message me."

"Ok, so when he can't, he'll hopefully move on to someone else. Hey, you're gorgeous but not that gorgeous," she jokes, trying to lighten my mood.

"Yeah, I guess, but you know what? I think I'll get those security cameras on the shop like you suggested a while back." Marta has fitted security cameras on my home and has asked me if I'd like her to do the same at work. My home is a fortress, but I've neglected security at the shop. Now seems like a good time to take her up on the offer.

"Good. I'll get the same ones that we used at your place and get them up as soon as I can."

"Thanks. I'll feel better with those up, especially when we're working late."

"Ok, I need to get back to work. Are you ok? Do you want me to come around later or something?"

"I'm ok. Cinta's coming around after work so I should be fine. I told her last night that I was on this online dating site, and she wants to hear about Guy."

"Oh, you told her? How did that go? And you haven't told me what he's like yet either."

"She seemed fine, and he seems really nice. I was on a bit of a high after meeting him and now this has brought me back down to earth with a crash. I'll tell you all about him soon though. Off you go–I'm really sorry to have bothered you at work–but so glad to be able to talk."

"You know I'm always here–well, when you can get hold of me anyway!" she laughs.

CHAPTER 20

Night Moves

Before my first night shift at Burmont, I packed an overnight bag to take with me. Russell wouldn't give up on talking me into staying over at his place for the week, so I finally agreed to go to his house after each shift, sleep there and go back home when he left for work each morning. Otherwise, I would have been bored silly sitting around someone else's house all day. Besides there was a lot of stuff I needed to do at home during the day.

My other proviso, in order to make sure that his mates didn't presume that we were 'sleeping together' was that I used the little room at the end of the verandah. I could see the disappointment on his face when I insisted on that condition, so I added, "There may be some visitation rights though. *As long as they're quiet.*"

I planned to do a lot of work in the garden during the week seeing as I'd have the whole day off before I was due to start work each day at four. I'd already started cutting back the bushes around the front pathway and had constructed a big pile of offcuts, but there was still a lot more to do. I felt much happier about the areas that

I'd cleared, and much safer. Once I'd finished the front, I planned to really get stuck into the trees around the back of the house.

I arrived at work a few minutes early, catching Noel and Geoff to say *hi* and *bye* as they were signing off on the day shift. I looked around, hoping not to see the boss. I hadn't had to face him since submitting my report a few days ago, blatantly ignoring his instructions. Thankfully, it seemed that he'd left for the day.

Geoff called out to Ray who was already sitting at his desk busily poking away at his typewriter with his index fingers, "Have fun with the new girl mate."

I didn't appreciate this comment, not only because of the inuendo but because he was calling me *the new girl.* It sounded dismissive. In the scheme of things though it didn't come close to some of the names I'd been called since putting on the pale blue uniform. Both by colleagues and members of the public. At one station I was called *the fluff* or *the skirt* and at another, a *dyke.* The first time a member of the public called me a *pig* I felt insulted, but I soon learned not to let those cheap insults affect me. I knew it was the uniform they were trying to rile against, so after a few years I'd almost become used to names such as *sow, oinker, filth* and *dickless tracy.*

Ray turned around and waved to the guys, then turned to me and said, "Don't let him get to you. He's just a stirrer."

"Yeah, I've figured that out already," I said, dropping my gear on my desk.

Senior Constable Ray Neuman was my partner for the next five late shifts. We hadn't said more than a couple of words to each other up until that point, so I felt a bit awkward about the prospect of spending all of that time with him. I also recalled that Noel and Nicki said he was quiet, so that made me dread that having conversations with him might be like trying to get blood out of a stone. I was glad that at least I knew that he had a wife and a little boy. Perhaps I could ask him about them if we were stuck for something to talk about.

I was encouraged by his opening words though, so I continued the conversation asking, "Any jobs left over from day shift for us?"

"Probably just the shitty ones they didn't want to do. There's a couple of jobs on the log there," he pointed in that general direction and turned back to his typewriter prodding. "Give me a few minutes. I've got to finish this report."

When everyone else had left, the station felt too quiet–almost eerie. The only sound was the painfully slow tap, tap, tap of Ray's typing. I often had to resist the urge to put some of these guys out of their misery by offering to type their reports for them. What took them an hour, would take me about ten minutes. But I knew that would be a silly thing to do. It would make me look like a secretary and give them a sense of superiority.

So I decided to block out the sound by starting on some paperwork of my own. I didn't get very far before we were disturbed by the phone and the first of several jobs on a busy night for the little country town.

* * *

After four nights of working with Ray, I felt much more comfortable in his company. Yes, he was quiet, but he had begun to relax around me a bit and started telling me stories about his little boy and the silly things he got up to. Most nights hadn't been as busy as the first night when we had an accident with serious injuries to attend, some complaints about hoons to follow up on, and a disturbance at the pub, which resulted in the town drunk spending another night in our cell.

On nights when there was not much happening, after we'd come back from our regular patrols, we would play backgammon. I was fiercely competitive and so was Ray, so we ended up having some hard-fought battles. I really enjoyed it. I shouldn't have been worried about how the night shifts would go–they were much more fun than the days.

Having more time at the station, with less people around I'd been able to do some checking into Brian. Russell's mate Brooksie came through with a surname for me, so I'd been able to see if he had any kind of criminal record. I wasn't quite sure whether I felt relieved or disappointed to find that there was no record of him on file. I was half-expecting to find that he'd been charged with some kind of harassment or assault.

The night shift week had been uneventful in that regard. I'd had no new notes in my letterbox and no sign of anyone hanging around during the day when I was at home. I couldn't help but wonder if it would be different if I were going home to my place after my shifts, and whether there would be noises in the night or someone lurking in the shadows when I unlocked my front door. I allowed myself to be cautiously hopeful that maybe these things would stop happening, but I still thought it would be wise to find Sue Ryan and see if she would talk to me.

To this end, I tracked down the station that she was transferred back to and rang in my official capacity, to ask if I could speak to her, if she was on duty. I was told that she no longer worked there, and that in fact she had resigned. Apparently, she had given notice on her first day back at the station, served out her minimum two weeks and then left town. I asked if there was some way that I could contact her. After assuring the officer that it was about official police business, I was given a phone number. I hadn't quite worked out exactly how to approach her, so I hadn't called the number yet. I also didn't want anyone else around when I talked to her.

Each night when I went home to Russell's place, I made sure to walk along the verandah up to the little room at the end, in case anyone was listening, and then quietly tip-toe down to his room a bit later to snuggle into his warm, sleepy body. He was always the first one up in the mornings, so I knew that I could sneak back to 'my' room before anyone saw me. Russell kept telling me I was crazy, but I just felt better, keeping up the façade of propriety.

Ahead of my final shift of night duty, I felt some disappointment as it would be the last night with an excuse to go to Russell's. It would seem quite strange going back to my own bed at night and to be sleeping alone again. I found that I was getting used to sharing a bed and felt reluctant to change that, especially after the previous night.

Russell was awake when I'd snuck into his room that night and we talked in hushed voices and kissed for what seemed like hours. Every other night, we had kissed a bit and cuddled a lot, resisting the temptation to take things further. This time though, his soft whispers and tender kisses and hard, warm body melted my resolve and our clothes somehow disappeared without any effort. We explored each other's bodies in the soft light of the three-quarter moon until I felt like I might explode with desire, and then we made love with an urgency and need that had been simmering since that first time we kissed.

The next morning, I felt like just lying in his bed with him all day and luxuriating in the memory of our intimacy–*and reliving it.* Russell didn't want to leave either and offered to take a sickie so we could stay in bed all day. Then he remembered that he had an urgent job that his uncle needed him to finish by lunchtime. We reluctantly dragged ourselves out of bed and dressed.

* * *

That same night, in that same three-quarter moonlight, a shadowy figure moved stealthily around the back of the little cottage on Millhouse Road.

He wished it were darker and cursed her for clearing away many of the branches and bushes that had previously afforded him cover.

Counting on the fact that the neighbours would be asleep and there were no dogs around now to alert the residents to his presence, he set to work–laying the groundwork, so that when the time came, he could move quickly and quietly. He would need to be quick and methodical. He couldn't risk being seen.

He knew that she was not inside the cottage. She had proved that he was right about her. She was sleeping at the boilermaker's house now, sleeping with him.

She was just like the other one–like all of them. Sluts.

CHAPTER 21
Terror

Working out in the garden before my last night shift, I found myself continuously daydreaming and savouring those wonderful hours of closeness that Russell and I had shared in the night. After another long idle period, I brought myself back to the clearing of the branches at the back of the house, a task I'd been working on since I'd arrived home at around seven that morning. I should have had it finished long ago, but my constant distraction had slowed me down and sapped my motivation. At lunchtime I decided to call it a day and take some time out to relax before work.

I ran the shower and started undressing, almost reluctant to get into the shower and wash off the faintly lingering scent of Russell, but I knew I must–I had to go to work in a couple of hours.

Wetting my hair so that I could wash it, I wondered if I heard a clunking noise at the side of the house. I wiped my eyes with the towel and listened but couldn't hear anything, so I reached for the shampoo and worked it through my hair. Then I heard another noise–much closer this time. *It sounded like it came from inside the house.*

I reached for the towel on the rack next to the shower, but a vice-like grip halted my arm and pushed it downwards, causing me to half crouch and struggle to retain balance. I screamed and tried to open my eyes. Stinging, and an impenetrable veil of shampoo the only result. I couldn't see anything. My throat was on fire and my mouth full of the vile, soapy taste of shampoo–I presumed I was screaming but couldn't hear anything except a pounding in my ears that must have been my own heartbeat. I reached for my eyes with my other hand, trying to clear the suds–struggling to see.

I clawed at my eyes, trying again to open them, and finally I could see some blurry outlines of a person. What I saw in that moment became burned into my brain–branded–never to be *un-seen*. Forever haunting me in my dreams and nightmares.

A dark shape… Tall… Bulky… Black balaclava…Sunglasses… Thick navy pullover… Jeans… Black boots… Black gloved hands holding a white cloth. The stinging made me squint and blink–I didn't want to lose sight of the shape, but my eyes wouldn't cooperate. I kicked awkwardly from my half-crouched position, toward what I blearily presumed was the groin of the shape, just as some kind of cloth covered my face. I felt hard pressure over my mouth and nose. I tried not to breathe. My lungs burning, I had to inhale. I smelt something foul. I struggled and squirmed. Suddenly the thought that I was naked hit me like a bolt of lightning. I intended to struggle harder but then my world blacked out.

I opened my eyes. I knew I was opening them because I could feel my lids and lashes hitting something as I strained to find some light or shape through the heavy blackness that was pressing down on my eyes. My mind was fuzzy, and my head pounded relentlessly, but I knew I needed to reach up and pull whatever it was off my eyes.

I engaged the muscles that would normally do that, but my arms did not move. I momentarily wondered if I was somehow paralysed, until I felt the resistance against my wrists. They were bound, but I discovered that I could move my fingers. They searched for something to identify by feel. Mattress, timber bed frame, mine I thought from the feel of it.

Legs. I remembered them and struggled against the restraints that I could feel holding them. To my horror, I then realised that they were spread wide. I could feel the air on my skin. I gasped, struggling to remember what had happened, hoping that somehow I was clothed–but knowing that I was not. The attack in the shower was vivid in my mind but after that–nothing. I felt like I must be strapped to the corners of the bed. A Vitruvian man flashed through my brain and I whimpered at the thought.

My sight useless, I tried to hear but there was no sound. That prompted me to try screaming. Only when I attempted to open my mouth did I realise that it was also covered and clamped shut–the effort causing my jaw to crack and begin to ache and my head to pound even more painfully. I tried to scream without opening my mouth but found that only made an ineffective noise that would not carry even to the next room. I tried to form words but failed.

I felt sure that there must be someone there, but they were making no sound, so I couldn't gauge their position. They had not spoken, and although I felt my hearing must be super-sensitive to make up for my lack of vision, I could not hear breathing or movement of any kind. The only sound a car passing and a bird call in the distance. *How could there be everyday sounds like that just carrying on as normal while this was happening to me?*

Then I heard it. A zipper, I was sure. The sound was short and crisp and filled me with dread, imagining jeans or trousers as the source. I struggled and made as much muffled noise as I could before a forceful blow hit the side of my face, jolting my head sideways. I braced myself for the unthinkable onslaught that I imagined would follow, all the time trying to squeeze my legs together. The best I could manage was to bring my knees slightly towards each other.

Then another sound reached my ears–a shutter snapping. New and different horror joined the fear of sexual assault or rape.

I was being photographed in that state–naked. I felt so totally helpless that tears began to leak from the sides of my eyes. I felt unable to breathe. The disturbing sounds continued–*click–click–click–my muffled cries–click–click.* I tracked the sound from my right side, to down near my feet. I struggled more to pull my knees together, twisting my body sideways, imagining the explicit nature of the photographs from that angle. With the tiniest measure of relief, I heard the clicking move to my left. There was still no other sound–not a word from the sick and cruel creature.

Then a pungent smell transported me back to the shower. I had smelt that before–when the cloth covered my face. Pressure over my nose–then blackness again.

* * *

I awoke with my stomach heaving and rolled quickly to the side, vomiting on the floor beside my bed. My head felt like my brain had doubled in size and was pounding the sides of my skull with force in time with each heartbeat. My first thought was my nakedness. I grabbed the sheet beneath me to cover myself, even though I sensed that I was alone. I was no longer bound, but I could see no sign of the ties or tape that must have been used to restrain and blindfold me.

I rolled to the other side of the bed and felt pain in other parts of my body, my head, my right arm, my wrists and ankles, but I did not feel any of the pain or tenderness I'd expected to confirm my worst fears. He hadn't sexually assaulted me. I felt so relieved–until I remembered the camera sounds. Someone had taken photos of me, totally naked–sprawled and exposed in that vulnerable position. I was mortified. My brain whirling with images. I couldn't bear to think about what this person was going to do with them.

I could see that my room was clear so I carefully moved into the tiny hallway, listening for any signs that someone might still have been in the house. Furtively, I checked the other bedroom and forced myself to enter the bathroom, at least far enough in to check that there was no one hiding in there, before stepping down to the back annexe and checking the laundry and toilet. I found no one there, but it became obvious how the intruder had broken into my house. Several louvre blades were missing from the toilet window. He must have removed them and climbed through while I was in the shower with the water running to muffle any noise.

I continued to quickly check the house, finding it empty and nothing else out of place, except that the front door was wide open. I presumed that this person had brazenly walked out my front door and down the path to the street and freedom. The knowledge that they had taken my dignity with them and a film with explicit photos of my body, burned in my chest like a hot coal, its heat flushing up through my neck and face and bringing tears to my eyes. I slammed the door shut and collapsed in a heap on the floor, sobbing and hugging my sheet tightly around me.

As I sat in my cocoon, the whole episode played out in my mind over and over. I tried to think about what I saw and heard. I found myself trying to force some memory of words spoken by this person, of their voice, even though I knew they didn't speak a word. I wondered why. *Did they think I would recognise their voice? Could it even have been a woman?* I pieced together the blurry images of the figure that attacked me in the shower. Something was nagging at me–some little detail, but I didn't know what. I felt sure that it was a man though. The size and strength could not have belonged to a woman.

Suddenly I realised that I'd been having a shower because I was supposed to be going to work. Although it was still daylight, I had no idea of what time it might be or how long I had been unconscious. I moved to the bathroom in search of my watch and again felt reluctant to go into that room, even though I knew it was safe. I wondered how I might ever feel safe in my own house again.

I desperately wanted to have a shower. The thought that someone had their hands on me, gloved or naked I didn't know–I just needed to wash it off. But there was no way I could coax myself into that shower. I tried, but I couldn't even reach in and turn on the tap. At that moment, I couldn't imagine a time when I would be able to do that again. I located my watch and checked the time. It was just after two-thirty. I felt like it should be much later–so much had happened in just over two hours. I knew that I couldn't possibly go to work. I needed to get to a phone to call in sick. Then, there was another number I needed to ring.

CHAPTER 22
Building Blocks

I drove to Russell's knowing he'd be home from work soon. Tama was there, so he let me in. I told him I would wait for Russell in his room, all the while keeping my face turned to the side so he wouldn't notice the bright red mark on my cheek and hoping that my sunglasses masked the slight swelling to my right eye. Thankfully he seemed busy and didn't want to stop for a chat. He closed the front door and left me alone to gather my clothes and toiletries. I packed my overnight gear back into my bag and sat on Russell's bed waiting for him to come home. I planned to have a very quick shower at Russell's and then drive to Agnes Water straight away–to see Sue. My leg jiggled uncontrollably as I sat waiting, and my mind wouldn't stop replaying the attack. I really needed to talk to Sue–I couldn't help wondering if she might know exactly what I had just gone through.

I knew Russell would be supportive, but I also knew he'd want me to stay. I felt like I couldn't just sit around and not be doing something to find out who broke into my home, assaulted me and took explicit and embarrassing photos of me naked like that. I couldn't think about it without rage filling me and my stomach churning. The bleary images of that shape flashed through my mind, while my brain struggled to identify the nagging feeling that something from those images should scream at me. That I was missing something important.

I heard someone pull up and looked out the window to see Russell about to start up the stairs. I ran to the door to meet him and threw my arms around him before he could get through the door.

"Oh God Russ, I'm so glad you're here," I muffled into his neck.

"*Hey.*" He hugged me but then pushed me out to arms' length so he could see my face. "What's wrong? Shouldn't you be just about at work by now? Whoa, what's happened to your face?"

I shushed him and led him into his room and closed the door, my demeanour indicating that I was not doing so with romantic intentions, my face and voice serious as I told him about my ordeal. I held myself together for most of it, and at the times when I broke down, his arm around my shoulders comforted me and gave me the strength to finish.

I could see he was seething. "Honestly, I just want to find this Brian creep and punch his lights out!" he said as he stood up and slammed his fist onto the top of his chest of drawers. "Can't I at least do that?"

I'd told him that I'd ended up telling Noel and his wife about the notes and earlier incidents but that I hadn't put in an official report yet. "Surely now you have to make this official? Give the police that description and tell them about Brian."

I had to admit that I wanted to, but whilst my description could fit Brian, it was just a shape–it could be anyone. Male or female. Then there was the embarrassment and shame, even the thought of explaining the details of my position–*those photographs*, to a man–a colleague–even Noel, was too embarrassing a thought to tenant. I needed to talk to a woman–*one woman in particular.* I tried to explain this to Russell.

"Well at least don't go heading off this arv, it's too late in the day. Stay tonight and go find her in the morning. Does she even know you're coming to see her?" I could see his point–my rational mind had been telling me the same thing. It would be silly to head off so late in the afternoon. I'd arrive just on dark if I did. After more comforting and convincing from Russell, I finally agreed to wait.

"Ok, you're right. I should wait until morning, plus if you've got a hammer and some nails, I'd like to board up that window until I can get it fixed. I've been thinking that I should also go and see Mrs Vescovi and ask her if she saw anyone around my house today, but I needed some time to compose myself before I faced her. This person left by the front door–maybe she saw something. I'm not going to give her any details though. I'll just make up something about someone busting the louvres. But before that, I really want, and need to have a shower and I can't bring myself to do it at my place. Can I have one here?"

"Of course. I'll find you a towel."

"And another strange request. Would you mind waiting around outside the door for me?"

"Mate, that's not strange at all… considering. Of course I will." I was sure that under normal circumstances he'd have been offering to come in with me, but he obviously understood that this was not the time for that.

I showered as quickly as I could, feeling extremely uncomfortable in someone else's shower, but I felt the need to clean and scrub myself thoroughly, so it took me a while. I would even have liked to wash my hair, but that would be something that I'd have to approach slowly. I'd have to find a way to do it where I could keep my eyes open.

When I emerged, Russ was standing guard as promised. "You look squeaky clean babe," he said and raised my chin so that we were looking right at each other, his sea-green eyes scanning my face. "That looks like it's going to bruise up," he added as he ran a gentle finger down my cheek.

I leaned gingerly into his chest, saying, "It doesn't hurt too much so I'm hoping it doesn't bruise too badly. Thank you… for this and for being so understanding."

"Understanding? Bloody hell, I'm spewing. I just wish you could tell me that it definitely was Brian so I could go around and beat the shit out of that little prick."

"Yeah, me too. But it might not be him if he didn't even know Sue, or it's less likely anyway. We need more proof and hopefully she can help me to find some."

He walked with me back to his room and collected his keys and sunglasses. "Are you ok to come with me to board up the window or would you rather not go back there? Maybe you could see Mrs Vescovi and then wait in the car?"

"No, I need to go in. There's stuff I need to get from there, and I want to have a better look around for any kind of evidence."

"Ok. We'll have to stop off and get a piece of ply or something at the hardware on the way. I'll grab my tools and we can get this done so at least the place is secured."

We stopped firstly at a public phone booth and I called Sue's number for the second time that afternoon. Her boyfriend answered and passed the phone to her. The vague background that I had on her indicated that she'd moved in with her boyfriend at Agnes Water after her resignation.

She agreed that it would be better to go out there in the morning, so we planned for around 10am. She still didn't ask for any more details of why I wanted to see her. *I felt like she already knew.*

We stopped again on the way to Millhouse Road, at the hardware store. I stayed in the car while Russ ran in to pick up some supplies. At the best of times, hardware stores made me feel claustrophobic with endless shelves of unrecognisable *stuff,* and that musty smell–like a combination of dust, chook food, rotting potatoes and rat wee. The prospect of being confined in those little aisles with that smell was too much to even contemplate.

Instead, sitting there waiting, I again wondered what was going to happen to the photographs. Every time I thought about them my face turned red and I felt overwhelming embarrassment and a sense of total helplessness. It frustrated me that I couldn't just fix this. That's what I normally did when I had a problem–just fixed it, but this time, I didn't know how to do that.

I'd come to the conclusion that this person must have a darkroom of their own. A roll of film with photos like I imagined these were, could not be dropped at the Chemist for development like normal films were. I was also aware that there were particular chemical solutions that you needed to set up a darkroom and process your own films, so I felt a slight hope that in starting to know something about this person–their interest in photography, that would give me some direction on where to begin. Some research would tell me what chemicals and equipment were needed and where someone might buy them locally. It would be unlikely that they could be sourced in a small town like Burmont. I decided to start with some discreet questioning of photographic equipment suppliers in the bigger surrounding towns.

As we approached my cottage in the car, I felt like it had a dark grey cloud hanging over it, like a haunted house from a B-grade movie set. I had no desire to go inside ever again. But I had to.

Before we entered, we decided to have a look from the outside and make sure that Russell had bought enough timber to cover the window. He planned to put a barrier on the outside and one on the inside as well.

Walking down the side of the house, I wondered at the audacity of someone climbing through a window like that in broad daylight, and then I noticed that the pile of branches that I'd been building with my off-cuts had actually provided some cover, shielding the view of the toilet window from anyone in the street, and from Mrs Vescovi's house as well. I'd been trying to make it harder for someone to skulk or hide around my house and instead I'd ended up giving them a perfect screen.

I cursed my stupidity as I stood and waited for Russell to hammer the piece of ply over the window. Once that was securely boarded up,

I unlocked the front door and we moved inside. I hesitated to enter. Russell came and put his hand on my waist. "Come on, I'm here."

I'd left the house so quickly after I'd decided to go to Russell's that I didn't have a good look around for possible evidence. I was only focussed on making sure that there was no one in the house when I did my fearful checking. I needed to take my time and look at it differently, with my knowledge and training at the forefront of my mind, looking for anything unusual or suspicious.

We entered the small lounge and an overwhelming need to remove myself from the space washed over me. I found it hard to take a proper breath–my lungs felt like tiny, deflated balloons. I made the excuse to Russell that I wanted to see Mrs Vescovi first and scarpered out the door.

I could hear Russell hammering loudly as I knocked almost in rhythm on my next-door neighbour's door. Mrs Vescovi answered quickly, leading me to wonder if she didn't even need the knock on the door. She invited me in and offered me a cup of tea but I refused politely–telling her I was in a hurry. I wanted to get down to the reason for my visit without a lot of preamble. I left my sunglasses on to avoid the inevitable questioning that my bare face would have triggered.

"I was just wondering if you might have seen someone around my house just after lunchtime today. I found that someone had broken my louvres down the back and thought you might have seen or heard them."

She shook her head. "Oh that's terrible! No love. If it was after lunchtime I'd be having a little nap then. I didn't see anyone. Just you and that young man just now. Did they break in and steal anything?"

"No, nothing stolen," I replied stoically as I thought of all the intangible things that were stolen from me. "It might have just been kids, but you never know." I didn't want to scare her–I just wanted to get back to Russell and do another check of my house. Even with my best efforts, she kept me pinned with more questions for another five minutes before I could make my escape.

When I returned to the cottage, Russell was still scratching around and hammering in the toilet. The sounds of him helping me somehow fortified me with the courage to start my search. I slowly scanned each room. The fact that it was my house, and I knew where everything should be, would make it easier to pick up anything out of place. Even so, there was not a single thing of note, except for the louvre blades on the toilet floor. It struck me that this person had been meticulous in every way. They'd untied me and taken the bonds with them so that they couldn't be identified, and they'd covered every part of their body so that I couldn't describe them at all. Their skin, hair, eyes could have been any colour, their bulk or skinniness indistinguishable under that bulky jumper, the only tell-tale factor was their height, which seemed to be tallish, and their strength, which seemed to rule out a woman.

I'd been constantly trying to fathom their motive. *And why me?* It seemed obvious that it was about control but then I thought, *if it was a man, why did they not commit the most vile act of masculine control, and what I'd feared from the first terrifying moment of my attack–rape?* Of course, there would be the fear of leaving evidence and I knew from my training that even when rapists use condoms, there is usually other evidence left behind, such as hair, skin, dust or clothing fragments. But there could be so many other psychological, physical or external factors that I didn't know anything about. *How could I even begin to determine their motivation?* I felt my brain could explode from the number of competing theories that swirled around in my head.

Another theory that had just occurred to me was that his motive could be to shame and embarrass me. Possibly he even planned to use the photographs to blackmail me for money–or something else. I couldn't bear to think of anyone else seeing those photos. The threat of blackmail filled me with a new kind of dread.

Even though I'd found no evidence on my search of the cottage, I was mentally building a profile. This person was controlling, and also had self-control; they were cruel, clever, tall and strong; most likely male and interested in photography.

That was all I had to start with. I was hoping Sue could help me build the profile further. Although no one had mentioned that she'd experienced anything more than some creepy notes and the sense of someone watching her, I had a feeling that we had more in common than that.

CHAPTER 23
Road Trip

I slipped a cassette into the player in my Kingswood and The Angels blared out of my open windows. They suited my mood on this trip. Their album *Face to Face* was in your face and cried out to be played loud–but that was The Angels in general.

As I listened to the lyrics, I thought about how people often find meaning in songs, even just snippets, that suit what's going on in their lives at the time. Half the time I couldn't even make out the lyrics but when I turned the volume up even louder to listen to *Take a Long Line*, the words grabbed at me, *finger on a photo... shadow... called him agitator, spy and thief.* I thought of what had been stolen from me by this shadowy spy. My confidence had been shattered, my body had been exposed and photographed, to be exposed over and over again at this sick person's whim.

There I was, making my way on my own for the first time in my life and feeling so independent, and so happy about finding someone like Russell, who just felt like home to me already, but a very cute and exciting home. I had even started to hope that the person who was writing the notes and creeping around at night might have stopped, seeing as nothing like that had happened for about a week. How wrong I was.

The excitement of moving into my first place on my own, and the excitement of meeting Russell all now jaded by the attack. I was left instead with constant feelings of vulnerability, helplessness and fear. I distracted myself by singing along to another favourite on the album, *I Ain't the One,* hoping and praying that Sue would be the one to help me dig my way out of the hole that I felt I'd fallen into.

After heading east from Burmont, I reached the highway and turned south in the direction of Agnes. *Highway* was a generous term for the road, which was a major connecting road running parallel to the coast–with rare sightings of the ocean. It was only a single lane each way with regular potholes and bits crumbling off the sides, that always seemed to be located at exactly the spots where I met cars and trucks passing in the other direction and had to move toward the verge, feeling my wheels drop into ruts and gravel each time. Luckily there was not much traffic on the road at that time of day.

I'd set off at seven o'clock, even though I knew that the trip should only take about two hours. I woke up early, itching to get moving, to be doing something, so as soon as Russell left for work, I hit the road. We always had at least two days off after night shifts, so I felt good about the fact that this time I had three days off before I was expected to go into work again.

The minutes and kilometres ticked past amid the crispy brown landscape. Bordering the road were clumps of tall, brown grasses, flanked by bare tracts of land, occasionally dotted with paddocks displaying various hues of brown and yellow. The crops starved of hydration during the ongoing drought and the cattle looking poor and ragged, foraging for the little nourishment they could still find. Every now and then a green pasture appeared, with large overhead irrigation systems clearly showing the reason why. Farmers were doing it tough, but that was nothing new to them, working on the land in a harsh country like Australia.

The coastline was also starting to make more of an appearance now and then, and I knew I was getting close to my destination when I saw the sparkling blue ocean becoming a constant companion through my passenger side window. Following the signs to Agnes Water and the town of 1770, I pulled up at the service station on the edge of town and filled up. I also dug out my map and the directions that Sue had given me on the phone.

I started to feel nervous about meeting her and unsure about how to start what was bound to be an unusual conversation. I practised a few opening lines in my head. All I'd said to her on the phone was that I was her replacement at Burmont and I wondered if I could talk to her about some strange things that had happened to me. I also mentioned that I'd met Nicki. She seemed to hesitate for a moment before agreeing but didn't ask for any specifics of what had happened to me.

I'd presumed that she'd give me her address, but I could fully understand her reluctance to provide that to someone just ringing her out of the blue. Even if she was lucky enough to have escaped town without experiencing what I'd been through, she'd still had the notes and the feeling of someone watching her. She would no doubt feel the need to protect her privacy.

I stopped the car in an informal looking parking area just in front of a small park which was positioned right on the edge of the beach–our designated meeting spot. White sand stretched out to meet the sparkling blue ocean with diamond points of sunlight dancing on the surface and frothy little white waves lapping at the edges of the darker sand. The park had a picnic table, a slippery slide and a set of swings. Sitting on one of the swings, facing me–rather than the beautiful view, was a young woman that I imagined to be Sue Ryan.

Having never seen a photo of her, I had no preconceived ideas about what Sue would look like, but her size was a bit of a surprise to me. I could already see while she was still seated, that she was tall and solidly built. As I stepped out of the car and into the welcome cool sea breeze, she stood up and I got a better idea of her stature. She was a good six inches taller than me and while I wouldn't say fat, the old standby 'big-boned' came to mind. She looked like she could hold her own in a tussle. I couldn't help thinking that the guys would have preferred to have her as back-up rather than me.

She smiled and put out her hand, "Hi, I'm Sue."

"Hi Sue, Tess. Thanks so much for letting me come and see you." Her dark brown eyes met mine and her smile faded on her lips as she looked down and noticed the bruise marks around my wrist. I wondered if she could see the bruising on my face as well. I'd tried to hide it with make-up, but I knew some of it still showed through. My right eye was still red and slightly swollen from the attack.

We just stood and looked at each other for a moment–neither quite knowing what to say or where to start. I knew it should be me who said something first, as I'd driven all this way to see her, but all of my rehearsed lines deserted me. I looked away from the knowing look in her eyes.

Sue broke the silence by saying, "You're early. I've just walked down here from our place." She waved a hand up in the general direction of the slope behind me. "I'm sorry… I just wanted to meet you before I invited you to the house."

"No, that's fine. I don't mind at all," I said, sitting down on the other swing. Sue reclaimed hers and pushed herself slowly backward and forward with one foot on the sand. I did the same. This time we faced the beach and I looked up and down the length of it before saying, "It's so lovely here. It seems very peaceful."

"Yes, it is. Just what I needed after being in that shit-hole of a place."

I was surprised that she'd just come right out with that comment, and I could hear the aggression in her voice in the way she said *shit-hole.* I immediately got the impression that Sue was a straight-talker and that she might be prepared to talk to me about Burmont without too much pussy-footing around. Still, I felt reluctant to jump straight in and ask her what I'd come to ask. Instead, I nodded toward the ocean and said, "Looks like it would be great for surfing. Are you into that?"

"Nah, not built for surfin'," she said spreading her arms and looking down at herself. "Rick's mad keen though."

Unsure how to respond, and not wanting to comment about her size, I came up with, "I tried it once and nearly drowned, so it's not top of my list of things to do."

We looked at each other across the gap between the swings and I saw her eyes flick to my wrist again before lowering to my ankles.

Then we both turned at the sound of an approaching car. The crunching sound of the tyres on the gravel slowing to a stop as it reached the park. The back doors of a beat-up Valiant station wagon flew open and two kids bounded out of the back seat, headed in our direction. A woman in a see-through white crocheted dress thrown over a yellow bikini followed casually behind them, smoking a cigarette.

After a dark look from the younger child who it would seem was not happy about adults hogging the swings, Sue said quietly, "Look, I think what we need to talk about might be better done at home. D'you wanna come to my place? It's just up the hill."

I nodded.

"Come on." She led the way to my car. "You can drive us."

Following her directions we pulled up at a shabby, older-looking, high-set weatherboard that hadn't seen a lick of paint for many a year. I could glimpse some patches of pale green where the paint had tenaciously held on. The neighbouring houses all looked weather-beaten, some faring better than others in the salty wind spray that would have been prevalent on the headland. Several of the houses we passed were little more than shacks which appeared to have been hastily thrown together as a weekend getaway.

"Come on in. Wanna coffee? I need one." She walked straight into the kitchen without waiting for an answer. I followed, agreeing to have a coffee, mainly because I always found it easier to talk when I had something to hold onto, and I figured we both might appreciate that kind of prop pretty soon.

I sat at the kitchen table, while she filled the kettle and started on the coffees. Seeing that the ocean was also visible out the kitchen window I said, "This house is in such a great spot."

"Yeah, the house is pretty crappy but the view is great. Rick's been here for a couple of years now and loves it. Mainly because he can hit the waves after work most days."

She placed a bottle of milk and a sugar bowl on the table and then returned with the steaming mugs. She sat and faced me across the small wooden table. I felt like more small talk would be fruitless seeing as she didn't seem like a small talk kind of girl. She seemed very direct, and I really wanted to get down to the reason why I'd driven all this way to see her. I eased into the topic by asking her, "How long were you in the job, Sue?"

"Only three and a half years. I was never really sure where I wanted to end up. I liked general duties but also had half a plan to try and get into the mounted unit. But those options were pretty much taken from me. I couldn't continue in the job after what happened out there." She dropped her eyes to the table as she said the last sentence and gripped her cup tightly in both hands.

"How about you? How long have you been in?"

"Ah, around five years now. I'll have to start thinking about doing some more study and trying to get my first stripe, I suppose."

"So you think you'll stick it out?" she asked, her eyes scanning my face, noting the bruise and returning to look me in the eye.

I sighed heavily and answered, "Well, I'd like to think so, but I suppose that depends on whether I'm enjoying it into the future or not. You'd know as well as I do what a struggle it is at times, not just the work, but the extra scrutiny we have on us all the time."

"Yeah, it's not an easy job, but it wasn't the work that I had problems with, I mostly loved that. It was the chauvinistic bastards in the boys' club. All that so-called mateship and sticking up for each other–should just be called what it is–*covering up* for each other." She shifted in her chair, looking suddenly uncomfortable.

"I know. Some are worse than others though. For example, Bollington. Did he tell you to put an 'F' on your reports? After your name and rank?" I asked.

"What? No. You're *kidding*. He actually asked you to do that?"

"Yeah, but I'm refusing. And from what my old Sarge said when I rang him, there's no way he should be asking me to do that."

"Well, I shouldn't be surprised. He's a chauvinistic arsehole."

"Yeah, no argument there." I agreed, then continued, "You know, when I found out by accident from the Real Estate Agent that you'd rented the cottage before me, I wondered why no one at work had said anything about you, so I tried asking a few times and they all just changed the subject. It was only after I'd gotten to a point where I had to tell someone at work about the strange things that were starting to happen to me, and decided to confide in Noel, that he steered me toward Nicki, and I finally got some answers. She told me that similar things had happened to you." I looked at her, hoping she might elaborate on her experiences. She did.

"That cottage was so cool, I was really looking forward to living there, but that didn't last long." She took a sip of coffee and continued to cradle her mug. "On the first weekend that I was there, Rick came out on the Friday night to visit and stay over, then he left to come back here on the Sunday afternoon. Later that night when I was asleep, at around eleven-thirty, I heard noises out the front and got up to have a look out.

Those curtains are pretty flimsy hey? I could see straight through them. There was this guy standing near the gate–just standing there–looking in. I felt like he was looking straight at me, although with the lights out I doubt he could've seen me, but it felt like he could."

"That's almost exactly what happened to me. I replaced all the curtains with the heaviest fabric I could find, but even after that, he seemed to be able to find a way to see in. One night when my boyfriend was over, he must have seen us kissing on the couch through a little crack where the curtains didn't quite meet, then he wrote *slut* in big letters on that little front fence."

"Shit you got it on the fence. I got it on a note under the door." She hesitated a little and then continued, "If only that was the worst of it." She looked out the window and sighed heavily, appearing to consider how to continue, then faced me again. "Was it just me, or have you got something else…" she stuttered a moment then glanced at my wrists again and gave me a questioning look. I didn't need the words. I knew exactly what she was trying to ask.

I rescued her by deciding to tell her what happened only yesterday. "I feel incredibly embarrassed actually saying any of this out loud, but I know I can talk to you, and you'll understand," I rubbed at my bruised wrists distractedly, as I started on my story.

She gave me a closed lip smile of encouragement.

"So, I'd been on night shift with Ray this week, and yesterday was the last one. I went in to have a shower around lunchtime because I had to go to work in a few hours and I'd had enough of working in the garden. I'd been cutting down branches to try and clear around the back of the house because this creep had thrown a brick on the roof the week before, so had obviously been skulking around there. Plus, he killed the neighbour's dog… but I'll tell you about that later." Sue raised a questioning eyebrow.

I took a deep breath and told Sue about the attack, trying to include every detail so that I only had to tell it the once. She nodded as I recounted what had happened, but she didn't interrupt. I continued, "He strapped me to the bed. *I was naked and blindfolded…*" my voice betrayed me at that point, and I had to stop. Sue reached over and put her hand on my arm, "I know,

I know. *That fucking bastard.* It was the same for me." She dropped her head and took a big shaky breath.

Hearing her say that was such a relief, but straight away I felt guilty that I was relieved that someone else had to go through this. I put my hand over hers and squeezed it gently before removing it to gesticulate when asking, "But then the camera? The clicking sounds that I can only presume was a camera. And the way he moved around to different spots to get his sordid angle shots. Did you hear that too?"

"Yes, it was definitely a camera shutter going off. Over and over. When I think of the angles, and the photos that he's leering over, I feel sick."

"Sue, I hate to even ask this, but I have to. Did he assault you… sexually?"

"*No.* I was so relieved when I came to and found that he hadn't tried anything like that. I was also surprised." She gave me a questioning look and grabbed my forearm, *"You?"*

"No. Thank God. I've been wracking my brain to think why he didn't but there's so many possible reasons that it's all just going round and round in circles and driving me crazy. Apart from the risk of leaving evidence, even using a condom, maybe there's some other reason–physically unable or something?"

"Possibly, or maybe it's just not his motivation. As you would know, sex offenders usually attack from the need to control, but he could be doing this for other reasons. Whatever the motive, he's methodical and careful, and there's a reason…"

I cut her off as the thought hit me, "Oh my God. This all means he might have done this kind of thing before–*to someone else.*" I hadn't even considered this possibility before. I'd been thinking it was all about me.

"Yes, now that I know you've been through this too, it's a definite possibility that some other poor bugger has as well. Listen, we need to compare every single little thing that we can remember about this bastard. I have my suspicions, strong ones, but I'm not going to say until I hear every detail of your description of him. I'm surprised you don't already know who it was. It makes me think our experiences must have been different in a few details."

"Don't already know… what do you mean?" I asked, confused. "That you *do* know?"

"Pretty sure I do but I want to be 100 percent. If you give me your description of him–every single thing that you can remember–then we can put it all together. Trust me."

I steeled myself to allow the image of that dark and menacing shape into my mind so that I could relay an accurate and detailed description to Sue.

"And don't forget smells and sounds," she prompted.

Smells. I hadn't thought about smells. I know my other senses seemed to be on high alert when I couldn't see, but I really didn't remember smelling anything, except that cloth. I really wanted to know what Sue knew. If she remembered smells, then there might some *other* differences as well.

"Maybe we should write this down and then compare, so we don't influence each other?" I suggested.

"Yeah that's a good idea," Sue agreed. Then as she was scratching around in a drawer of the dresser, I couldn't help asking her if she'd met Brian.

"Look maybe I *do* know who it was. Did you meet a guy called Brian when you first arrived in town? Blonde guy, good-looking but a bit weird? He pounced on me as soon as I hit town and he is my first suspect, but when Nicki said you'd not mentioned him, I began to wonder."

"Nope, never met a Brian." She handed me a piece of paper and a pen and sat back down with her own implements.

After a few minutes of frantic scribbling to get it all down, I checked my list to make sure I hadn't missed anything. I looked up and found that Sue had also finished and was waiting on me. We swapped lists and read intently.

Body shape and height matched, clothing, gloves and balaclava matched, boots matched but Sue had written, *black boots with dirty brown marks on sides,* whereas I remembered the boots being black and clean. Then I remembered Nicki telling me that Sue had said something about boots just before she left town.

"Boots. Sue, you said something to Nicki about being able to smell shit on some boots. Is this what you meant?"

She looked surprised that I knew she'd said that. "Yeah. I am ninety-nine percent sure I know whose boots they were. And if you look down on my list, you'll see that I distinctly remember a smell. A smell like cow poo. And he whispered something in my ear."

I gave her an incredulous look and spread my hands in a gesture of despair. "He spoke? What did he say–why didn't you tell me this before?"

She lay both her hands on the table and clasped them in front of her. "I wanted to know about your experience first. I was hoping your description would help to reinforce what I already know." She raised her clasped hands to under her chin and rested her head there. "And it does."

She looked me in the eye as she asked, "If you knew who this was, what would you do to them?"

"I'd report them. I'd love to arrest them myself, but that wouldn't work, so yeah, I'd report them and get Noel or someone to arrest them."

"Well, guess what? I did report him. I reported him to the Senior and he got me transferred out the next day."

"What do you mean? I'm not following. Why would he do that?"

"Boys club."

My mouth must have dropped open because I had to bring my jaw back up to form the next word, "What are you saying? That this was a copper? One of *us*?" My tone was incredulous, and my mind was flicking through the limited number of people that she could possibly be talking about.

"One of *them,* as it turns out. There is no *us.*"

CHAPTER 24

Riding High

Tuesday has finally arrived and I'm a little concerned about whether Guy will even turn up. Since taking down my profile, I haven't been able to contact him to confirm that I'd still be here for our surfing lesson. Neither of us had given out our mobile numbers either, so that's not an option. I can't help wondering what he's inferred from my profile disappearing and I was even tempted to reinstate it briefly so I could send him a message and then get off again quickly, but I couldn't bring myself to do it. The unpleasant feeling of Marcus out there watching and waiting, or someone else like him, loomed over me every time I thought about going back online. Even though I reassured myself that my fears were probably unfounded, I figured it wasn't worth the anxiety it caused me. Besides, I told myself that if Guy was keen, he would turn up.

As I sit on the sand waiting and hoping, I survey the waves with my untrained eye, deciding that there is not much swell and wondering if there is even enough of a wave to push a board along. I'm grateful that it's not a rough day and there is only a gentle breeze. I can feel the enticing warmth of the sand under my feet, so I spread my towel out to lie down and enjoy the warmth on my back as well. There are other towels and people scattered along the beach, but only a few with boards, none of them Guy.

Lying with my head propped up by my arms, I run my eye along the length of my body, prompting me to pull my tummy in. After three kids, one a caesarean, gravity and the passing years, my bikini days are over, but I think I still cut a decent figure in a one-piece. Today, I've chosen my navy swimsuit because I think it's the most flattering, and teamed it with a pink floral, long-sleeved rashie. I figure we might be out in the water for quite a while trying to get me vertical on a surfboard, so I'll need the heavy-duty sun protection.

As the minutes pass, I feel more and more concerned that he's not going to show. Having just checked my watch again though, I find it's only 8.28 so he's not even late. I am just uncharacteristically early. With the water starting to look very tempting and the heat of the sun beating down I consider just going in for a swim, but vanity holds me back. I don't want to look like a drowned rat when he arrives–I want to look my best, so I decide to wait.

I lie back and watch the seagulls hover above in that magical way that they have where they appear frozen in mid-air, an illusion of white magicians on the backdrop of a pristine blue sky. Then I follow their path as they squark and fly off to my left and into the distance. I look back just as a shadow creeps across my face. I turn my head to find that the source is Guy, standing just behind me with a very long surfboard, which he is proceeding to prop in the sand beside him.

He has a big smile on his Zinc covered face and is wearing sunnies and bright blue board shorts. I prop myself up and say, "Hey, how are you Guy? If it *is* you under all of that."

"Fantastic," he laughs. "Yes, it's me." He leans over to place a Zincy kiss on my cheek, then gently wipes the white smudges away as he straightens up and says, "So, welcome to Guy's surf lessons–which, by the way, include gals as well." He performs a flourish with one arm along the length of the board.

"Well I'm very glad to hear that. I just hope these lessons are not too expensive, and that the teacher has a lot of patience."

He sits on the edge of my towel near my tucked-up legs. "Hmm, let's see. The price today will be to have lunch with your instructor, and as for the patience, we shall have to see," he laughs.

"Deal. But honestly, if I'm really unco and driving you nuts, just tell me and we can stop."

"I haven't had a failure yet, so I don't think you'll be my first. I brought along my best learner board. You'll be up on it in no time."

"Ok, I'll believe it when I see it though. How is it out there today for a learner like me?" I ask.

"Pretty perfect really. But we'll start on the sand, getting you used to popping up into the right position, then when you get a handle on that, we'll move into the water. You ready to get started?"

"For sure. Let's do this." I jump up and brush the sand from my legs.

Guy lays the board down on the sand and says, "I'll give you a demonstration first and then you can copy, ok?"

I nod, "I reckon I might need a few demos though."

He lies down on the board and runs me through a commentary of how I should be lying, how I'm going to paddle onto a wave, where my hands should be placed once I'm on it, where my front foot goes, where my back foot goes and a half a dozen other instructions that have just passed straight through my head.

"Ok, whoa, whoa. Can you run through that again and just stop about half-way or so where you started talking about front foot and back foot? You lost me there. How do I know which is which?"

"Ah, well you will have to feel it. You can try both ways and see which one feels more comfortable."

"Doesn't it go by whether you're right or left-handed or something?"

"You can try that theory, but if you're left-handed it's really just going to come down to feel. Right-handed people are usually regular but sometimes they're goofy as well." I have to laugh, even though I know he's using some kind of surfing jargon, with his accent added in it sounds hilarious.

"Well, I'm right-handed but also quite goofy, so let's try this." I lie on the board and Guy talks me through the routine. I find that doing it is much easier than thinking about it and quickly get the hang of popping up. This is where we need to get into the water. It's all very easy standing on a board on solid sand but trying to balance on water is going to be the big challenge for me.

"So now remember when you get onto the wave and pop up, you need to keep your knees bent but not your upper body, straighten up and keep that strong. And look forward, not at your feet. They'll look after themselves." He's holding the board in the water, while I'm lying on it and listening to these extra instructions. I know I won't remember everything, especially as his brown, muscular chest and strong shoulders are taking up most of my attention, but hopefully some of it sticks.

"Are you ready to have a go?" he asks, looking behind to see if there are any waves coming.

I look too and see that they're still less than half a metre high–probably the best waves I could hope for to have my first go at standing up on a surfboard. I figure it's now or never. "Yep, I'm going on the next one," I say as I start paddling and feel the board receive a little push from Guy to help me on my way.

I get on the wave, I push up, I bring my left foot forward and then as I try to bring the other foot through to my hands, I lose balance and fall in. The first of many failed attempts. But I keep at it and Guy keeps telling me what I'm doing wrong until finally I have my first little wobbly ride where I actually get to step off the board at the end rather than getting dumped. Now that I've done it once, I want to feel that feeling again. Even though I was shaky and awkward, it felt great being embraced by the wave and propelled forward like that. It almost felt like flying.

"You did it. *That's fantastic,*" yells Guy, waving to me as I paddle back out to him. I sit up on the board as he holds it close to him. He raises his hand for a high five and I reciprocate. We're both grinning like schoolkids, and I can't remember ever feeling so elated and relaxed at the same time. I slide off the board and into the water in front of him and he reaches out and puts one arm around me and pulls me closer, while he holds the board with the other. "I'm so proud of you–my star pupil," he says. "How about a couple more and then we call it a day? Your legs are going to be like jelly after this."

He's right. They already feel that way, but I think it might also have something to do with being so close to him at this moment. I climb back onto the board and have a couple more slightly less-wobbly rides, plus a couple more fails before we call it a day.

Walking up the beach to my towel, I can really feel how tired my legs and hips are. I'm glad Guy's the one carrying the board because I don't think my legs could handle the extra weight of that right now.

At the carpark, Guy loads the board onto a dark grey, newish X-trail, while I rinse off under the outdoor shower. When I re-join him he says, "So, lunch at mine? Yes?"

"Yes, that sounds wonderful. But be warned. I'm not going to be offering to help cook. My legs feel like they're about to fall off."

He laughs, "Just as well it's all prepared. Would you like to follow me?" He looks toward my van, reminding me again of how visible it is, and bringing the dark cloud of Marcus over my carefree morning.

I follow Guy the short distance up to Battery Hill. After a couple of turns and a steep climb he stops at a striking house with sharp angles and a mixture of building materials, colours and textures. It looks very modern and very much like it was designed by an expensive architect. A black garage door opens in the grey and natural timber section on the left, and Guy noses halfway in. I park in the driveway behind, leaving enough room for him to unload the board easily.

"Your house is beautiful, Guy. Did you build it?" I ask, admiring the façade.

"Thanks. Yes, about three years ago now. I love it. My dream home. Come in–I'll do the board later." He leads me through the massive timber front door, through a wide hallway into a big open room with glass doors all along one wall–looking directly over the ocean. It's breathtaking.

Guy lays out a simple but delicious lunch of prawns and salad and we eat at the breakfast bar, facing the panoramic view. Artistically positioned at the end of the breakfast bar is a large, clear vase with pale pink peonies and blue-grey gum leaves. It caught my attention as soon as I walked in and my eyes travel back to it now. It's very tastefully arranged. I wonder where he bought the flowers–slightly jealous that another florist must be getting his business.

He notices and says, "What do you think of my taste in flowers–from your viewpoint as a florist?"

"I love peonies. They're one of my favourites, but then I have so many favourites that I can never settle on just one. Where did you get them?" I ask, my curiosity getting the better of me.

He smiles and gives a little laugh, naming one of the local florist shops and promising to come and see me for his next arrangement. After eating, we move out onto the deck to enjoy the views and chat about surfing and the best beaches in the area. Then he changes the topic. "I saw that you are no longer on the Wings site. I wanted to send you a message on Sunday, but you were gone."

I wonder how much detail to go into about my reason for disappearing offline so abruptly. I opt for very little to start with. "Yeah, I'm really not comfortable being on there. I like my privacy a bit too much, so decided it was time to take it down. How about you? How do you feel about all of that?"

He looks at me with a considered look and rests his chin in his hand for a moment, like he's making a decision of some kind. Flashbacks of that same kind of look on Perry's face just before he told me he'd lied about his age pop into my head. *Oh no, here we go again.* I steel myself for what's coming.

"I am no longer on there myself. I need to tell you something and I hope you won't be upset or take it the wrong way."

I feel dread working its way up my spine and have a sinking feeling in my stomach. "Go on," I manage to croak.

"You will remember my field of work? Well, I also do research and conduct various studies, and have written and published some papers on my findings. However, my latest research is in the field of community connection, personal relationships, and the changes as the result of technology in the last ten years–with a specific focus on online dating."

All of a sudden I feel like a fool. A minute ago I felt happy and optimistic, now I'm a lab rat, running on a wheel in a cage, with a magnifying glass examining my every move.

"I'm research? A lab rat?" I ask incredulously. I wonder how I could have been so gullible. But then I suppose this *was* too good to be true.

"No, no, no!" He holds up his hands to stop me but I'm too outraged.

"What number am I then? How many other poor gullible women have you researched in your... your... study?" I spit the word out like it's poison.

"No, no, wait. My study isn't about the women. I needed to explore the options and avenues open for people to meet other people, and I needed to understand how online dating sites worked, as a part of that." He throws his hands up and says, "No, let me try to explain again. In order to write with any authority, I needed a better understanding of how these processes work."

I look at him with wide eyes and say, "And that's supposed to make me feel better?"

"I do want to make you feel better because this..." he points from me to himself and back again, "is real. It's not part of a study. Only the process was. As it happened, I truly did want to meet someone, and the timing just worked. And now I've met you and I want this out in the open, so you know that you can trust me. No secrets."

No secrets. I think that is a big ask, especially this early in a potential relationship, but I suppose he is telling me about *this* early on, and I should appreciate his honesty. "Look, I appreciate you telling me. I would have been even more disappointed to find out later… if there is a later."

He reaches for my hand and says, "I hope that there is. I hope we can put this behind us and get back to where we were. I was feeling optimistic and happy at meeting you. Today has been so much fun, I didn't want to spoil it, but I didn't want to delay the truth either."

"It has been fun, and I loved learning to surf, well, starting to learn anyway. You've thrown me a bit with this revelation I have to say. I'm not a hundred percent sure how to feel about it. On the one hand it's great that you've told me but on the other, it's raised a few doubts, you know?"

"Of course. I plan to show you that I'm genuine though–if you'll let me." He looks at me with those vibrant hazel eyes and I find it hard to be suspicious of them.

"Time will tell, as they say. I suppose I just need a little time to get to know you better so I can judge for myself how genuine you are."

He stands up and goes to the big, black double door fridge. Opening one door he says, "This should count for something. I've made sticky date pudding especially for you." He disappears into the fridge and then leans back around the fridge door so I can only see half of his face and adds, "And I don't do *that* for just any old lab rat."

I look around for something to throw at him, feigning insult, but also can't help but laugh, enjoying his sense of humour. Even though today he's given me some pause for thought–a moment of doubt and a reason to put up a little guard rail around my heart, I am enjoying the parry and the dance that is part of getting to know someone. I just hope what I discover can lead me to trust as well.

CHAPTER 25

Just Looking

I arrive at work early on Wednesday morning to open up the shop. I'm also keen to see how the girls went yesterday on my day off. As Ros has today off and Sally will come in around midday for a half-day, I'll need to set up on my own.

Opening the front door, I see that the shop looks spic and span and I pop my head into the cold room to see what delightful bouquets and arrangements they have left over from the day before. Expecting to see mainly yellow and oranges from those two girls, I'm pleasantly surprised to see that even though those colours are prominent, they're mixed with blues and purples, making vibrant and joyful looking displays.

At the front counter, the receipts are all neatly filed and the takings for the day look very healthy. This is encouraging. *Maybe I should take a day off during the week more often,* I think. I certainly could handle spending Tuesday mornings (and as it turned out yesterday, most of the afternoon) with Guy. After our hiccup at lunch at his house, we relaxed on his expansive deck and talked over a glass or two of wine for a couple of hours.

I discovered that he is divorced and has been on his own for three years. Hence the new house. The family home was part of the settlement for his ex. He didn't speak about her a lot but answered any questions I posed. I think I would be a bit concerned if someone who was divorced wanted to go on and on in detail about their ex to someone they'd just met. I found out that he has two grown-up kids and a grandchild on the way. His face lit up when he was talking about his daughter and how wonderful a mum she'll be.

I talked about my kids and answered his questions about my ex as well. I kept the conversation away from the past as much as possible though. He was keen to know about my business and surprised me by telling me that he and his wife used to grow gerberas and foliage to supply to florists and the markets. Finding that common ground was great. We went on to talk for ages about flowers and plants, growing methods and gardening, the environment, climate change and a million other things. Conversation flowed easily and time seemed to slip by quickly. I all but forgot about his confession regarding his research.

I thought about it later at home though, concluding that if he's just using me as part of a study, he's a very convincing liar. I still believe that people's eyes give them away when they're lying, and his tell me that he's genuine. At the Police Academy we learned about body language as part of some basic studies in psychology. These skills are useful in helping to identify when someone is lying, but if the person doing the lying also has training and knowledge in these areas, then they can become quite adept at masking the usual tell-tale signs that liars display.

This whole online experience has caused me to doubt my judgement lately too. I decide to still be cautious, even though I really want this to work out with Guy. Already, I've started to imagine introducing him to my kids and to Marta and Helen and other friends. I pull myself up when I find I'm doing this and tell myself to slow down.

When I was leaving his house, he asked me if I'd like to go to dinner on Friday night. There was no question–I accepted. He gave me the double-cheek kisses and a hug to send me on my way, along with a container holding a big piece of sticky date pudding.

* * *

Now, having set up the shop and downloaded the orders for today, I start to work my way through them, placing them in order of required delivery time. Joe will be delivering the late afternoon orders today, but I have one that needs to be out by twelve-thirty for a funeral, so as soon as Sally arrives, I'll get her to drive that one over to the Funeral Parlour. Gone are the days when I had to put a sign on the door saying 'Back in 10 minutes', and race out and back with urgent deliveries.

Sally arrives with her usual bright and cheery greeting, props her bag on the table in the back room and pulls out a sheet of paper with her words of wisdom for this week. I follow her as she sticks it up on the wall and read this quote, again credited to Jim.

We've all had that feeling of being somewhere we don't want to be. Maybe for work, maybe for family. That feeling that there is something else more pressing and more important that you should be doing for yourself, but you stay, out of duty. When in fact your heart and mind are not there–you're distracted and not present. Most of us live our whole lives in this way–denying our true self because we want to appear 'normal' and 'nice'. Fearing that someone might think badly of us. Be true to yourself. Be present in all your actions.

"Honestly Sally, you seem to find the most amazing quotes these days. Not that your old ones weren't good, but you know." I shrug and look back to re-read the quotation.

"Thanks, Yeah, when I look back on some of those, they were a bit lame. Well, you all know it's Jim's influence, but I've started reading more philosophy now and I even find some good ones of my own." She moves her bag to the floor in the corner and rubs her hands together, saying, "Right, what have we got on this arv?"

I point to the large casket spray of natives in gold, white and green that I've spent most of the morning preparing. "This one needs to go out straight away for a funeral. Has to be there by twelve-thirty. Are you able to pop out and deliver it?"

"For sure. I'll go now." She carefully gathers the arrangement and I attempt to pass her the keys to the van and a note with the address for delivery. Her hands are fully occupied with the flowers, so I pop them both in her back pocket and open the door for her.

Once alone again, I return to a bouquet of a dozen champagne roses that I was half-way through arranging. There hasn't been much foot traffic through today, only three walk-ins so far, so I'm hoping the lunch period might prove to be a bit busier. As I tie the ribbon on the roses in the workroom, I hear the shop door open. I know it's too quick for it to be Sally coming back from her delivery, so I walk out to greet the customer.

My breath catches in my throat and my legs stop mid-stride. I think I recognise the man stooping over, looking at one of the purple and yellow bunches prepared by Ros or Sally. He looks up as I approach and I immediately recognise the glasses, confirming that it's him. Dark lenses mask his eyes, a small smile touches his lips.

"Hey Tess," he says, moving toward me. I fear he might be thinking of kissing my cheek, or giving me a hug, so I slip behind the counter. I stiffly return his hello and ask if I can help him with something.

"Just looking," he says as he turns away from the flowers and moves closer to me. "You left so quickly the other day that I didn't get your number, so I thought I'd call in and see you."

I don't know how to respond straight away, but I know I need to confront him about how he knew where to find me. I might have been willing to treat this as a coincidence but he's not even trying to make it look like a coincidental meeting. I'm very conscious of not wanting to be blatantly rude or upset him, because I'm here on my own, and in theory I should give him a chance to explain himself, so I adopt a friendlier tone.

"So how did you know where to find me?"

"You told me you worked here, remember?"

"Ah, no I didn't. I would have remembered that."

"Oh well, I must have seen you arrive in your van," he says dismissively.

"Well you were at the table when I arrived. Maybe it has something to do with the photos you took of my van when I was leaving?"

"Oh that's right. What's the matter? Don't like photos?" The way he says this and the look he gives me make me freeze for a second. A deadweight drops into the pit of my stomach and pushes the contents upward, threateningly close to my throat. I look down at his hands.

I'm unable to speak, so he continues, "I tried to send you a message, like we agreed, but your profile has disappeared. What's going on there?"

This conversation is way too confrontational. I desperately hope for another customer to enter, or for Sally to return from her delivery, but neither happens and I start to feel more and more uncomfortable.

"Oh, sorry Marcus," I say, getting my voice back and trying to sound casual–like it's no big deal. "I deleted it because I've decided that I'm not ready to find someone right now. It was a mistake and I'm sorry I wasted your time." I figure this is a kind and impersonal way of putting an end to the matter, but he doesn't accept my explanation.

"You just think you're too good for me, don't you? As soon as you saw that ankle monitor I had on, you changed. I told you it was all a mistake and it's gone now. Don't you believe me?" He's up close to the counter now and props both hands on top, his fingertips white from the pressure he seems to be putting on them. He almost looks like he's about to do a set of push-ups.

"No… look, yes, of course. But I've explained that I was wrong in thinking I was ready to get out there and meet someone so let's just leave it at that hey? I really have a lot of work to get done, so I need to get on with that." He doesn't move or say anything, so I try again. "I really hope you meet someone Marcus, but I'm out of that whole scene, so please, I need to get back to work."

"I hope you're not lying to me. I really don't like it when people tell me lies." He reaches over the counter and grabs my hand before I can pull it away. He squeezes it saying, "Fine, I'll give you a bit of time then. I might come back and see you another day."

My throat constricts and goosebumps creep up the back of my neck. I pull my hand away and give it a rub. It hurts from where his fingernails have dug into my palm. "Really, I don't think that's a good idea. I will put my profile back up, if and when I'm ready, so you would be able to check that way rather than coming into my workplace."

"Well it *is* a public place isn't it? I might want to buy a bunch of flowers so why shouldn't I come in here?" he asks confrontationally.

Mercifully, the shop door opens and Sally walks through, glancing at me and then Marcus as she passes us, offering a quick 'Hi' in our direction. Her arrival is enough to break the tension like a beam of sunlight penetrating the invisible, weighty fog that had begun to engulf the room. I suddenly feel like I can breathe again.

He turns and begins to walk toward the door. Stopping with his hand on the handle and turning back to me, he says, "See you in a little while then," and gives me a smile that makes my skin crawl.

I grab my water bottle from under the counter and take a swig. I follow that with a few deep breaths to calm myself, silently wishing Marta had been able to install my security cameras so that this episode could have been recorded. Maybe he wouldn't have even come in if they had been in place. Then I realise that I may have missed an opportunity to see what kind of car he drives. "*Shit,*" I say as I run to the front window. I see his retreating back as he almost reaches the other side of the road. He stops at the driver's door of a white, older model Toyota Camry. It obviously doesn't have central locking because he bends to unlock the door manually. As he opens it and begins to step into the car, he turns fully to look back at the shop. I duck back out of view, hoping that he didn't see me watching him.

When I risk another quick peek, I catch the last two digits of his number plate–AZ, as he drives off. I can also see that he has a decent scrape along the rear side panel. I commit these details to memory and turn around to see Sally staring at me from the doorway to the workroom.

"You ok?" she asks.

"Yeah, I'm ok, but I need to tell you something about that guy that was just in." I realise that my behaviour must look quite odd, and I can't just fob her off. I also realise that I have an obligation and a responsibility to look after my staff. The possibility that he could be aggressive to any of them is unacceptable. I'm going to have to start from the very beginning and let Sally know how I know this person, and how my online experience has been very different from hers. I also need to talk to Ros and Joe. I feel like I'd rather only go through all of that just once though, so an idea forms in my mind.

"You know what, I think we need to have a staff meeting. How about I give Ros a call and see if she can pop in this arv around closing time? That way Joe will be here too and I can explain this to all of you at the same time. It's a bit complicated."

She gives me a raised eyebrow look and a tilt of the head, saying, "Yes, of course. You're sounding very mysterious though. Are you sure you're ok?" Her concern is touching. I'm also sure her curiosity is killing her.

"Let's just say, I was very glad to see you come back, he was not a pleasant customer." Changing the subject and hoping to lighten the mood I hold out two order slips and ask, "Do you want the $80 arrangement in natives or the new baby basket in pinks?"

CHAPTER 26
The Stench

I reached over the table and grabbed both of Sue's arms with my hands, "Who? Tell me. And what did he say to you?"

"Steady on, you're digging in."

I released my grip which had become much firmer than I had intended. "Sorry mate. I just need to know. *Who?*"

"First, now that you know that the option of reporting him is off the table, tell me, what would you do to him if you knew who it was? I need to see if we're on the same page with this."

I clasped my hands up to my mouth and bit into my finger while thinking about what I would do to this person. I recalled a case from a couple of years ago where a rape victim cut off her assailant's penis. When I'd heard about that, I was glad I didn't have to be the one arresting her for GBH. I could almost understand that kind of revenge. The victim wanting to ensure the rapist could never use it again to hurt someone in that way. But of course, as a law enforcement officer, I couldn't condone it. Now, as a victim of a different kind of assault, I thought about what might stop this assailant from repeating this kind of horrific intrusion and assaulting and humiliating someone else. *He'd already done it twice–at least.*

"Cut off his shutter finger? I don't know." I scratched my head and added, "You know the one thing that just sticks in my mind is, *what is he planning to do those bloody photos?* All I can think about is finding them and destroying them. Then think about what to do with *him.*"

"*Exactly.* Me too. But I want to *hurt* him. I want him to remember me in a different light–not as a helpless victim. I'm constantly imagining that sick fuck leering at those photos, plus God knows what else he's doing with them, and I want to tear my hair out–no, I want to tear *his* hair out–I want him to suffer for this. It's *so* not over." Her voice raised to a higher pitch and her eyes glistened from the emotion, tears welling and threatening to spill over. Watching her and listening to her, I felt mine filling up as well.

"I totally get it." I paused then as a feeling of certainty spread over me. My mind had been working tirelessly in the background, recalling every conversation, every look or hint that could possibly reveal which of my fellow officers could be this devious and cruel. I'd finally come to the conclusion that there was only one person on staff capable of this kind of behaviour to the women that he worked with. His words echoed in my mind, *Have fun with the new girl.* I recalled his questioning of me about my actions at the B&S ball. *It all fit.* As I asked the question, I already knew in my gut what the answer would be, "It's Geoff, isn't it?"

She nodded slowly and continuously, her eyes narrowed and her brow creased at the mention of his name. Measuring her words, she said, "That bastard–creeped me out from the start. The snide comments about women, commenting about my weight even, the chauvinistic jokes, always needing to be the centre of attention and the 'funny' guy. And then they rostered me on *night shift* with him. Thanks a lot Don."

"I imagine Don wasn't to know. No one could have. How did you know for sure though? That it was Geoff."

"This all happened on the last day of the late shifts–same as you. I wasn't in the shower though. I was sleeping. He'd obviously worked out my patterns on night shifts. I always take ages to unwind, so don't end up going to bed until around 3am, and then sleep til around eleven. I don't know what time it was, but I didn't hear a thing until I opened my eyes and saw this black shadow leaning over me and the cloth just in front of my face. As he pushed it onto my nose and mouth, he pinned me down and pushed my head to the side. That's when I first spotted his boots. I tried to yell but don't even know if I did because I must have blacked out then." She stopped to take a big breath.

I used the pause to ask the question I'd been wanting to ask the whole time. "I don't get how the boots make you so sure that it's him though. How do they prove anything?"

"*The cow poo.* He hadn't even bothered to clean his boots from the night before. Dirty bastard. We had a call out to a farm early in that shift. Another bloody domestic out at O'Rileys. Anyway, he stepped in cow shit and dragged it back into the car with him. I had to put up with it for the rest of the shift, even though I asked him to do something about it–several times. He just ignored me and said, *Suck it up,* then another time when I asked him to clean his boots off he muttered, *Bossy fat bitch,* under his breath."

"Bastard." I whispered.

She continued. "After he'd blindfolded me and tied me to the bed and I'd become conscious again, I was struggling, trying to yell out… trying to talk… to reason with him, but he'd stuffed something in my mouth and taped it shut. He hit me then, hard on the side of my head. I pretended to be knocked out, but I could hear him taking the photos and moving around. That's when I smelled it, when he came up close to my head and that's when he whispered really, really, quietly, *Fat bitch.* He probably thought I didn't hear." She shook her head and breathed in through her nose, almost as though she was smelling that unpleasant aroma again.

"The stench of it took me straight back to the patrol car and those exact words–I couldn't believe it, but I knew it was him. The smell was less potent but still recognisable, and the boots, when I saw them earlier, had the brown marks on the sides–there's no doubt they were his." She balled one fist and covered it with the other hand, like she wanted to smack something.

I was dumfounded, my mind whirling with memories of my own ordeal mixed with the new details of Sue's. Something was grabbing at the edges of my memory, but I couldn't quite pull it into full focus.

When I didn't say anything after a second or two Sue carried on. "Mind you, at this stage, I didn't realise I was naked because I'd worn knickers and a t-shirt to bed as usual. I was lying there dreading the moment when he'd touch me, but the only touch was that cloth going over my face again and then nothing. I didn't realise how graphic those photos were going to be until after he'd gone, and I came to. Then I found I was *naked.* I searched for my undies but they were missing and my t-shirt was ripped apart. *Sick prick.*"

"Oh my God, Sue. I need to think about this–get it to sink in." I knocked on my head with the heel of my hand. "It's so hard to believe that a police officer would do something like this." And then it hit me–the thing that had been niggling at me since that first blurry, stinging snapshot of the dark shape that grabbed my arm in the shower. *It was the boots*–not because they were dirty–they weren't. They were police issue! I saw them every day so they didn't stand out but now they stood out to me like a flashing beacon. *Those boots should not have been in my bathroom–in my house.*

I bounded out of my chair and smacked my palm down on the table with the shock of the realisation. "Sue, it *was* the boots. I finally realised what my brain has been trying to tell me. They were police issue. They were clean, but they were *coppers'*."

Sue leaned back in her chair, tilting her head back and raising her arms in the air, like some kind of hallelujah. She sat back up and said, "I'm so glad you remembered. I was hoping for some extra confirmation from you. Not that there's any shadow of a doubt for me that it was him. You even picked him, once I said it was one of them. Then there's the fact that he's into photography. He even told me that, on one of those night shifts. Said he photographs birds and has some you-bute camera with this that and the other thing. I didn't pick it up at the time, but he probably thought he was so clever, telling me he photographs *birds* and giving it a double meaning. Has he still got those photos of an eagle up on the wall near his desk?"

"Yeah, I've seen those. I hate to admit it but they're actually good."

Sue continued, "Well, the kind of photos he took of us can't go through a lab so he must develop them at home. He must have a darkroom set up."

"Yes, that's what I figured too."

I drained the remains of my lukewarm coffee and asked, "What about Bollington though? Did you actually name Geoff?"

"Oh I named names alright."

"Tell me exactly what you told him."

"Shit, I can't remember word for word but something like, *I've been assaulted. Tied up and photographed naked and I know who did it.* He asked me who and I said Geoff. He asked if I was sure, if I positively identified him and I told him I couldn't see his face but I knew it was him. He seemed relieved. Then he stood up and basically stood over me and said, *This never happened–it's a fabrication. I've known that officer for seven years and you for five seconds. This is what your lot do. Come in and cause trouble.* I was speechless. I had marks on my wrists and ankles and a black eye, for fuck sake!"

I was feeling speechless after hearing that, but managed to ask, "When was this, that you told him?"

"This was straight after it happened, about two in the afternoon, so I knew Watts wouldn't be around yet. You can imagine how nervous and embarrassed I was, even going in to speak to Bollington about this, and I suppose I was in shock too, after what had happened.

Then to have him say that to me? I can't put into words how that felt. I just didn't know where to turn."

"God, Sue, I can't even imagine."

"Then he says something like, *I hope you're not planning on throwing a sickie–you're on duty tonight and we're short-staffed.* That's when I got my voice back. Blood rushed to my head and I exploded. *You expect me to work with him? You expect me to sit in a car with him–to speak to him? Are you fucking crazy?* Now that I think about it, I think he was deliberately riling me up so I'd give him an excuse to get rid of me."

"Where were you through all of this? Did anyone else hear any of it?"

"In his office. No, the door was closed. Unless they heard me right at the end because I lost my shit."

"So obviously you didn't go to work. What happened then?"

"It happened before that even. While I was still standing there in his office, after I'd called him fucking crazy, he said, *Start packing luv–you're out of here.* Him calling me *luv*, set me off again. I said, *Don't call me luv you ignorant old dinosaur.* Then I turned around and opened the door and said, *Fuck you and fuck this job!* and walked out. Now, I'm pretty sure Don and Derek heard that because neither of them would look at me and they seemed incredibly busy with paperwork when I walked past them."

"What did you do? Did you have anywhere to go?"

"Well, I had four rostered days off coming up and there was no way I could stay in that house on my own, so I started packing straight away to come out here and stay with Rick. I needed his support so much then."

"So you just left town and never went back?"

"Yeah, pretty much. I called in and saw Nicki briefly but even though she's lovely, I just didn't know her well enough to talk to her about this, plus she's married to a copper and Noel and Watts seem like they're friends. I was probably pretty incoherent when I dropped in on her. Couldn't wait to get out of that friggin' town. The whole place felt sordid."

Sue stood up and paced around a bit, then looked at her watch. "Come on, let's get out of here for a while and go back down to the beach. I need to shake all of this off."

So we walked the short distance to a quiet spot on the waterfront and sat straight on the sand with no towels. The fresh air and smell of the ocean felt cleansing, the sun warm and refreshing. Our conversation had been deep, dark and all-consuming, so I appreciated getting outside and into nature, where I felt I could breathe again.

We both enjoyed a few moments of quiet and I felt a strong sense of companionship and solitude with this similarly broken and disillusioned woman. Sensing that we both needed some extended time out, I looked over and asked, "Hungry? You got a good fish 'n chip shop here?"

"Yeah man, I could eat a horse," she replied, "Let's go."

After eating, with the food spread out on the paper on the sand, sharing and talking now and then, but also comfortable in shared quiet periods, we packed up the rubbish and walked back up to the house. Neither of us had touched back on the reason for this visit but I'd begun to watch the time because I knew that it would take a few hours to get back home, and I wanted to do that in daylight. So, hiatus over–we needed to get back to business.

As soon as we re-entered the house, it was as though that was a signal to return to the discussion of our dilemma. Our conversation resumed where we'd left off, Sue picking up the threads, "Rick was so great when I told him about what happened. He straight away suggested that I move in here and helped me make the decision to quit, officially."

"Yeah, that was a big decision. I can understand it, but did you consider going to someone else and reporting both of them?"

"Of course, I considered it. And if I knew anyone with some seniority that I could have trusted, I might have done that, but I'd only been in the job for three years and hadn't formed any good working relationships with any Sergeants or higher. I had no one. Especially after being treated like that by Bollington, who I'd figured would do the right thing as the officer in charge of the station. How could I trust anyone? I felt like I was banging my head against a brick wall." She smacked herself on the side of the head for effect.

"It killed me because as I said, I loved the work, but even worse than that was the feeling that I was running away–defeated. That's not what I do. That's why I need to get back at him. I need to let that piece of shit know that he hasn't won. I haven't just disappeared like a good little mouse."

From what I'd learned about Sue, she seemed very unmouse-like to me, but I understood the metaphor. "We're both not good little mice," I said, grasping the old nursery rhyme and twisting it, "he tried to turn us into two blind mice, but we've managed to see–and we may turn into the farmer's wife instead."

"If there's a knife involved and we're cutting something off, I'm in." Sue added.

I wasn't sure if she was playing along with euphemisms or if she might have been serious. I searched her face for some indication. None the wiser, I asked, "In the end Sue, what *are* we going to do? For me, it's all about getting hold of those photos."

"All of this time, I've been rolling around scenarios in my head. This was before you rang me and I realised that he'd done it again. I had plans to go to his house–break in and search for the photos. Find that darkroom. Because not only do we need to find the photos –we need the negatives as well. I'd basically decided to go ahead and do that, on my own, but the one problem with that plan was–*he doesn't get hurt*–he doesn't feel the fear–there's no deterrent to him doing it again, *and again.*" Sue's anger was evident as she stood up again and started pacing.

"Hold on Sue. Surely if there's two of us now to go together and report him that would make a difference. Obviously not to

Bollington–not anyone in Burmont–somewhere else. My old Sarge Bill, is really nice. We could go to him."

"Think about it mate. Do you want him, and a couple of hundred other coppers pawing over those photos of you? *I sure don't.* Even if your Sarge went ahead with an investigation, which I'm not sure he would when he hears a Senior Sergeant is somehow involved, but even if he did risk his career and go ahead, could you handle the exposure?"

I sighed heavily, knowing that she was right. To ask Bill to take something like this on, that could affect his career, would be a big ask. And then thinking about all of the people who would have to look at the evidence–*those photos–displayed in a Courtroom,* sent a cold chill shuddering through my bones, and a hot flush flooded my face. I dropped my head into my hands, forgetting about my bruised face and winced at the pain.

Sue sat down again and said, "We can do this–together. We can sort it without involving anyone else and without the humiliation and embarrassment of having to flash photographs of our fannies and boobs at all and sundry."

I looked up and met her eyes. I could see the anger and passion raging in there and it scared me a bit. I felt the anger myself, and the need for some kind of revenge, but mostly the need to protect myself and to put an end to the fear. I couldn't see any other option that would achieve that–Sue was my only hope.

"Ok," I said resignedly, "but we need to plan this–meticulously."

CHAPTER 27

Staff Meeting

I look across the workbench at their expectant faces, Sally's more concerned than Ros and Joe's who are sitting on their stools beside each other, chatting. Now I'm wishing I'd had some time today to compose what I'm about to say to them, but the day got quite busy as it went on. At least that served to prevent Sally from asking me about the customer who was in the shop when she returned from the Funeral Parlour.

We don't really have regular staff meetings. We just usually chat about upcoming weddings and other information that needs to be communicated. But if there's a major issue or some changes like when we changed the EFTPOS system, then we do get together and go through the details. This one is a little bit different though.

"Guys," I say, to get Ros and Joe's attention. "Thanks for staying, and for coming in in your case Ros. As you know we don't make a habit of staff meetings, but there is a possible safety issue that I need to talk to you about." At the mention of safety, they look at each other and me with more concerned expressions.

"It's a bit of a long story, one which I wasn't quite ready to share, but I don't have a choice now. I need to start by giving you some background, so you can understand what this is all about. You'll all remember some weeks ago when Sal broke the news about her and Jim, well not long after that I figured I might have a look online and see who was out there." I see a look of surprise cross the three faces surrounding me.

I address Sally with, "I suppose you sounded so happy, and it all sounded so easy that I thought I could do the same." Sally says, "Aww," and gives me a closed-mouthed smile and sympathetic look.

I reflect her smile and continue. "Well, as I soon found out–it's a crazy jungle out there. There are some *strange* people online, but I worked out ways to avoid most of them and started to wade my way through a few possibilities. My friend Marta helped me a bit, especially with the photos because I really hate being photographed, and she gave me some moral support. Anyway, long story short, I've met up with a few guys and one of them was not very nice. We met up in a café last week and almost from the first moment, I knew it was a mistake. He spoke badly about his ex-wife and he was wearing an electronic ankle monitor."

"Wait, doesn't that mean he's just got out of jail or something?" asks Joe in a conspiratorial whisper.

"Yes, exactly that. You guys know my police background, so of course for me it set off alarm bells and I hoped that after leaving that meetup, I would never have to see him again. I took down my online profile and we hadn't exchanged numbers or anything, but because he saw me driving the van, he knew where to find me. Straight after I'd left the café he came outside and stood there taking photos of the van, and probably me, in it."

"This guy sounds really dodgy," says Ros.

"Was that him that was in the shop today?" asks Sally. The others turn to look at her.

"Yes Sal. Now you know why I was so glad to see you. He didn't do anything, although he grabbed my hand quite tightly, but he just won't take no for an answer by the looks of things. Said I think I'm too good for him and that he knows I don't believe his story about why he had the monitor."

"Why did he have it?" asks Joe.

"From my experience, it would be a fairly serious offence but he's trying to tell me he just went back to his old house, which now belongs to his ex-wife, and let himself in to get something. Says everyone else is lying–you know the usual bullshit. Anyway, even if it was *just* Break and Enter, he wouldn't end up with a monitor, so I'm presuming there was aggression or violence involved. He also said his ex has turned the kids against him and won't let him see them or the grandkids. All red flags to me."

"Gees Tess, I'm glad I came back when I did too," says Sally. "What can we do? Do you think he'll come back?"

"I don't know. He said he was going to check back in *'in a little while'*. I tried to tell him I'd made a mistake and wasn't ready to meet someone after all and that's why I took down my profile. Then he basically told me I'd better not be lying. I asked him not to come back but I have an awful feeling that he will."

"Shit mate, you poor thing. Are you ok?" Joe's voice rings of concern. None of them knows what I went through in the past and I'm not about to tell them now. I can imagine there would be even more concern for me if they knew.

"Yeah, I'm ok thanks. Really my main concern is that he doesn't bother any of you. I am going to take steps to increase everyone's safety here in the shop. My home is already a fortress, with security cameras and screens. I've organised for Marta to come and put cameras up outside here, but I am going to get her to put one up inside as well–a very obvious one that might act as a deterrent." I reach into my bag, which is at the foot of my stool and grab my laptop.

While I fire it up, Sally asks, "Do you think we should limit the times when anyone is here on their own? Just for a while until you know it's safe?"

"Yes, my thoughts exactly. As it is, it's not often that one of us is here on our own but let's try to make it even less often. The other thing I'd like to do is make you more visible Joe."

Joe points to his chest and says, "Me? I'm no heavy. Well, I've got the size but nothing to back it up."

"I don't expect you to have to do anything, but I think seeing a guy here will be a bit more of a deterrent. It might also be good if you can answer the phone most of the time when you're in, if that's ok with you?" I look at Joe and raise my eyebrows, hoping he's happy to take on this role.

"Of course. I'll put on my most masculine voice. *How does this sound?"* he asks, doing a Barry White impression.

"Hmm, we might end up with a few more customers if you're answering the phone like that," I laugh, then become serious again as I turn the laptop to face the group, especially Ros and Joe who haven't seen this face before. The photograph is the best of the ones I could download, but still masks his eyes.

"This is what he looks like. And he always seems to be wearing those glasses. They make it hard to see his eyes, but he called himself *Blueeyes* online, so I imagine they're blue. He said his name is Marcus but who really knows?"

"What about reporting this guy?" asks Ros. "To the police."

"Yes, I'm going to do that on my way home. I can give them a copy of this photo and he should even be known to police already. Then, even if his name isn't Marcus, they would be able to ID him–if it comes down to needing to do that. For now, I just want them to have a record of my concerns. I don't want to have him charged with assault or anything for grabbing my hand. If he doesn't get the message to steer clear, then I'll push for some action from them."

"What about on the dating site? Did you report him to them?" asks Sally.

"No. Good idea though. I was in such a hurry to get offline and become invisible that I didn't even think of that. I will though. I don't want other women to have to go through this too."

Sal gives me that sympathetic smile again and says, "I'm so sorry that it hasn't worked out for you the way it did for me. It sounds like I was just very lucky."

"Did you meet any that were half-decent?" asks Joe.

"Oh, kind of. One guy who's an accountant and has offered to do the books at a good price," I give a little laugh and add, "but he's definitely just a friend."

Sensing there is more, Sally prompts me, "And…"

"And another one who I've only met up with once but seems nice enough." I'm not sure why I lied about only seeing him once, but I suppose it's because I don't want a whole lot of questions about him, especially as I'm still working out if he's genuine or not.

* * *

After our meeting, we all leave the shop and I head to the local Police Station to make my report. The officer on the front counter is a young constable, tall and dark-haired with a baby face that makes me feel incredibly old. He introduces himself as Constable Michael O'Mara. He takes down my details and a record of the conversation with Marcus, along with my description of him. I allow him to print a copy of the photo from my laptop and he assures me that he will log the incident and start a file. He's polite and efficient and hands me a card at the end, telling me to let him know if I have any further problems with Marcus, or call 000 if it's urgent.

Once home, I kick off my shoes and put my feet up on the couch with Lola curled up by my side. Then I call Marta to update her with today's events. After our greetings I get straight to the reason for my call.

"Hey, you know that *Blueeyes* guy that you rescued me from the other day? The creep with the tracker taking the photos of me in the van?"

"Yes, of course."

"Well, he turns up at the shop today and starts on about me thinking I'm too good for him and not believing his lame story. He actually grabbed my hand at one point and his manner was aggressive. I was on my own and didn't feel very safe."

"*Shit Tess.* What did you do?"

"Well, thankfully, Sally came back while he was there and that was enough to get him to leave, but he said he'll be back. I asked him not to but don't think he'll take any notice."

"So it definitely was you he was taking a photo of then. Does he still have the tracker on?"

"He said it's off now, but I don't know... I just went to the local station and reported him, just so it's on record."

"How did that go?" she asks with a cynical edge to her voice.

"No, it was good," I assure her. "The young constable seemed interested enough. I also got the gang together at work and told them so they can take extra precautions, and I showed them a photo so they can recognise him if he comes back." I take a breath and try to get his face out of my head.

"I was ringing though to see if you have any spare time to maybe do those cameras at work, sooner rather than later? And I want to put a really obvious one inside the shop so he can see that he's on camera."

"Good idea. I'm working tomorrow but the day after I'm off. How's that? Will just need to buy some equipment and then I can head over around ten. I should be able to do it without disrupting business too much and I'd rather get it done before the weekend. Helen and I have a bit on, plus the sooner the better by the sounds."

"Yeah, Friday is fine." The mention of Friday makes my tummy do a little flip as I remember my date with Guy. "I'm seeing Guy again on Friday night," I say. I've told Marta about the bombshell he dropped on the surfing date, and I've already told her we're going out on Friday night but can't resist mentioning him again.

"Yes, my dear. You did mention that. Sounds like you're looking forward to it."

"That obvious hey? Yeah, I am. Trouble is I have to get through dinner on Thursday night with Perry," I say, sounding considerably less enthusiastic.

"Oh the fibbing accountant? You should probably just let that one slide. Up to you, of course, but you don't want to give him false hopes."

"I reinforced that it was just friends, and that we should go Dutch. Anyway, we'll see. He's offered to help with the tax return for the business and I could really use some help with that, especially from an accountant."

"Using him?" she suggests.

"Maybe a little. He's good company though. I *should* look forward to having dinner with him. I suppose it just fades a bit when I think about having dinner with Guy."

"It's such a shame that other creep had to spoil things for you. Otherwise your online experience would have been pretty good hey?"

"Yeah. Should've stopped while I was ahead. I keep wishing I'd pulled the pin on that meeting with him, but I was trying not to be rude. Ugh, *bloody stupid.*"

"You weren't to know. Honestly though, what are the odds?"

"Incredibly high for me for some reason. I wish I knew why I attract them."

"Hang in there. We'll get you all wired up and spook him out with technology. See you Friday."

"Thanks Marta. See you then." I end the connection and call Jacinta. She knows about Guy but now I think it's time she also knew about Marcus. I feel a strong need to protect everyone around me who could be in any way vulnerable.

CHAPTER 28
Planning

"You know what they say–well what my footy coach always used to say… Get the five Ps right because proper planning prevents poor performance, or in our case… proper planning pinches pervert's photos." Sue's mood visibly improved once I committed myself to the cause. She ran our cups under the tap and filled the kettle again as she spoke. I had a visual of her on the footy field, running with the football tucked under her arm. I would get out of her way.

"We have about an hour before Rick gets home so we need to start to form a plan on how we're going to do this," she continued as she sat back down.

"Yes, and I need to hit the road soon too," I said, checking my watch again. "Ok, we need to think about the *when* first, then the *how*. We both obviously want those photos in his hands for the least amount of time possible, so *soon* is my suggestion. I'm talking the next few days–but we can't rush into this. I want to be sure we've covered our arses before we do anything."

"Absolutely. And you have more to think about in that regard if you want to continue in the job. I'm out now but I still don't want to get caught breaking into someone's house, especially a copper's. As I said, when it was just me, I started out thinking along the lines of waiting until he was at work on a dayshift and watching to make sure he'd dropped Leah at work as well, and then breaking in and finding that darkroom. That would've given me enough time to do a thorough search while they were both at work. But, with that plan there's no reason for him to stop, plus there's the possibility that I wouldn't be able to find the photos or negatives and I'd need him there to *convince* him to cough them up. Now there's two of us though, we can work out a much better plan."

I couldn't help wondering what kind of *convincing* she might be talking about. I suspected there were other holes in her plan, so I questioned her further.

"Hang on, how do you know that he drops his wife at work every day?"

"He used to have to run off for 20 minutes on the late shift to pick her up at work and drop her home, so he had to explain those absences to me, or take me with him."

"Why on earth don't they just get a second car?"

"She doesn't drive. I only realised later that he'd love that because it makes her totally dependent on him. Nicki said she seems quite timid and doesn't socialise much."

"Ok apart from that, I don't want to have to actually break in. That's a crime in itself–let's keep *those* to a minimum. We'd have possible neighbours' eyes on us too, and what about a dog? Oh wait, they couldn't possibly have a dog and do what he did to Mrs. Gordon's dogs over the back. Do you remember them? He baited them because they went for him when he took off from my place late one night through her yard. The poor little one died and the big one was really sick but survived."

"An all-round shit human being, Constable Watts," Sue muttered. "I can't call him Geoff anymore by the way, it sounds too familiar for a creature like him."

"I agree. Saying his name gives me the creeps too. Look, I reckon we do it when she's at work and he's home alone. We walk right up and ring his doorbell or knock or whatever and that in itself will catch him by surprise, then we can push our way in if he tries to stop us. He's so arrogant that he probably won't even see us as a threat."

"Ok, say we do that, and we ask him nicely for the photos and negatives and he says, *Fuck off*, what then?" Sue asked.

"That's where it gets a bit hairy," I paused, finding it hard to propose the next steps that might be required.

Sue stepped in and did it for me, "Well, obviously we're not going to oblige and just *fuck off*. We can't fail at this because it will probably be the one and only chance we get. We need to be prepared to get physical because I reckon he'll just laugh off any threats we make."

I knew she was right. I just didn't like the idea of having to use violence, even though I knew that this person had used it against me, and Sue. He'd invaded our privacy and robbed us of our dignity, perhaps even more–that we didn't even know about. I felt the anger and resentment, but I didn't feel the same need to inflict hurt that Sue obviously did.

I said, "Let's presume we get the photos and negatives without having to be too hands-on. How are we going to make sure he doesn't do this again? Can we threaten to make the photos public or tell his wife or something?"

"Would he fall for that? I don't know." Sue thought for a moment then added, "He'd probably know that we wouldn't want them to be public, and how do we even prove that they're his photos?"

"We need to take photos of everything as we find it–like a proper crime scene search. Have you got a camera? Of course, we'd have to say he invited us in and told us where to find things, *willingly*."

Sue nodded, "Yeah, I've got a Nikon with a good flash." She turned over her sheet of paper from earlier and started writing on the back. "Camera and flash," she read as she wrote, "gloves, torch, hammer…"

I interrupted her, shocked. "Hammer? What do we need that for?" My imagination was sending me disturbing images.

"Just in case we end up having to break in–might bring a screwdriver as well," she answered, still writing. "Duct tape, windcheaters–I think we should wear windcheaters with hoods in case the neighbours are sticky beaks. Try to be as unidentifiable as possible. Sunnies too. And we should have our gloves on before we arrive and keep our hands in our pockets until we're in. Maybe even turn our backs to the door so he can't see us 'til he opens it. Once he sees we're wearing gloves, he might shit himself a bit though. I say we grab him as soon as he opens the door, get inside quickly and lock it–just in case he tries to make a run for it."

"Shit Sue, even talking about doing this stuff is scaring me. Are we going to be able to go through with this?" I couldn't believe she was so into the detail already, and so calm about it all.

She looked up in surprise and said, "*We bloody well better.* Don't go all soft on me now. Do you want those photos back or not?"

"Ok, ok, I know." I looked at my damaged wrists and felt the still raw bruising on my ankles. Outrage filled me again as my mind tried to imagine what those stolen images of me could possibly look like. I felt like I wanted to throw up. I quickly grabbed my empty mug and filled it under the kitchen tap. Taking sips of the cool water helped to settle my stomach enough to sit back down and continue our planning.

The more detailed our planning became, the more I started to think we must be crazy. Each action was allocated to one of us so that we knew exactly what our responsibilities were under pressure. We couldn't afford to slip up by expecting the other person to do something that was part of our role.

Ensuring the door is locked (by me) and both facing him, Sue would move to our right and I would move to our left. We'd stick to these sides whether he was facing us or turned his back on us. We'd grab one arm each and pin them behind his back, pushing him to his knees. We both knew this move well from our training. Sue would have the tape in her pocket and tape his wrists together, then we'd walk him to the nearest suitable chair, tape him to it and question him. If he tried yelling, I would jam the kitchen sponge that I'd have in my pocket into his mouth and Sue would tape over it. At this point our plan stalled. Sue added the sponge to the list and then chewed on the end of the pen, thinking.

"Now, either he tells us or refuses to. If he co-operates, one of us stays and guards him while the other goes to where he says it is and finds the stuff."

I knew which of those roles I wanted so I volunteered to do the searching. There was no way I wanted to be left alone with him–tied up or not.

Then I asked the question that we'd both been skirting around, "What if he just won't tell us where everything is? I'm thinking it would all be in the darkroom but that might not be the case. He might have some sneaky little hidey hole where he keeps all his sick stuff. He couldn't risk his wife finding it."

"Yeah, if he won't tell then you'll just have to hope we can find the darkroom and search it. If what we're after's not there, I might just find another use for that hammer."

I looked at Sue and she stared back at me with a look that told me she was not joking. She raised an eyebrow and her dark eyes squinted slightly as she said, "Get used to it. There's a distinct possibility that he'll think we're no threat to him–won't take us seriously. He will probably take a little convincing, but I'm only talking about a smack on the kneecap or elbow or something. Although, if a little smack doesn't get him talking, then maybe a slightly harder one will."

I felt nauseous again and started sipping my water. Sue noticed. "You throw up in his house and we're stuffed. You need to focus on the goal, get your moves clear in your head and don't think about the other stuff. I'll handle that. We need to walk out of there with what we came for."

She sounded so matter of fact. Like it was a football match or something. She wrote on the list again saying, "Plastic bag. Make sure you've got one of those in your pocket too–just in case you need to puke."

I swallowed hard and sat up straighter, willing my stomach to settle. It co-operated partially–enough for me to sound confident as I said, "I'm pretty sure that he and Mark went straight onto night shift when Ray and I finished ours, but I'll need to double-check the roster, then I'll call you. Ideally, this needs to be in the next couple of days, while I'm still on my days off."

Sue agreed, "Yeah, I'll have to drive in early that morning so he doesn't get a chance to see my car around town. Don't want to give him any reason to be on guard. And we need to be careful when we park in his street. Will have to stop up the road a bit and walk down."

That comment made me realise that I didn't even know where he lived. "I take it you know his address then?" I asked.

"Yeah, he took me a couple of times when he was dropping Leah home from work. 27 Highgrove Street." She stood and fetched another sheet of paper and started drawing. "Here, I'll draw you a sketch of what the front of the house looks like, so you know what to expect. It will be too risky for you to check it out by driving around there–just in case he sees you."

She described everything as she drew, including lines of trees and bushes around the house. She then handed me the drawing, saying, "How about I meet you at the Ampol garage on the way into town at eight-thirty? Assuming he's on night shift day after tomorrow, let's aim for that."

I sounded calmer than I felt as I agreed. I then copied Sue's list of essential items onto the back of the sketch she'd just given me. We cross-checked the lists, allocating each item to the person responsible for bringing it along on the day. Just as we ticked off the last item, we heard a car pull up outside. Our eyes met and I pocketed my list as Sue said, "Talk about timing."

Hearing Rick coming home made me think of Russell. I felt uneasy knowing that I couldn't tell him anything about what Sue and I were planning to do. I nodded in the direction of the street and was about to confirm that it was the same for Sue, when she beat me to it, "Not a word–to him or your guy." She gave me a serious look from under her dark, knotted eyebrows.

I nodded, "Of course. They can't be involved."

Sue stood up and gathered the mugs into the sink. I took that as a signal that I should be on my way, so I stood as well. We headed toward the door just as Rick was about to enter. Sue did the introductions, and I met a short, stocky, brown-haired guy of around our age, dressed in what were probably once navy overalls, but which were mostly blackened with grease. I presumed he was a mechanic or something but realised I hadn't even asked Sue anything about him. We said a quick hello and I turned to Sue, "I'll call you soon." *An innocent enough sentence with a huge hidden meaning attached in this instance.*

On the drive home I realised that we didn't get to discuss in any kind of detail what we planned to do to instil the necessary fear that would prevent Watts from just going out and doing what he had done to us again, to someone else. Then another chilling thought hit me. *What if he tried to get back at us afterwards? To have his revenge. How were we going to avoid that?* I knew there needed to be an extremely strong deterrent to any kind of retribution as well as stopping his current pattern of behaviour. I tossed ideas around as the kilometres disappeared under my Michelins and the sun threw out its last feeble golden rays, like fingers losing their grip on the land over the edge of a cliff.

* * *

Russell had been expecting me for the past hour and seemed relieved to see me when I finally arrived home. I'd started to think of it as home because it was going to have to be my home for a little while at least. Going back to live in the cottage on my own was just not an option.

"How did you go?" he asked, moving in close for a kiss.

Now it starts, I thought. I didn't want to lie to Russell, but I had to limit the information that I gave him. I knew that if I were to tell him who attacked me, he would be itching to go around there and do something to him–even though he was a cop. Apart from his concern about me, he also had a stake in this because of the attack on him and there was the likelihood that his assailant could be one and the same, although I couldn't reconcile why he would've attacked Russell on that first night. Still, I could not involve him in the plan that Sue and I had agreed upon.

"Pretty good," I answered. "She *did* have a disturbingly similar experience and she and I are going to put our heads together again soon and work out who did this to us." I knew it sounded lame, but it was the best I could come up with, without blatantly lying.

"Well, I suppose two heads are always better than one, but do you think you'll be able to? What about the police?" His mention of police rocked me for a moment, until I realised that he meant reporting it to the police.

"No, she couldn't bring herself to and she's adamant that she still doesn't want to. You know how I feel about that, so we're going to do our own investigations for now." I felt like my face must be glowing red from lying to him and I wanted to change the subject, so I asked, "Would you mind coming around to my place so I can pack some more things? Oh, and by the way, would you mind if I move in with you for a little while?"

He laughed, "I figured that was a given. No way you should be on your own until this is all sorted and this bastard is locked up."

Going back into my house felt strange. It felt like a deserted house to me now–no longer the cosy little cottage where I'd planned to make an independent and exciting, new life for myself. I packed a lot more of my clothes and gathered up any food that would go off in the next couple of weeks. On the way out, I stopped at the letterbox, thinking that I should check, but not really wanting to open it in case there was a note in there. I really couldn't face something like that after the long drive and mentally exhausting day.

I flipped it open and found some advertising material and a letter from Mum. I was so relieved to see her writing on the envelope that I almost cried. Seeing the letter made me feel incredibly homesick– like just packing up the car and leaving all of this behind me. But I knew I couldn't do that, and I knew that I would not be leaving Burmont until I had those photographs, and the negatives in my possession.

In Russell's car, after leaving my place, he said, "I hope you're hungry. Tama's cooking tonight." Apparently, everyone in the house had turns cooking dinner and it was Tama's turn.

I hadn't thought about dinner but the mention of it made me realise that I was hungry. I was also a little nervous about having dinner with his housemates and letting them know that I would be staying for a while. I'd asked Russell not to tell people about what happened yesterday, but I knew he had told them about some of the earlier incidents. I started to wonder exactly what they did know.

"So how much have you told the guys and Letitia about what's been going on? Will I need to explain about why I'm staying?" I asked.

"Well, they know about the brick on the roof. I told them that's why you were staying after your late shifts. Other than that, I told them about the necklace and the first note, but not the second one, or the fence, and obviously not the break in and photos because you asked me not to. Of course they all know about Daz's car–he went on for days about that. They're all concerned for you, and both of us really, after me ending up with concussion. It was Letitia who found me on the doorstep, bleeding and out cold. Scared the shit out of her she said. So yeah, they'll understand."

I put my hand on his arm and he covered it with one of his. "Thank you," I said, "I don't know what I would have done without you."

I later realised I'd spoken too soon. Over dinner at Russell's that night, I once again felt like running home to my mum.

* * *

Tama was a Kiwi, from Hamilton, and he was a big guy. The dinner he'd prepared looked like it could feed the All Blacks, maybe for a week. Along with a platter of massive steaks that would do Fred Flintstone proud, were trays of roast veggies and a big saucepan of gravy. I feared the steak would be tough, so I searched for the smallest piece available. Surprisingly, it was quite good, and we made a bigger dent in the smorgasbord than I'd expected.

During dinner the guys were telling stories about their days at work, but I felt like I couldn't contribute much about my day. I told them I drove to Agnes Water to see a friend and raved on about how beautiful it was there. I also thanked them for letting me stay.

Darrel said, "Maybe you'll like it so much you'll want to take over Russ's room when he leaves for Europe in July. We'll be looking for a couple of new housemates with him and Brooksie gone." He smiled and looked at me expectantly. The look on my face must have conveyed just how badly he'd put his foot in it. He fumbled on, in a much quieter and uncertain voice, "Unless you're going too, I guess." Again, he looked from Russell to me and back again before deciding he should probably just shut up.

Russell grabbed for my hand and I resisted the temptation to pull it away. I didn't want to put on a display during the first dinner I'd had with his friends, but I really just wanted to get up and leave. July was less than two months away. I wondered just when he might have been thinking about telling me this little piece of news. The meal sat heavy in my stomach, and I felt increasingly uncomfortable. My one last bastion of stability, the person I trusted most, had lied to me. Worse, tricked me. I would never have slept with him if I'd thought he was leaving town in six weeks' time. *He should have told me.*

"We need to have a talk about that yet," Russell offered into the silence that had descended over the table.

Tama reached through the awkwardness and picked up the tray of potatoes in an effort to rescue the dinner, "Come on guys, don't hold back on the food." He passed the tray around the table.

The conversation slowly picked up again with everyone holding their tummies and assuring him that they were stuffed. Pretty soon we were all chatting fairly normally, but the topic of overseas trips was not raised again.

After clearing up, Russell and I headed to his bedroom for what I imagined was going to be a very interesting conversation.

CHAPTER 29

Dinner and Dinner

Marta has finished fitting the camera inside the store and is giving me a quick rundown on how it works. She's positioned it in a prominent spot, high up in the corner behind the front counter. People would hardly fail to see the large black camera with its glowing red light showing that it's filming. She also has a sign for me to stick to the door, telling people that the premises has surveillance cameras in use. Again, pretty hard to miss as you enter the shop.

Now she takes her ladder and moves outside to fit two cameras out there, to cover all approach angles. I go with her to act as her TA, and so that we can continue to chat. I've told her all about the dinner last night with Perry, with a course-by-course description of the meal, but it seems that what she really wants to know is if I've taken her advice about letting him 'slide'.

"Did you set him free?" she asks. "Or at least tell him that you've met someone else?"

"Actually I did tell him. When he dropped me home, he asked if I'd like to go for a picnic this weekend, which seemed a bit keen to me, so I figured you were probably right that he might still have hopes of something that's not going to happen. I told him I'd met someone just recently and that I wanted to see where that goes."

"And... how did he take it?"

"He did look a bit crestfallen. So, although it was hard to see the disappointment in his face, I was glad I followed your advice and got that message through loud and clear. I thought I already had, but obviously not. He was nice about it though."

"What about the picnic then? Are you going to still hang out together?"

"Yes, but I suggested that we catch up next weekend instead. He wants to go somewhere dog-friendly so he can bring his dog Benson and I'll bring Lola. Let them have a *play date.* His dog sounds gorgeous–it's a dalmatian. You know me and dogs–I'm kinda keen to meet Benson so yeah, we'll do that next week."

"Poor old Perry. Another Tess Merlin reject. At least he's not the stalking kind. Speaking of which, that creep will have to be thick as two bricks to try coming back here when all of this is in place." Marta grabs her drill from me and points it toward a spot on the wall. "Here ok?" she asks and when I give my approval, she begins attacking the wall.

In the quiet after the drilling stops Marta says, "So, dinner out two nights in a row. You decided what you're wearing tonight?"

Even the mention of it makes my tummy do a little jump and a smile arrives at my lips. "I know. I feel very spoiled. And no. If I had more time, I'd go shopping and buy something new but I'm just going to have to drag something out of the wardrobe."

Marta smiles at me and says, "That wardrobe? That's as good as going shopping. You must have a dozen outfits in there that you've never even worn." Then after a second she adds, "Are you tempted to tell him about this other jerk or are you afraid that might lead to having to tell him a bit more about your past than you want to at this stage?"

"Good question. I am tempted, and he said *no secrets,* but it would be only part of the truth if I told him about this without him knowing the background. And then there's the fear of him seeing me as a *case*."

"Yeah. It's tough. You will have to tell him eventually though–if this is a goer."

"True. That's what I need to work out first though–if this is for real. You know sometimes I think he's just too good to be true and then I start looking for reasons to hold back, like the fact that we met as part of his research project."

"Well, if it's real, will it really matter how you met?" She gives me a questioning look with a little smirk like she's proud of herself for making the point.

I know it's a good point and I should give him the benefit of the doubt, but my life has been dotted with instances where I did just that, only to be let down and taken advantage of. The fear of being used or let down again is very real and being vulnerable will not come easily to me.

"You know the kind of trust issues I've had in the past and how hard it was for me to even trust Bernie enough to go out with him, and eventually marry him–and we all know how that ended up. There hasn't been anyone that I've been able to trust implicitly–ever." Realising that I'm talking about romantic relationships but haven't quite made that clear, I add, "I mean in a partner. Of course there's you and the kids..."

Marta interrupts, "Yeah, I know exactly what you mean. It won't be easy, but it might be worth it." She changes the drill bit, and screws the camera into place before climbing down the ladder. She puts her arm around my shoulder and says, "Hey, try not to overthink it. Have a great night out and see how things feel." She gives my shoulders a squeeze and moves her ladder to the next installation point. Before she climbs up, she turns and says, "And if it feels good, bring him over for dinner to ours soon. You know we're all busting to meet him."

* * *

Guy has made reservations at a restaurant near his place called The Jetty, which he told me has amazing seafood. We arranged to meet outside at six-thirty, and as I walk along the footpath beside the ocean, my eyes search for his shape amongst the people gathering and walking near the shops. *The Jetty* isn't on a jetty, but from the window of the Uber on the way I saw that there was one close by. I admired it as we passed, timelessly spanning the sand and only just touching the darkening waters of the low tide in the fading light.

As I move closer, I can see him. He's waiting a few metres away from the entrance. I wave as I see him look up and spot me. I feel my pace quicken along with my heartbeat. He's smiling broadly as I reach him. He pulls me in for a hug.

"It's so good to see you," he says close to my ear.

"You too," I respond as we break apart and I take a good look at him. He's wearing a light grey, long sleeved, close-knit sweater in the style of a t-shirt with no collar. It hugs his chest and arms, accentuating his pecs and biceps along with the relatively flat stomach that many men his age would be so jealous of. He's teamed this with pale denim jeans and brown Vans. His unruly blonde hair looks to have been tamed somewhat but is still natural enough to look casual. I'm impressed by his dress sense and realise that this is the first time I've seen him in anything other than boardies and his garish Hawaiian shirt.

I tried on about seven different outfits before I settled on a brown and white spotted wrap dress that is very figure flattering as well as being comfortable to wear. Even though I'm in my fifties (a fact that my brain finds hard to accept), I can't bring myself to dress like someone in their fifties. I like my dresses above the knee to show off my still impressive legs, and I've finally developed enough confidence to just wear what I like, rather than what other people might think is appropriate. I've occasionally tried going down the path of dressing my age, shopping in the more conservative sections of department stores and even trying some of those 'old lady shops' as Cinta calls them, but anything I've ended up buying from them has sat in the wardrobe, unworn.

This one is a bit of an old favourite because of the way it clings to my figure and just shows the right amount of cleavage, plus I usually get compliments when I wear it. Keeping up that tradition, Guy says, "You look amazing. Love the spots."

"Aw, this ol' thing?" I say and do a half twirl holding out my skirt. "Thanks, you look pretty amazing yourself," I add.

We enter the restaurant and are ushered to our table by a dark-haired young lady who seats us and introduces herself as our waitress for tonight–Mimi. She hands us each a large one-sided menu and assures us she will be back shortly to take our drinks orders, then heads off to fetch water for our table.

The atmosphere is one hundred percent marine inspired. There are fishing nets strung just below the ceiling, running the entire length of the room, and the lights are in the style of boat lanterns. Blues and greens cover the walls, along with beautiful murals of sea creatures, and anchors and old ship wheels adorn the internal pillars. Even though it is quite early on a Friday night, the restaurant is already packed, which I take as a good sign of it being able to live up to Guy's glowing recommendations.

The only negative for me is a big glass tank that I spotted on our way in, holding lobsters that I imagine will be killed and eaten tonight or sometime soon. Luckily, I'm facing away from it, but even if I'd been considering having lobster, I couldn't face it now. I can't help reflecting on how little we think about where our food comes from and the processes that go into it ending up on our plate.

I mention this to Guy and he glances over at the tank replying, "Yeah, I read a book recently about octopuses and how intelligent and complex they are. They sometimes even form relationships with people, like the woman in this book. After reading that I haven't eaten octopus again–never will."

After ordering our meals–mine scallops followed by tempura battered barramundi, and his crab rolls followed by grilled snapper–we spend a lot of time talking about food and our likes and dislikes. When our entrees arrive, I have severe food envy for his crab rolls.

"Oh, they look fantastic," I hint not very subtly, and he offers me one as a swap for a scallop. I feel at ease and comfortable about sharing food with him, like an old married couple.

As we start on our main courses, the conversation turns to our experiences with online dating. As it was me who brought up the topic, I don't have to be concerned that this may form part of his research. Guy has me in stitches about some of the names and profiles that he came across, especially one calling herself Playful Bunny whose inuendo was as subtle as a sledgehammer as she promised to *jump into 'gear' and hop on for the long ride,* finishing off with, *you know what we bunnies are like…*

I tell him about *Funtimepete* with the gold chains and the oil and the poor old snake, and a few others that are good for a laugh, and then get a bit more serious when I ask, "Have you had any really strange or unpleasant ones?"

"To be honest, I've only met up with you and one other lady. She was supposed to be fifty-three and in the photos her hair was brown, and she looked quite attractive. When I arrived at the café, I was about to walk straight past her when I heard her call my name. She stood up from the table that she was waiting at and said hello. Seriously, in real life she looked about sixty-five, her hair was mostly grey, and she was rather on the plump side."

"How did you handle that? Did you stay and go through the motions?"

"Yes, I couldn't just turn around and walk out but I felt a bit cheated and was tempted to say something. I just couldn't figure out how to do that without being blatantly rude. In the end, after a decent amount of time I started to talk about leaving and she asked if I wanted to get together again. Put me on the spot that did, so I said that she wasn't quite what I'd expected from her photos. It was very awkward."

"That's so annoying. I don't see the point in lying about your age and putting up old photos. It's not as if the person you're meeting is not going to notice that you're suddenly about ten years older and probably less attractive as well. I had a guy lie about his age but other than that he was very nice. I thought we could be friends, but he was hoping for more."

"Oh?" he prompts.

"Actually, I had dinner with him recently and it seemed like he was still hoping for more than friends, so I told him I'd met someone."

"And who might that someone be?" he asks with a tilt of his head and a smile. I just smile back. "I'm hoping you were talking about me," he finishes.

"Yes, I had this nutty professor, surfer dude in mind when I said that."

He reaches across the table and holds my hand saying, "Ah, that's nice to hear."

* * *

As the dinner goes on, I'm starting to feel like I can talk to Guy more openly now, and maybe the second glass of wine is also having an influence on that, but I decide to tell him about Marcus. I leave out my past experiences and concentrate on Marcus only.

By the time I bring him up to date with all of that and tell him about Marta and her photographic skills and her sidelining as a security tech, it's starting to get late.

"That's really concerning. Are you sure you're ok? What about your home, is it alarmed and safe?" Guy seems genuinely concerned.

"Yes, Marta has done her magic there too. Plus, I have Lola." I'd told him about Lola during our long conversation on his deck on Tuesday. He said he'd love to meet her.

I look around to see that the restaurant patrons are thinning out. I nod toward the clearing and wiping of tables going on behind us and say, "It looks like they might want to close up shortly."

"Yes, let's go. I'll go up and pay," he says as he reaches into his pocket for his wallet. I decide to let him pay without arguing because I plan to ask him over for dinner at my house soon–just the two of us.

"Would you like to walk up to my place? I would be under the limit by then and I could drive you home," he offers as we leave the restaurant. "I'd love to see you home safely."

I'm really quite tempted, not for the safety aspect, more for the extra time together, but I resist. "Oh, thanks but I'll just grab another Uber. I'll be fine," I say as I start the process of ordering my ride home before I can be swayed. "Thank you so much for dinner though. It was so good."

"Yes, the food was incredible and the company even better."

"Ha. Charmer," I say. "I was wondering if you'd like to come over to mine for dinner soon. You can meet Lola then too."

"I'd love it. Should we go surfing again soon too? How about Sunday?"

"Ok. We can go for a surf in the morning and then maybe we could have dinner Sunday night?" I wonder if I'm sounding a bit too keen but Guy replies quickly, "Fantastic."

We make plans to meet up again at the same spot on the beach and I check my phone for an ETA of the Uber.

"It's only three minutes away, apparently," I say looking up at Guy.

He touches my upper arm and says, "Before your ride comes, we should say goodbye properly so you're not in a rush. Can I kiss you goodnight?"

By way of an answer, I lean toward him and go up on my tippy-toes and gently kiss him on the lips, pleasantly surprised by their softness. I then descend to my normal height and enjoy the buzz that the kiss has given me. I look into his eyes and say, "That's a yes."

He gives a little laugh, and as the Uber pulls up beside us, I add, "That Zinc cream is doing a good job of protecting those lips by the way."

He leans close and opens the rear door of the car for me saying, "Are you sure? Maybe you'd better just check their condition one more time."

This kiss is longer and more sensual and sets a few little butterflies loose in my tummy.

CHAPTER 30

Plan in Action

Russell held both hands up in front of him, palms open at shoulder height, like he was facing someone with a gun. Instead, he was facing me–only armed with that one burning question.

I asked it before he had a chance to speak. "When the hell were you considering telling me that you're pissing off to Europe in a few weeks?"

"Tess, look, I'm sorry, alright? I've been wanting to tell you but with all of this other stuff going on in your life, I just couldn't bring myself to do it."

"No. Not good enough. You *could* manage to bring yourself to sleep with me, but you couldn't manage to tell me that? What kind of chicken are you? Or are you just a user, a... a conman, *a bloody liar*?" My outrage kept building, fed by the feeling that I'd been duped and used by him.

"I don't blame you for being upset, but I was hoping that you might wait for me–be here when I get back. We'll only be gone for six months." He tried to hold my hand, but I pulled it away from his grasp.

"*Six months...* How the hell can you expect me to trust you now? Do you seriously think I would believe that you'd stay true to me while you're backpacking around Europe all that time, and meeting all sorts of exotic girls? That I would just sit around here waiting and hoping for you to come back to me? *You've got to be joking.*"

I kept talking as I dragged my suitcase out from under his bed and started throwing clothes and other belongings into it willy-nilly. I'd only just unpacked them before dinner.

"Especially after you couldn't even be honest with me about this to start with."

Russell grabbed my shoulders from behind and tried to hug my back but again I pulled away. "No, don't touch me. I need to go."

He dropped his hands, looking dejected, and said, "Please, just wait, babe. I don't want to lose you. Could you just try and see this from my point of view?"

"Don't *babe* me! I'm not your *babe.*"

"Ok, sorry, Tess. But you can't go home. Even if you're really pissed off with me, you can't go back there on your own. What about you just stay here in the little room up the verandah until you settle down?"

"Russell, there'll be no settling down. I need to go. You don't need to worry about me anymore," I said as I slipped past him and collected my keys from the top of his chest of drawers. I opened the bedroom door and thankfully there didn't seem to be anyone close by who might have heard our raised voices. I couldn't have faced seeing anyone at that point. I could feel the tears threatening to betray my steely resolve, so I hurried to the front door with my bag.

"Tess," Russell called, but I didn't turn back toward him. If I did, I knew I'd open the floodgate, and once I started crying, I wouldn't be able to stop. The hurt and disappointment vied with the shame and embarrassment of being used. I started down the stairs quickly but soon had to slow my pace and hold the handrail as my vision blurred and finally my eyes turned to pools of tears.

Once in the car, I let out a huge sigh and rubbed my eyes to clear them. I felt alone, heart-broken, and so, so tired. I had no home to go to, no warm, familiar bed and no comforting hugs or words from another human being. Another wave of sobs engulfed me as I allowed myself to register how lost I felt–like I'd been cut adrift with no life raft in a dark and threating sea, in the midst of a wild and unpredictable storm. My trust severely misplaced and abused.

After a minute or two of self-pity, I pulled my thoughts together and wiped my eyes. I started the engine and headed for the only sensible option–for that night at least. The Two Flamingos Motel, near the Ampol garage on the way into town.

* * *

The next morning, in the public phone box, I hung up the receiver from calling Sue, with trembling hands. My legs felt like jelly. The full realisation that we were actually going to do this thing had hit me like a ton of bricks.

I had gone in and double checked the roster, confirming that Watts was definitely on a late shift the next day. I dreaded going into the station in case I ran into him. I feared that my face would betray me and alert him to our knowledge. I was pretty sure that he wasn't there though. I'd checked the carpark and had only seen Derek's car and the patrol car there. I parked my car down the street where I could see the station and waited for the patrol car to leave the car park as always at 7.45am to go and pick up Senior Sergeant Bollington from his home and deposit him at work. Somehow Officers in Charge of stations seemed to think they were entitled to their own personal taxi service. Obviously, we chauffers couldn't argue with that.

I needed to be absolutely sure Bollington would not be at the station. I would've had almost as much of a problem facing him as I would have seeing Watts. His treatment of Sue and his effectively ending her career–all in her time of need, left me seething every time I thought of it.

I dressed in long sleeves and jeans, to cover my wrists and ankles and applied a substantial layer of make-up over the bruise on my face. I had my excuse ready in case anyone asked why I was checking the roster, *I wanted to see when my next days off were so I could plan a trip home to see my family.*

Only Don was in the office, so I said hello briefly and made my way to the roster pinned on the wall near the front counter. I was in and out of there in record time and scampered away like a rabbit that had dodged a bullet.

I left the phone box and returned to the motel via the local BCC supermarket, picking up a sponge and a roll of tape, along with some food items so my purchases didn't look too strange. Once back at the motel, I attempted to occupy myself by reading a book that I'd found in their activities room, but I felt too wired up and jumpy to sit still and concentrate. Possibly choosing a Stephen King book was not a good idea. *Night Shift* was a collection of short stories and the first one already had me creeped out half-way through. I tossed the book onto the chenille covered bed in my tiny room and wondered what else I could do to pass the time.

I reached into the pocket of my windcheater and retrieved the list that Sue and I had made, checking that I had gathered all of the items attributed to being my responsibility. I ticked each one off mentally, then hid the list at the bottom of my suitcase.

While I had the suitcase open, I looked through my meagre possessions for some inspiration–finally pulling out my running shorts and a t-shirt. I decided that maybe if I went for a run, I could sweat off some tension and tire myself out so that I had a possibility of actually falling asleep later.

I ran at a good pace for ten kilometres, however, each time my foot hit the pavement, the impact jolted through the tender area around my ankles and instead of relaxing me and loosening me up, it only served to ignite my anger and fuel my enthusiasm toward our plan. I mentally played out my upcoming role many times before I slowed my pace and began my cool-down.

Showering for me was becoming a very quick and furtive undertaking. The motel room being so small made it easy for me to check that I was alone and that the only three points of entry–door and two windows–were secured. I showered like a deer taking a drink from a waterhole in the forest–ears and eyes alert for the slightest sound or intrusion.

Around three o'clock, when Russell would be finishing work, I started to wonder if he might try to come and find me. I half-hoped and half-dreaded that he would, but there was no knock on my door.

The afternoon dragged by until the slim pickings of daytime television made way for the News and *A Country Practice.* Re-runs of *Charlie's Angels* then took me through until I started to feel my eyelids becoming heavy and I decided to tackle the daunting task of finding sleep. I battled with flashbacks of the attack, replays of the break-up with Russell and imaginings of our future encounter with Geoff until I finally fell into an exhausted, fitful sleep.

* * *

I waited for Sue at the Ampol as arranged, parked off to the side so that it didn't look like I wanted to buy petrol. Sitting in my car, I was jittery and nauseous. I wanted to get out and move around but I felt that would only get me noticed and we didn't need that, so I sat and picked at the already red and painful quicks around my fingernails.

I kept thinking that even with our careful planning, there was still the possibility that he might not be home. He might have made plans for the morning, or for the whole day before he was scheduled to start work at four. What then? We couldn't sit outside doing surveillance in one of our cars. He'd spot it straight away when he did eventually come home. He'd know our cars–just like I knew his–a silver Ford Escort. I pictured his car in my mind and then had another lightbulb moment where I remembered that first day, moving into my cottage, how I saw a tiny bit of a silver car driving off. This was another link in the chain that helped me to assure myself that he was in fact the one who had done these gruesome things.

Tucking my hands under my legs so I had to stop picking, I heard a car approach. I looked up hoping to see Sue's old blue Datsun 240Z that I'd seen parked outside their house in Agnes Water. Instead, it was a cream-coloured Ford Falcon driving toward me. The driver gave me a wave and I recalled the car as the one Rick came home in, when Sue and I were finishing off our planning.

Sue parked beside me and motioned for me to join her. I grabbed my windcheater and keys and swapped cars. As I slid into the passenger seat her greeting was, "You good?"

"Far from good but I'm ready," I said patting my pants pockets to show that I had everything I was supposed to have with me stashed in them. "How about you?"

"I'm up for this. Bloody ready alright. Just hope the arsehole is home and I haven't come all this way for nothing."

"Yeah, I've been fretting about that. Only one way to find out I suppose," I said sighing heavily and putting on my seat belt. "Good idea bringing Rick's car."

"I figured there'd be less chance of being recognised in this. Told Rick I didn't trust my little Datto on the longer trip and that his has a better sound system, which it does."

"Have you got everything?" I asked, knowing that Sue would have made sure of this already but still wanting to be re-assured.

"'Course," she answered, indicating a bag on the back seat. She was already wearing her windcheater, so I unclipped my seat belt while we were still stationary and put mine on too. "Do you need to run through the plan?" she offered as I struggled with dressing in the confined space.

"Yeah, let's do it once–just to be sure."

"Right from the start though, I think we need to make one small change," she began, making my heart beat a little faster for fear that it was going to be something unpleasant. "I was thinking it might be better if you're standing at the door on your own and I'll crouch down and be doing up a shoelace or something in case he has a spy hole in the door. What do you think?"

"Why?" I asked.

"Because if he looks through that or even looks out the window and sees two people with hoods over their heads he might get spooked, but if he just sees you, he'll just be super curious rather than on guard. Are you happy to ditch the hood as well, once we reach the door?"

I got where she was coming from. I had been thinking that two people in hooded jackets facing the other way might raise some concern so I had to agree that this slight change to the plan might give us a better chance of him opening the door.

"Sure. He's gonna see my face soon enough anyway."

We completed a run through of the other details and grabbed our gloves and stuffed them into our jacket pockets. She turned the ignition key and the V8 came to life. As she let out the clutch and we took off, I felt my stomach lurch, knowing that what I was about to do would change the rest of my life–one way or another.

Sue pulled up several houses away and reached for her sports bag on the back seat. It looked quite bulky to me, and I couldn't help wondering what she might have put in there other than the tape and hammer. Maybe she'd put a towel in to make it look like a proper sports bag. It didn't feel like the right time to start questioning her, so we put on our gloves and walked silently toward the house–as casually as we could manage under the circumstances. I wasn't even sure if my legs were moving or not, but I seemed to be keeping pace with Sue, so I figured they must have been.

The houses in his street were all on large blocks, at least half an acre by the look of the yards. I could see his house ahead of us.

I took in the tall palm trees casting their spidery shadows over the tiled roof, and then the thicker, greener trees and shrubs closer to the house. It was a sprawling, low-set brick construction that loosely resembled Sue's sketch. Relief and fear flooded my brain in equal portions, and goosebumps rose on my arms and the back of my neck as I saw the silver Escort parked in the driveway. He *was* home. The thick greenery afforded us some cover as we quietly approached the front door.

* * *

The doorbell rang as Geoff was half-way through his second set of bench presses. He was in his gym. In reality the third bedroom, which he'd recently converted to his workout space. His gym and his darkroom were his escapes from Leah. He was looking forward to the day when they could buy their own place, so he could build a proper shed and move his weights down there, along with his other prized possessions. He swore as the doorbell sounded a second time, then walked quickly toward the front door.

He looked through the peep hole and saw a smallish person in a dark windcheater and jeans. He squinted, trying to identify the visitor. It strangely appeared to him to look like that new policewoman, but he figured it must be the distortion of the lens as he couldn't believe that she would come to his house. Curious, he opened the door and then started as another shape in an identical outfit rose from a crouched position right in front of him. Then he saw *her* face. His ears began to ring from the blood that seemed to be suddenly pounding his eardrums and temples.

"What the hell?" He grabbed the door and pushed, trying to shut them out, but they were prepared for just that and pushed back with their combined strength. He backed up a little as they jostled inside and closed the door behind them, one of them locking it as he frantically thought about other possible escape routes. He couldn't decide whether to run or to just stand there and face them–see what they thought they're doing in his house, but before he had a chance to make a decision, they moved on him–one on each side. Instantly, his arms were locked behind his back. He struggled but they already had the upper hand. He couldn't break free. He felt his wrists being bound with some kind of tape.

They know, he thought. *Shit, they know.* He couldn't think how they could be bold enough and certain enough to undertake something like this attack on him even if they suspected him. *It's the fat bitch,* he thought. *My one mistake was calling her that–but I thought she was out to it.*

"What the hell...?" he started but didn't get to finish his question as a gloved hand clamped roughly over his mouth.

He was being physically pushed into the kitchen and down onto a wooden chair. He struggled as one of his assailants held his head back and the other one bound his thighs, tightly securing them onto the seat of the chair. *Smart move,* he thought. *I would have head-butted you into next week if you didn't have that vice-like grip on my head.* Next his ankles were being bound together, despite his struggling. That ensured he had no chance of even doing a bent over chair shuffle to try and escape. His brain working frantically to come up with ideas. He figured he could talk his way out of this if he could just be allowed to speak. He came up with no other options, so at least he had to try–play dumb and make them doubt what they thought they knew.

The hand over his mouth released its grip but hovered nearby. He seized the opportunity to speak. "Girls, what the hell do you think you're doing? I could start yelling and have the whole neighbourhood over here in no time," he bluffed, although he knew that his closest neighbour was at work and the other side was unlikely to hear much because they were on a bigger block and their house was too far away.

The big one showed him the roll of tape and the other produced a sponge from her pocket. One moved to each side of him, in perfect sync.

"No, no. I won't yell." He struggled with his bindings and tried the innocent act again, "I don't know why you're doing this to me. I'm a police officer–we're all police officers. We stick together."

The women looked at each other and Sue gave a cynical laugh, the first sound either of them had made.

Then she said, "Oh yes, we're well aware of how police officers stick together, only trouble is you seem to need a dick to be a part of that little circle. Right. Enough crap. Where are they?"

Geoff wrinkled up his brow and put on his best dumbfounded look, saying, "What the fuck are you talking about? You two need to get out of my house–now. Do you know what kind of shit you're going to be in when I report this?"

One grabbed his face and shoved his head back. Now he could only see the ceiling. He heard the other one walk off and then return a minute later.

"Nothing," she said, then to him, "I'm asking you nicely for the last time. Where are the photos? Where's your dirty little darkroom?"

Fuck, they know I've got a darkroom. He started to panic and struggle frantically with his arms and legs. He tried to stand and started to rock the chair sideways but was held back by the hand gripping his jaw even more tightly.

"Get fucked," he murmured through his clenched jaw.

Suddenly there was a cracking noise and his knee exploded in a shower of pain. His yell cut short by a thump to the side of his head. He heard his neck crack and his vision blurred.

* * *

"Shit Sue. Is he still breathing? Have I broken his neck?" I asked, looking at the limp figure slumped in the chair, head back and mouth open. I was shocked that Sue had so quickly resorted to violence with the hammer, but as soon as he started yelling, I knew I had to stop him somehow. I just hoped I hadn't broken any bones.

"I thought there would be a longer questioning process. You took me by surprise with that knee move."

"We haven't got time for his bullshit. He'll live. He'll come round in a minute. Grab some water and throw it on his face. That should do the trick." I turned to the sink and filled a glass that I found on the dish rack while I reported the result of my quick search of the house, "I didn't find a darkroom. I checked every room–nothing."

I threw the water in his face and he started to come round. Coughing and groaning, he shook his head. He immediately regretted the sudden movement, wincing in pain.

He looked at his knee and then at Sue and said, "You're a nasty bloody heifer. I'll get you for this."

His threat was like a red rag to a bull. Sue moved toward him again with the hammer, incensed by his insult.

"Wait Sue," I warned and then looked at him, "let's give him one last chance."

I took a step closer and said to him, "Talk and you might save yourself a lot of pain. Where are the photos and negatives, you slimy little creep?"

"What's this? Good cop, bad cop?" he feigned a laugh. "Still don't know what you're talking about you stupid bitches."

"Wrong answer," I heard from beside me where Sue was standing. The hammer was now gone, replaced by some other kind of tool that she'd dragged from her bag.

"*Sue,*" I whispered, "What the…?"

She held up the weapon so that he could get a good look at it. I also had the opportunity to register exactly what kind of tool it was. *A pair of bolt cutters.* I couldn't think of any current need for a pair of bolt cutters–at least not one that didn't involve cutting off a body part.

She advanced toward him, snipping the blades together a couple of times for effect, the metallic sound causing goosebumps to form all along my spine and neck. "How 'bout now? These jog your memory at all?"

Just as I was about to bottle it and stop Sue from doing something drastic, he caved. "Ok, ok, I do have a darkroom. Just put those bloody things down and let me loose and I'll get the photos you want."

"Wrong again. You tell us where the darkroom is, and we'll find them for ourselves. You're not getting out of that chair arsehole." Sue moved around to the back of his chair, saying, "Now are you left or right-handed? Let me try and remember..." She grabbed his right index finger and looked up at me. "You reckon we should do all those other women out there a favour? I think this one might be his shutter finger." Then back to him, "Now, if you're thinking you could learn to shoot with your middle finger, well you'd have to still have a middle finger to do that."

I could see the panic on his face. Sweat beads gathered on his forehead and upper lip and the armpits of his grey t-shirt were sprouting big dark balloon shapes. He struggled to move his feet, rocking the chair again in an effort to stand, but Sue stopped the movement with a heavy whack on his trapezoid with the bolt cutters.

He groaned and swore, "*Fuck's sake.*" He sounded close to crying as he croaked, "Out the back." He hesitated and then growled–a deep and primal sound like a beast in pain. "The shipping container." Then dropped his head onto his chest, his shoulders indicating that he was sobbing silently.

Sue stepped over closer to me, eyes still on Geoff and asked, "You want to go look and I'll stay here and guard him?"

"Of course." There was no chance I wanted to be left alone with him inside the house, but I fleetingly wondered if it might be unsafe to leave her alone with him. I was not as concerned about something happening to Sue as I was about her doing something else to him while I was gone.

"You're cool, right? Don't do anything 'til I come back hey?"

She nodded, "I won't hurt him unless he tries anything." Her warning intended for his ears as well as mine.

This only slightly reassured me, but time was ticking, and we needed to get what we'd come for and get out of there. "I'll be back in a minute," I said as I dug Sue's camera out of her sports bag and headed for the back door.

I *was* literally back in a minute. As soon as I saw the dark green metal shipping container under the shade of some Lilli Pilis, I spotted the padlock on the door. I had a quick look at the other sides, just in case there was another door, but there were no other openings. A sealed little box of depravity.

"*It's locked.* Did you not think I'd be back to get the key?" I directed this at him and then to Sue, "He's stalling, hoping for some miracle to come and save him if he wastes enough time."

That was enough to set Sue into action. She grasped his jaw tightly, emphasising the pain already throbbing there from my earlier blow. Her voice was eerily calm as she leaned over him, "Last chance. No one's gonna save you so quit wasting our time. The key, fuckwit."

He looked her in the eye and started to try and move his mouth, like he was going to speak, but instead he spat. It emerged as more of a dribble than a spit because of the way Sue was holding his face, and it didn't reach its target of Sue's face, but it served to enrage her, nevertheless.

She grabbed the bolt cutters from the floor and resumed her previous position behind the chair with his right index finger in her hand. He tried to curl it and wriggle it from her grip, but she was strong enough to hold it. Letting the bolt cutters slide to the floor again she fished out the duct tape from her pocket and said to me, "Here, give me a hand with this."

I grabbed the tape, not sure of what she wanted me to do. None of this was part of our planning–it was all ad lib on her part. She pushed his finger onto the edge of a rung on the chair's backrest and indicated with a circling motion that I should tape his finger there. His struggling made the simple task really difficult–the gloves added to my clumsiness in trying to apply the tape.

Once done, I stepped back and Sue fiddled with the tape a bit so that part of his finger was exposed, just below the top joint. "The key or the finger? Your choice," she hissed into his ear.

"You're bluffing. You wouldn't do it. I told you, I'll get the photos if you just untie me."

"The key or the finger?" she asked slowly, like she was talking to a simple person.

I was impressed by her bluffing. I'd have believed her if I were him. Also niggling in the back of my mind was the possibility that she may not be bluffing. After her readiness to inflict pain with the hammer to his knee, I felt like she was a more impulsive person than I'd previously thought. I swallowed hard and wondered if I'd strapped myself to a loose cannon by joining forces with her on this mission. If she were to go off script again and inflict grievous bodily harm and we got caught, I'd be charged with it as well because I'd helped.

GBH was a serious offence–in fact–a crime. To be *grievous*, the injury involved had to be permanent and I was pretty sure from my studies at the Academy that having a body part amputated qualified as *grievous*. Serious jail time was a distinct possibility for something like that.

I wanted to make sure she was bluffing but I couldn't say anything that would give it away to Geoff. If we couldn't get the location of the key out of him, we would be totally stuffed. The whole charade would have been for nothing, only serving to make him angry and hell-bent on revenge. Our lives would be a nightmare–looking over our shoulders forever.

Too late I heard him growl, "Fuck you." Immediately the words were out of his mouth I heard a sickening sound–a crunch, then a scream. I leapt forward and threw my hand over his mouth. He tried to bite, forcing me to let go but I quickly grabbed the sponge with my other hand and held that over his mouth under my gloved hand. The sponge provided enough padding to prevent his teeth from penetrating, and to cut off his next scream.

From my vantage point I could see the blood pouring from his severed finger stump. On the ground about a metre away was the top inch and a half of his finger, lying there like a fat grub, forever isolated from its life source and its long-time companions. The object looked so out of place that my brain didn't want to believe what my eyes were telling it. My stomach churned. Sue quickly grabbed a tea towel from the oven handle and put it over the ugly stump, then wrapped tape around it tightly.

She seemed calm while I was a raging tornado of fear, adrenaline and too many other chemicals and emotions to register. Sue seemed to be on some kind of auto-pilot, because her next actions seemed oddly robotic. She picked up his severed body part in her gloved hand and left the room. Seconds later I heard a toilet flushing. I dry reached at the thought. He grasped this as an opportunity to make another bid for escape and started struggling violently. I pushed him hard into the chair and applied extra force to his mouth.

Sue returned and went directly back to her position behind the chair. She grabbed his middle finger, right next to the poor battered and permanently shortened index finger, and said, "Now, what were we saying about taking dirty little pictures with mister middle finger?"

I felt his head shake from side to side under my grip and his repeated muffled word was clear enough for me to understand, "No, no, no, no." He was sobbing and his body was heaving under my pressure. I was afraid he might throw up and choke on it if I pushed the sponge too hard down on his mouth. I released the pressure slightly and he sucked in a shuddering breath.

"*Tim. Doom. Mim. Bim.*" He was trying to say something through the spongy layer but I couldn't understand what the words were.

Sue could. "Gym? Whereabouts in the gym?" she asked.

I released the pressure and stood ready to reapply if he tried to scream. "Under the mat near the squat rack," he whimpered, then added with more assertion, "The middle box only. All of your stuff is in there. Leave the rest of my things alone." He closed his eyes and let his head drop back onto the backrest of the chair. "I need an ambulance," he sobbed. "Now that you've got what you want. *I need an ambulance.*"

"Well, we haven't actually got it yet, so you're just going to have to wait a bit longer. Your own fault. You could have saved yourself all of this if you'd just co-operated," Sue patted him condescendingly on the shoulder.

She nodded to the camera over my shoulder saying, "Don't forget to document it all." Then she started pointing down the hall, "Go. Quick."

I passed the sponge to her and ran down the hall. The key was where he said it would be. I photographed that. I grabbed the key, looped the camera strap over my shoulder again and rushed out the back door for the second time. With shaking hands, I photographed the container door and the lock. I fumbled and missed the keyhole but slotted it in on my second effort. The key turned and the shackle popped out of the padlock base. I threw it on the ground and moved inside, reaching for the torch in my jeans back pocket.

The pungent smell of chemicals hit my nostrils and clawed at my throat as soon as I entered. There were no windows, so I wondered if he ventilated it somehow when he was using it. It seemed a very unhealthy environment–in more ways than one. I felt like I didn't even want to breathe in there, or at least I needed to limit the time I was inhaling those fumes.

The torch beam found a table lamp on a workbench along one wall of the container. I flicked the switch and the space was lit by a dim red light, enough to see my way around and to identify the shapes surrounding me. There were tubs all along the other side wall, filled with some kind of liquid, and on the far end wall were several lines stretched across the space, like clotheslines. Click, flash, click, flash. The irony of taking photographs in a photo developing lab was not lost on me.

Pegged to these lines with little clips were rows of photographs. I shone my torch on them, hoping to find the photos of me, but cringing at the same time for fear of confronting the images that my imagination had plagued me with for the past three days.

They were birds–rosellas, plovers, a kookaburra and a family of ducks, flying just above my head in one single stage of flight, forever frozen in time by his lens. I photographed them as well.

I shone my torch into the corners and the sphere of light picked up the end of a row of black plastic boxes lined up under the drying line. There were three boxes, all identical, with no labels. I knew he said only the middle one, but surely he couldn't expect us to respect his wishes, or to believe that he wouldn't have more stashed in the other boxes as well. I needed to look in them all. I photographed them all in situ.

I pulled out the first one–on the left–and opened the lid. It was almost full to the brim with loose photographs. No albums or folders. No packets because the images had all been developed in that stinky little room rather than at a lab. I spilled them out onto the floor so I could sift through more easily. More birds, some cows, landscapes and seascapes were all I found.

I grasped the middle box and slid it toward me. Squatting on my haunches, I lifted the lid, letting it fall down behind the box. What I saw caused my legs to give way under me and I fell to the ground, flat on my bottom. I trained my torch on the contents. The ability to breathe had abandoned me when I caught sight of the contents, but I eventually gasped in the stinging fumes. I desperately needed to get into some clean air so I could take a full breath. I dragged the box with me to the door so that I could check it more thoroughly in the daylight, while I filled my lungs. My head had started to ache from even a few short minutes' exposure to whatever was in those tubs, permeating the whole environment inside.

Neat stacks of photographs, each consisting of about thirty to forty photos, lined one end of the box. The top one was of me. I gasped and looked away briefly to catch my breath again, then forced myself to look back and record it on Sue's camera. I lifted one stack, and another–all me, but some of them were me in the street, fully clothed. Me going into the Drapery store, me getting into my car, me sitting in the car waiting for Russell at the hardware store–photos of my everyday life that I didn't even realise were being taken. These had as much of an effect on me as the naked ones. *He'd been watching me and photographing me–and I'd been oblivious!*

Finally, I found some photographs that looked to be of Sue. Her face was contorted and difficult to recognise, but I thought it was her. Beside these stacks of photos were long snake-like lines of negatives, most neatly curled but some breaking free to slither around the bottom of the box. I picked up one of these and again saw the person that I presumed to be Sue.

I was very aware of the time that was passing and of the increased danger with every passing minute, but I felt the need to be thorough. I needed to retrieve the third box. I covered the sordid contents of the second box with the lid and pushed it further out onto the grass.

I dreaded going back into the fetid little room but flicked my torch back on and filled my lungs with clean air, before heading straight for my target. I pulled out the last box. It felt very light as I carried it out the door and opened the lid. I found it was almost empty except for a brown bag, some lenses and some little canisters that looked like they would contain film. I pocketed those just in case they contained negatives rather than unexposed film.

I picked up the brown paper bag, expecting it to contain more negatives or photos, but it felt soft and light. After lifting it from its spot in the corner of the box, I saw that there were more photos hidden underneath. I peered inside the bag first, shining the torch in before I was game to put my hand in and touch whatever lay within.

I gasped in shock at the contents but also felt a strange surge of delight. I then flicked through the photos and fought my mouth as it started to form a smile–*this is not the time,* I told it. I ignored the lenses and transferred all of the other contents of this box into the one waiting on the grass. I quickly re-entered the shipping container and scanned the rest of the room for other boxes or shelves. I found none but I did see a very big, very fancy camera sitting at one end of the bench. I picked it up and opened the back to see if there was a film still in there. It was empty. With a feeling of satisfaction, I tossed it sideways into one of the tubs containing the liquid chemicals. I rushed back to Sue with the black box tucked under my arm, and with a feeling of renewed confidence and almost joy.

The bag, and the photographs secreted beneath it were more than I'd hoped for. Getting the photos of Sue and me back was the goal–and providing we could get out of the house undetected we'd achieved it. But this discovery… this was the super bonus, double jackpot, cherry on top.

CHAPTER 31

Late Home

The Uber smells of air freshener and the seats are covered in a kind of plastic coating. I'm grateful that the driver has the windows open so that I can lean toward mine and enjoy the fresh breeze as it hits my face. As we turn into my street, I see a white Camry parked about fifty metres from my house. My senses are immediately on alert and the memory of Guy's lips that had been occupying my thoughts recedes as I scan the rear panel of the Camry. I spot the scrape, then try to see if there is anyone in the driver's seat but by the time I move my attention from the rear of the car to the front, I miss my chance.

I think quickly enough to say to the driver, "Keep going. Please don't stop." He slows because we are almost at my house. "No, no, *please don't slow down.* Keep going." He speeds up again and asks, "Isn't this the address you gave? Where to now then?"

"Could you turn right at this next street here and go around the block please?" I indicate the corner that is quickly approaching. "I'm sorry, yes, it was the address, but I just need a minute."

He looks in the rear-view mirror at me, probably wondering if I'm drunk or just weird. I give him a reassuring smile and fix my eyes back on the road to make sure he's going to turn at the right street to do a loop. He puts his indicator on at the appropriate spot and turns right, then right again, and again, almost ready to turn into my street for the second time to complete the square.

"Could you go past my house again please, and just keep a constant speed of around 40 k's an hour?" I am aware that this sounds very demanding and just hope he is fine with it. I don't want to have to go into detail about why, I've too much to think about right now. "And please don't stop at the address this time either." Another look, slightly darker than the last is cast from the driver's eyes to mine via the rear-view mirror.

I prepare myself to get a good look at the car as we go past again. If Marcus is in the car, that's a concern. That means he's watching my house, unless by some peculiar coincidence he's waiting on someone who lives in my street. Then if he's not in the car, maybe that's an even bigger concern. *Does that mean he's in my yard, in my house?* Or again is there an innocent reason for his car to be parked where it is. *And what do I do–either way?*

This time around I have a chance to check the rear number plate as we approach. The last two digits are AZ–it's definitely his car. I also memorise the full registration number. As we cruise past the front of the car, I cover most of my face with my hand in case he's looking our way. I look directly at him. I feel we almost locked eyes, but it's dark and my face was obscured. I can't tell if he's recognised me or perhaps has noted the fact that this car has gone past him twice in the last few minutes.

On the circuit, I've been tossing up what to do depending on whether he was in the car or not. *Do I go to the police station, or just call?* In my wallet I have the card that Michael O'Mara gave me but the number is a central number, not the local station. There's no direct line these days–the job would have to be allocated from the communication centre and in all honesty, it wouldn't be considered urgent. Back in my day people just rang the local station and if it was unattended, the call was diverted to comms. This is not a triple zero kind of emergency either, so that's not an option for me.

Knowing that he's in the car, I could quickly get inside and lock up. I'm confident that my house is safe, but I am also very aware of being alone with just Lola, who I hope would have a go at an intruder, but as I haven't trained her to do that, I can't be sure that she wouldn't just lick them to death. If I don't get out at my house this time around, I'll have to ask this driver to take me somewhere else or wait with me for what could be ages before a patrol car is sent out to investigate.

I have to make a decision. "Could you take me to the local police station please? Do you know where it is? I can give you directions."

"I know it. That's ok." He gives me another, less annoyed look in the rear-view mirror, then returns his eyes to the road and ferries me to my new requested location. I ask him to wait while I check if the station is attended.

"That's ok," he repeats. I close the car door and run up the stairs two at a time. The front door opens as I push it, so I know there's someone here. I move toward the front counter and a policewoman approaches from her side. I blurt out my delight at finding the station open and rush back to the door telling her, "I'll be back in two seconds."

She spreads her hands in a questioning gesture as I turn my back and leave. I quickly dispatch the patiently waiting driver, thanking him several times in the process. He will get a glowing review.

I hurry back inside to where I find the policewoman now accompanied by another officer who I'm relieved and happy to recognise from my visit earlier this week. Michael recognises me too and says, "Hey, it's the flower lady. Is everything ok?"

"Michael, I'm so glad to see you. No, it isn't. You know the guy that I reported who'd come into my shop and kind of threatened me? Well, he's parked in my street. Just sitting in his car, about fifty metres down the road from my house."

"You're sure it's him?"

"*Yes.* Remember I mentioned to you the other day that I got a bit of a look at his car–white Camry with a scrape on the back nearside panel, and the last two digits of his plate? Well now I've got the whole rego. It's definitely his car. When I spotted it from the Uber, I got the driver to do a lap. The second time around, I could see him inside."

"Well, that's good that you came here and didn't go into your house." He slides a piece of paper and a pen across the counter. "Here, can you write down the rego for us? I'll do a check." He tilts his head toward his offsider and says, "This is Constable Sandy Winter, by the way." I share a quick smile and continue writing the registration number.

He takes the sheet of paper and sits at a desk where he starts tapping on a keyboard–a proficient touch typist by the looks. I say hello properly to Sandy and tell her my name, so she doesn't have to call me *the flower lady*. She offers me a seat in the waiting area. No sooner do I sit than Michael returns with his results. I hurry back over.

"I can't tell you who this vehicle is registered to, but their name is not Marcus. Well done getting the rego number. Not everyone thinks to do that."

I figure now might be a good time to let him know the reason for that. "Some things you learn at the Academy never leave you," I say, hoping that this might relax the protocol a bit so I can find out the real name of the person who owns the car.

"Oh, you were in the job then?" he asks.

"Yeah, a lifetime ago," I laugh.

"Well, in that case, I don't see a problem in letting you know this guy's got a record. I just checked when I got his name from the registration. Milton Watts. Break and Enter with Intent, GBH and Assault and he did time last year. Out on parole with the monitor–like you mentioned. Still has to report but monitor removed six days ago." All of the words coming out of his mouth after *Watts*, seem to be reaching me through a blurry cloud of distraction.

"What? *Watts*? Are you sure?"

My mind flicks through the two encounters with Marcus. His hands on the table in the café, eating the mille feuille, leaning on the counter in my shop. Ten fingers, every time, so it can't be him. *Of course it can't be him*! But there was something familiar about his face, his stance. *Could this be his brother?* I tell myself not to be ridiculous. Watts is a common name. Over the years, every time I hear it, I get stupid, even if it's old Daphne Watts being called for her appointment at the Doctor's surgery. She makes me wonder what kind of mother Geoffrey Watts had. What kind of childhood and other influences might have contributed to his behaviour later in life.

Michael and Sandy are both looking at me strangely. Michael says, "Yes, of course I'm sure. Why? Does the name mean something? A collar from years ago?"

"No, no. I didn't arrest anyone by that name." I regain my senses and say, "Right. Thanks for that. What do you reckon now?" I ask, hoping they're going to suggest driving me home and confronting him if he's still there.

"Let's take a drive over there and see if he's still scoping about. Sandy and I might have a quiet word to him. You'll have to wait in the car though."

"You bet. I don't want to see him, and I don't want him to see me, that's for sure."

"Give us a minute to lock up," Sandy says as she moves out from behind the counter to lock the front door. When she returns, she says, "Come through the back way to the car with us."

I feel strange and oddly reminiscent getting into the police car, but I also don't relish sitting in the back seat, where I know that all sorts of drunks, offenders and others would have sat. The station is only about three kilometres from my place, so we reach my street quite quickly. As Sandy steers the vehicle around my corner, I see that the Camry is still parked in the same spot. She pulls up a good ten metres behind and she and Michael exit the vehicle. Both officers are armed, and Michael is carrying a small container with him.

As they approach the Camry, I see the brake lights come on and hear the motor start up, but Michael has already reached the driver's side window. I have my window wound down so I can try to hear some of what's being said. I slide down low in the back seat.

Michael knocks on the car window and then I hear him saying, "Turn the engine off and step out of the vehicle please."

The door opens and he emerges from the vehicle. Milton or Marcus or *Blueeyes* or whatever else he calls himself–*Watts.* I'm relieved that he doesn't look in my direction but I still sink lower in the seat in case he does.

Michael continues, "We've had complaints from the residents about a man sitting in a white Camry. Do you have any reason to be loitering in this street?"

"It's not against the law is it?" he retorts.

"Well that depends on your intent. So how about you tell me what you're doing here."

Milton looks up and down the street, obviously trying to think up a good excuse, then comes out with, "I got lost, ok?"

"Doesn't explain why you've been sitting here in the car for so long."

"Who reported me anyway?" he asks.

"As if we're going to tell you that," Sandy interjects. "Do you know anyone who lives in this street?"

"No."

"Where were you going when you got lost?" she continues to fire questions at him.

"Home."

"So you don't even know your way home? And where would home be?" She reaches into one of her pockets and produces her notebook and pen.

She stands, pen poised waiting for an answer. When he doesn't respond she asks, "Can I see your driver's licence please?"

"But I wasn't even driving," he protests.

"You are in charge of a motor vehicle and technically you were driving because you had the motor running, so I am asking you again. Can I see your driver's licence please?"

He reaches for his back pocket and both officers watch him on high alert, Michael saying, "Slowly. No sudden movements." A wallet emerges and he flips it open and scratches around inside, struggling to pull the plastic rectangle out of its slot. He eventually hands it to Sandy. She shines a small torchlight on it briefly while asking him to recite his name, address and date of birth. She records the details in her notebook and returns his licence to him.

I reach for my phone while I'm waiting in the car. I'd really like to ring Marta or someone, but I don't want him to know that I'm in the back of the car, so talking is out. I could text but I'd need to turn the screen display right down so the light isn't visible from outside. I take a look at the time and reconsider even texting. It's ten-forty. A bit late to be bothering her now. I put my phone away and concentrate on the conversation around the Camry.

"Have you been drinking tonight Milton?" asks Michael.

"No."

"I now require you to provide a specimen of breath for a breath test," he says as he produces the kit and opens it.

"This is harassment. I'll report you."

"I very much doubt that," says Sandy as Michael begins the instruction process to obtain the sample.

After a couple of minutes, Michael informs him that the test is negative.

"Of course it is. I told you I haven't had a drink."

Sandy steps forward and says, "I am directing you to move on Mr Watts. We will be doing patrols in this area and we'd better not find you hanging around again, otherwise you will be arrested. Is that clear? As a result of your behaviour tonight, we have your vehicle details, your full name and address and these will be going on record at the station. Any further interaction with us may affect your parole. You do know that don't you?"

"So you've checked me out already. Bloody coppers, can't leave me alone. Of course, I know all that parole shit, but I haven't done anything wrong." He spreads his arms like an innocent man, wronged.

"On your way," says Michael, "and don't come back."

Sandy and Michael walk back to the police car as the Camry drives off into the night. We crawl the fifty metres or so to my driveway and I ask as Sandy parks, "Do you want to come in? Would you like a coffee or something?"

Michael replies, "Not for me thanks," and looks at Sandy who shakes her head. He adds, "But I'll walk you to your door and just check that everything looks normal to you–no sign of someone trying to break in. Unless you want us to take a look around inside as well?"

"No, no. I'm fine."

Sandy doesn't look like she's going to get out of the car so I thank her and walk the short distance with Michael to the front door. Everything looks to be as I left it, so I slip the key into the door and open it to find Lola sitting on the mat waiting for me.

"Oh you've got a dog–that's good," says Michael.

"Yeah, she's getting on a bit but she's great company. Although how she knows when I get home, I don't know–she's pretty deaf now."

"They seem to sense it somehow, hey?" He reaches past me and gives her a pat on the head saying, "Good girl. Hello you." He's obviously a dog lover as he starts giving her a very welcome scratch under the ear.

"Great watchdog–she's putty in your hands now." We both laugh.

He straightens up. "Well, don't hesitate to call us back if you see his car around again or get worried. Might pay to call triple zero next time. This will be on report, so they should get someone here quickly. Did you hear our conversation? You'd have dealt with people like him before in the job."

"Yeah, nothing new there, just unsettling when it's aimed at me," I smile. "Thanks heaps for this."

"De nada. Hopefully we've put the wind up him a bit and he won't be back." He looks up at my CCTV cameras and says, "Looks like you've got the place well under surveillance. Even a bozo like him couldn't be stupid enough to try anything with that lot."

"Sometimes their stupidity knows no bounds."

"Tell me about it!" He starts to walk back to join his partner and turns back saying, "We'll do some patrols up and down here during the night. Sleep tight."

I wave and call out, "Thanks, that'd be great."

He was true to his word, I'm pretty sure I heard every car that went past during the night. Early on, I got up and looked out the window each time, catching sight of the blue and white a few times, but later I just felt too exhausted to move. Sleep evaded me though. Every time I felt I was drifting off, I'd hear a tiny noise, or a car going past, or even Lola's gentle snoring on her bean bag, which usually comforted me, but which tonight, was only serving to keep me from falling into a proper, deep sleep.

Next morning, the person looking back at me in the bathroom mirror in the harsh light of day seems to be me, digitally remastered to represent how I might look in ten years' time. I splash cold water on my face and steer my exhausted body in the direction of coffee.

CHAPTER 32

Not so Pretty in Pink

Carrying the incriminating black box in front of me with both hands and Sue's camera slung over one shoulder, I hurried back into the house. I placed the box on the floor in front of Geoff and Sue and beckoned Sue to come and have a look. "I think I got it all–and more. I'll watch him. You've gotta come see this." I didn't need to move closer to guard him as I saw that Sue had covered his mouth again with tape. That didn't stop the moan I heard escape from behind the silver wrapping when I'd appeared with the box. Only his eyes and nose were visible–the eyes showing fear and pain. He squeezed them shut and moaned more loudly as Sue started digging around in the box. He knew what she was going to find.

"You need to see what's in that paper bag, and the photos next to it. The rest we can deal with later," I said, keeping one eye on him and one on Sue, waiting to catch her reaction when she registered what the items were.

"Woohoo!" she hooted. A huge grin erupted as she pulled a pink, lacy G-string out of the bag and twirled it around her gloved finger. In the other hand she held up a photo of Geoff, naked except for the tiny lacy fragment of pink fabric. His pose studied, leaning forward with his rear to the camera and looking back over his shoulder suggestively. His lips formed a pout that Marilyn Munroe would have been proud of. There was not much left to the imagination.

"Man, you're an even more perverted little prick than we thought." She dropped the undies and flicked through the rest of the photos that accompanied them. Suddenly she stopped at one and her jaw dropped. She held it up, showing it to him.

"*These are mine you disgusting worm.*" She looked at the photo again. "Oh my god. This is the grossest thing I've ever seen." Again, he was posing and looking directly at the camera with his pouty lips. This time, it was a front-on shot. He had a red bra stretched around his chest with the undies that Sue recognised–red bikini briefs with a black lace overlay panel at the front. He had them pulled up high in the front, exposing part of his testicles.

I took a quick look and wished I hadn't. "Spew," I said, looking away.

Sue started flicking through the rest of the photos of Geoff striking various poses in an array of women's underwear. She commented quite casually as she sorted through the compromising pictures, "You may not know this about me *worm*, because I wasn't here long enough for anyone to get to know me, but I happen to be good friends with some high-profile journalists." She threw a sideways glance at him and continued, "I did first year Journalism at Uni before I decided I wanted to be a cop and I made some great friends in that year. I think they would be very interested in these photographs. What do you think Tess, would these look better in print or on TV? I can't quite decide."

I knew she didn't actually want an answer, so I didn't bother. Geoff started moaning again and throwing his head around, desperately trying to say something. Sue loosened off the tape over his mouth, threatening as she did so, "You scream and you won't see daylight for quite some time."

He grimaced as she pulled the tape off his mouth and then licked his lips as though he needed to get some moisture on them before he could speak. I suspected he just needed time to think of a way to get the incriminating photos from us. "Please no. Look I'll do *anything.* Just leave those and take the rest. I won't report you." His tone desperate and pleading. "Am I bleeding? Are you going to get me an ambulance?"

"How the worm turns," Sue sneered. "Get it? *Worm?*" She'd amused herself with her new nickname for him. We ignored his questions.

"Maybe we should just send some of these anonymously to his wife, and his parents. Are your parents proud of you Geoff?" I asked. He turned to me with a frantic look in his eyes. Having been the one to find the underwear and photos, I'd had a bit more time than Sue to process the discovery. I'd rolled a few scenarios around in my head and this was one of them.

"No! She can't see those. *They* can't... Look, what do you want from me? Take the photos of you and go...*please.*" His head dropped again. His body shook with silent sobbing.

"Not an option–they're all coming with us..."

I cut Sue off there and surprised myself by saying, "Right, this is what you're going to do. Stop your snivelling and listen carefully–this is not negotiable." Sue raised an eyebrow at me but let me roll with it.

"Tonight, obviously, you'll call in sick. Let them know you've injured yourself with your... you got a chainsaw?" He nodded. "... with your chainsaw and will be off for a couple of weeks. Next, you submit your resignation–no questions, no explanation." He tried to interject but I raised my hand and continued over him. "I don't care what story you make up to tell your wife, but it better be good enough to convince her that you both need to leave town. Tell her you're cracking up from the job or something. Next, you need to move far away from here and start a new life somewhere else."

Sue joined in here with, "And if this ever happens to another woman, remember, we've still got you in your frilly underwear–and mine, and I can always get hold of a pair of bolt cutters, only this time, it'll be something you treasure more than a finger." She tapped his groin with the toe of her boot.

He tried to squeeze his legs together further, reminding me of how I struggled so hard to try and do exactly that, just a few short days ago.

Sue hadn't finished. "Your mate Bolly won't be able to save you this time. I reported you to him, but I didn't have any evidence. Now, we've got more than we need. You deviate from this roadmap for your life and you'll need to get ready for instant and widespread exposure."

He looked like he was weighing up his options before he spoke, "If I agree to resign and leave town, couldn't you give me those photos back then? I promise I won't try this again."

Sue scoffed, "*You promise? You promise?* Your word is lower than that cow shit on your boots. And by the way, if you have any thoughts of trying to get these back off us, you won't know where to look. One of my journalist friends has a special drawer for stories that are not quite ready to break. They sit in there safely stewing away until the time is right. I know there's space for these, and all it would take is one call, or for something to happen to either of us..." She waved a finger from me to herself and back again.

He sighed heavily and pleaded once more, "I need an ambulance. Maybe they can sew my finger back together if it's not too late."

Sue looked at me and then started stashing everything from the box into her sports bag. "We need to get out of here." Then over her shoulder to Geoff, "Trust me *worm.* It's too late."

CHAPTER 33

Rained Out

Why couldn't I have a job where I get the whole weekend off? I blearily wish. I'm so tired I'm not even sure I will be able to focus on work, and if it wasn't for the fact that I'd just told everyone to minimise time alone in the shop, I'd call up Ros and tell her I'm sick. I finish my coffee and do little more than walk through the shower as a refresher, apply deodorant and a skerrick of make-up and grab my keys. I look a mess still, but hopefully I smell ok and can manage to function without injuring myself with secateurs or scissors for around four hours–until I can officially close the doors and start my weekend. As I reverse the van out of my garage, checking the street carefully for any sign of the Camry. I grimace at the thought of how busy some Saturday mornings can be. Today I'd happily sacrifice the takings for some peace and quiet.

I spend the morning in a foggy haze, occasionally roused by a customer walking through the doors or Ros asking me something. Every now and then I feel wide awake and discover that Ros is half-way through telling me something, or I look in amazement at the flowers that I've been working on, finding that they've shaped themselves into beautiful designs and bouquets that I don't even remember being responsible for creating.

Most of the time I'm worrying and fretting about finding Milton Watts in my street last night and transposing my hazy memory of Geoff Watts's face over his. I've tried very hard to forget *that* face, but it emerges, and it fits. The rest of the time I'm thinking about what I'm going to cook for Guy for dinner tomorrow night and re-living our kiss goodnight after our date.

Ros asked me after the first half hour or so if I was ok and I told her about what had happened last night, but only from the part where I spotted the Camry in my street on my way home from *dinner with friends*. I still hadn't told them any more details about Guy.

Ros is very concerned for me and asks if I've considered moving in with Jacinta or Marta for a while, until things settle. I tell her that I have thought about it but feel safe enough at home. I think we'll both be relieved when the clock has two hands in a vertical position, and we can head to our respective homes. She to her family and me to my bed to try and wrestle back some of those stolen hours of sleep.

* * *

With the cranky old air-conditioner struggling to bring down the temperature in my bedroom, I manage to grab a couple of hours of sleep in the afternoon. I emerge from the cool environment into a steamy, locked-up house and make my zombie-like way around, opening windows and turning on the ceiling fans in the living areas. The humidity feels incredibly high, and I feel washed out–possibly even worse than before I had the nap. As I look out the large sliding doors in the kitchen, through my tropical birch trees I see clouds building in the east.

My watch tells me it's almost three-thirty. I sit at the breakfast bar and lay my head on my folded arms on the benchtop. I enjoy the cool feel of the marble as I think back to the events of last night.

I've been wanting to ring a few people and tell them what happened, but I couldn't find the energy when I got home from work, collapsing on the bed instead. Now I'm starting to feel the effects of having very little breakfast and no lunch. I force myself to get moving. I open the fridge and await inspiration–at the same time enjoying the blast of cold air on my body. I grab the yoghurt and track down a banana for a quick pick me up.

With some energy restored, I find my phone and start to call my list of nearest and dearest. Those who will be most concerned about me and want to know of this development. I try to play it reasonably cool so that they are not worrying too much but it's hard to sound cool about a convicted felon sitting in a car watching your house late at night. I especially need to tell Marta his name. She is the only one that that will mean anything to. The kids don't know the details from my past ordeal except that I was stalked for a while.

After my calls to the kids, Jacinta wants me to move in with her and Brad, and Dan offers to come and stay with me. I'm touched by their concern and thank them, assuring them that I will take them up on their offers if I feel at all unsafe. Now it's time to bring Marta up to date.

"Marta, you know I had the date with Guy last night?" I don't wait for an answer, "Well, it was great, but I'll tell you about it later. Listen, when I was almost home, I spotted the Camry–you know, *his.*"

"Shit, in your street?"

"Yeah, about fifty metres from here. With him just sitting in there large as life, so I got the Uber driver to keep going and take me to the station. The young guy that I reported the shop incident to was on again. I was able to give him the full rego this time and he did some checks. Marta, the guy's name is *Watts.* It's not Marcus either, it's Milton Watts."

"*Watts? No way.*"

"Yeah, and he's been inside for GBH and has previous for Break and Enter, and Assault."

"Right, you need to pack some gear and get your arse over here," she says, concern evident in her tone.

"No, honestly. I'm fine. You know how safe I feel here. The kids offered too, and I really appreciate everyone offering to have me stay or to help but you know how hard it is staying at someone's place for any length of time. It's like Franklin said about *fish* and *houseguests*–they both begin to smell after three days."

"I'll have to remember that if I ever come and stay at yours," she laughs. "Yeah I know you'd rather be in your own home, with your own bed and your own stuff. So would I, but if at any time you feel like it–just come on over. You've got a key. Let yourself in, even if we're not home."

"Thanks Marta. I do appreciate that. I'll think about it. But let me finish… Michael, the young cop and his partner drove me home and stopped and spoke to this Milton on the way. Gave him a breath test and sent him on his way, telling him he'd better not come back."

"Well, hopefully that puts the wind up him. Did he see you?"

"No, I sat low in the back of the car and he didn't even look my way. But Marta, *Watts*, his name is *Watts*. And there's something kind of familiar about this guy. I might be crazy but I even think he could be his brother."

"Ok, the fact that you said to me the other day that he seemed familiar, before you even found out his name, makes me think that's not so crazy. Look, forget the fish, I'd feel a lot better if you came and stayed with us for a while."

"I honestly will think about it. I'm too buggered today to even think about packing up and I've got Guy coming over for dinner tomorrow night, so maybe after that?"

"Sure. But be careful and call me anytime hey."

"Yep. I will."

"And don't hesitate to call triple zero."

"Yep. Will do."

We say goodbye and end the call. I look at Lola, who has decided it's way past her walk time and has dragged her lead from its usual spot beside the front door and placed it in front of me.

"Ok, I get the hint, girl. Let's go then." I attach her lead as she dances around excitedly. We head out on our regular route around the local streets. The sun is low in the sky, its burnt orange rays flickering through the trunks of the Tulipwood trees lining the street and hitting us at eye level as we depart, then kissing the horizon as we return home. Pink and grey clouds threaten to obscure the dying rays, and higher in the sky, thick bands of cloud are forming. It feels like rain.

As I search around with my fork for the good bits of my microwave dinner, I try to plan what to cook for Guy tomorrow night. We've discussed food quite extensively, so I know his likes and dislikes. I really don't want to be fussing in the kitchen while he's here though, so it needs to be fairly simple, but tasty.

I decide on salmon cooked in the oven, accompanied by a creamy, buttery mash, broad beans and pickled ginger, followed by my fool-proof lime coconut cake. Decision made, I make a list of items that I'll need to pick up tomorrow on the way home from surfing. I look again out the sliding doors and see little dark spots gathering on the paving outside. *Damn,* I think, *maybe there won't be any surfing lesson tomorrow.* I do a search on my weather app and see that the forecast is for heavy rain and a possible storm, clearing to showers by the late afternoon.

I think about ringing Guy. I've got his number now, but I've never rung him. It was only last night that I saw him, so I haven't really expected him to ring me either. I considered ringing him when I was ringing the kids and Marta, but I'd talked non-stop for an hour by the time I'd finished with them, so I felt all talked out. Now that I've eaten and started to feel a bit more normal, I think about how nice it would be to hear his voice.

I bring up his number and hit the green button. He answers after two rings, "Hey, I was thinking about giving you a call. I just saw the weather forecast. How are you going anyway?"

It's weird hearing his voice over the phone for the first time. Weird but nice. I picture him in his massive living room overlooking the ocean and the dark, threatening sky. "I'm pretty good. How are you?"

"Only *pretty good?* Are you not well?" he asks showing some concern.

"I didn't sleep much last night that's all. I ended up having to get the police because that guy I told you about was parked in my street." I add quickly, "Nothing happened and I'm fine–just a bit unsettling."

"I knew I should have seen you home safely. That's terrible. What did the police do? Could they arrest him or something?"

"They gave him a talking to but he hadn't committed any offences so they couldn't arrest him. They're keeping an eye on the place and I feel safe enough." I am getting a bit sick of telling everyone that I feel safe, even though I really appreciate their concern. Truth be known I *do* have concerns. I saw enough bizarre break-ins when I was in the force to realise that crims can be pretty inventive sometimes and find a way to get around even the best security systems. But I'm not going to share these concerns–that would only make everyone more insistent that I don't stay at home on my own.

"Well my little surfer girl, I don't think we will be going out tomorrow. The forecast looks pretty bad." He sounds disappointed.

"Yeah, I just had a look too. That's partly why I rang. I should give you my address seeing as I won't see you in the morning. Would you like me to text it?"

"Yes, perfect. What time would you like me to arrive? And what can I bring?"

"Say six-ish? Maybe some wine? We'll be having seafood, but I don't care what colour wine, unless you do?"

"How about a Pinot Gris?"

"Sounds ideal. I'm looking forward to having you over."

"Me too. Stay safe now."

"You too." I'm not sure why I said that–just an automatic reaction.

He laughs and says, "Always. See you tomorrow."

I hang up, smiling contentedly, then text Guy my address and add "looking forward to seeing you tomorrow". I flick on the TV and sink into my favourite lounge chair. Lola joins me in her usual spot and we both ignore the flickering box. Me lost in thoughts ranging from pleasant projections of tomorrow night with Guy to disturbing thoughts of men named Watts; and her asleep as soon as her head settles on my lap.

I maintain the charade of watching television for another hour or so until I can feel myself fading and drifting in and out of that pre-sleep zone where another world of reality seems to take over my brain. I nod myself awake, rouse Lola and turn off the TV. It's not quite nine o'clock but I know that the scant sleep that I had last night and today can't keep me going any longer.

I settle into bed and reach for my book on the bedside table. I find myself re-reading the same paragraph several times and not reaching the end before starting to drift off each time, when I hear a noise like something falling down at the other end of the house. I look at Lola, not knowing why I would expect a dog with a severe hearing impairment to have heard anything, but perhaps some small vibration or other instinctive reaction? Her tongue is lolling out the side of her mouth and her eyes flicker like she's dreaming.

I throw on my robe and grab my phone, then pad down the hallway. Part way along I hear another fainter sound coming from the rumpus room at the end of the hall. Moving quietly, I stop at the laundry and grab a can of insect spray before continuing. As I round the corner at the rumpus room, I feel for the light switch and turn it on. Standing directly under the missing skylight cover is a figure, dressed in black with a black balaclava. I flash straight back to the shower all those years ago and freeze. The figure is the same size, same shape, same colour.

I have no doubt who stands before me.

CHAPTER 34
The Exit

Sue drove us back to the Ampol. I don't think we said much during that drive, and to be honest, I couldn't remember anything after throwing the bulging bag onto the back seat of Rick's car and climbing in ourselves.

When we got to the garage, I saw my car waiting there, innocently. I suddenly felt a rush of guilt. Last time I drove it, I was an innocent person. Now. We had just broken into someone's house, assaulted a police officer and cut off part of his body and flushed it down the toilet. Admittedly Sue did most of the latter part of that, but I was along for the ride–and I hit him, threatened him, stole photographs from him and destroyed his expensive camera. I was as guilty of all of it as she was.

I asked myself, *Was there another way–a less violent way?* In the end I didn't think so. Reporting him was worse than useless–it got Sue transferred, and ultimately she had to quit a job that she loved. He did cruel and disgusting things to us and he was just going to walk away, and probably do it again. He was never going to cough up those photos without the threat of violence–and what good was a threat if the person receiving it didn't believe you'd follow through? *Were we justified in what we did?* We certainly had provocation.

Sue came back to my motel room with me and we quickly gathered up my stuff and headed to the cottage that we'd both once called home. *Could I call it that again now?* The coming days would determine that. If we did a good enough job on him, he would be gone soon enough.

Safely inside the cottage, and even though it was only eleven o'clock in the morning, I pulled a bottle of wine from the pantry cupboard and showed it to Sue with a questioning look. "You bet," she said as she hauled her sports bag onto the kitchen table. She took out her tools and my stomach lurched as I saw blood on the blade of the bolt cutters. She tipped the rest onto the table. Seeing the underwear land on my table I felt like I would have to disinfect it into next year before I'd feel comfortable to eat off it again. I wondered if that was academic anyway. Perhaps I wouldn't eat or sleep in the house again. I couldn't imagine when I'd be game to shower there–without someone standing guard.

That brought thoughts of Russell to mind and suddenly I understood what that saying of *tugging at your heartstrings* meant. It literally felt like there was something attached inside my chest and a tug of war was taking place. My heart torn asunder as a result.

My connection with him seemed so real and he seemed so genuine that I still couldn't believe how he'd deceived me. Plus, there were only two motels in town. Surely if he really cared, he would have tried to track me down and apologise. On top of that was another feeling that if I were to try and forgive him that, then I would feel hypocritical by keeping from *him* the new secret that Sue and I shared–*our mission.* I questioned whether I could even trust him with something that big. In reality, I had only known him a short time and as much as I wanted him to be perfect–he wasn't, *but neither was I.*

My brain couldn't deal with the complexity of our relationship after what Sue and I had just been through, so I decided to think about it later. I took a big mouthful of the wine and leaned on the back of a chair as I watched Sue sifting through the photographs.

"There are so many!" she exclaimed, "and some of them are doubles–look at these." She held up two photos of me from possibly the most graphic perspective. I needed to sit. I pulled out the chair and flopped into it.

"You don't think he was doing something with them do you?" Sue asked.

"Doing something–like what?"

"Selling, sharing, I don't know. Why would he need two photos exactly the same?"

I realised she was right. I stood and started digging through the photos with her and we roughly sorted them into piles of mine and hers. When we were nearly at the bottom of the mess, Sue straightened up one of the piles in front of her and said, "I need the loo. Back in a minute."

As I continued to dig through, I found a small bundle of about six photos with a band around them. I turned the little bundle over and found a scrap of paper tucked under the rubber band. 'Brian' it said.

I pulled the band off and quickly saw that all of the photos were of me. Disgust lodged in my throat and made it difficult to swallow–or breathe.

I sat and took this in for a moment. Then immediately began to fret that maybe he had already given Brian some others. Maybe these were a top-up. Or maybe he *was* selling them, and Brian had forked out for this selection. I couldn't stop my brain from going places I'd rather it didn't. *Had he already given or sold some to other creeps that shared his dirty little secrets?*

I forced myself to look at the photographs that he'd set aside for Brian again and I realised that none of them showed the binding on my wrists or ankles, but they all showed the rest of my exposed body, and my face–with no gag or tape on my mouth. In fact, the photos could be seen to be voluntary. My head was to the side in all of them and although it was obvious to me that they were taken when I was unconscious, it would be possible to believe that I just had my eyes closed at the time. The way that he'd developed and printed them did not give away his methods in obtaining them. His background story probably had me painted as a willing participant.

Sue returned and I showed the bundle to her. "Frickin' hell Sue, look at this. You're right. The slimy little creep had these ones set aside for his mate Brian."

"*Disgusting bastard.* So who is this Brian again?" she asked.

I described my first encounter with Brian and then the night of the B&S Ball and what happened to Russell, finishing with, "So he was the one I first suspected was writing those notes and things."

"Ok, that's why you asked me if I met a Brian when I arrived in town. Well, judging by this, he's a creep of a similar breed to Watts."

I sat and took another swig of my wine saying, "Let's rationalise this. We're both going to be wondering now if he's already given similar photos of either or both of us, to Brian or even other dirty bastards that are into this stuff. God forbid there's more of them lurking around but who knows?"

"Yeah and Watts will know that by now we'd have found this little package that he's put aside for Brian, so he's either going to think we'll confront Brian, or hold this information over him along with all of the other stuff."

"Right, so what *do* we do with this information?" I asked, feeling somewhat confident that he might not have had time yet to distribute photos of me and perhaps was just in the process of preparing to do so, but I had to respect what Sue wanted to do, because the photos of her were from months ago and he'd had all of that time to potentially spread them around.

"I say we just sit on it. We really can't risk confronting someone like this Brian, who at this point could be totally innocent. And from what you say, he maybe had a thing for you and wouldn't have been interested in pictures of me anyway."

I was relieved to hear Sue say that. The fact that there weren't any photos of Sue going about her normal life around town also made me think that the main focus of interest was me. "Yes, I agree," I said and then showed Sue a photo of me waiting in the car for Russell just a couple of days ago. "These ones are almost as disturbing…"

"Did you feel like you were being watched?" she asked.

"Well, ever since that first night I had that feeling, but I didn't see anything unusual. Now I know I had good reason to feel like that."

In silence, we finished piling up the sickening little snapshots of our torture and shame and the catalogue of my everyday life around town. We didn't count them, but there must have been close to three hundred photographs piled up before us.

"What on earth are we going to do with them?" I asked. "I don't want these lying around for someone to find, and to be honest I never want to have to look at them again."

"Me neither," agreed Sue. "We burn them–all except for one of each of us–just in case we need it down the track. Pick out a full length one that shows the gag and binding and isn't too graphic."

I reluctantly looked through them again and selected the most modest angle that showed all of the binding. I understood why we needed to keep *some* evidence but still wondered where I could possibly hide it and be confident that no one would ever find it.

Sue swept the remaining piles into her sports bag, leaving one stack of photos still on the table. The photos of Geoff in women's underwear. Beside it sat the brown paper bag containing four pairs of knickers and the red bra.

I pointed at the steamy little pile and asked, "Who wants to take responsibility for that lot?"

"Yeah, that's our insurance–we need to keep it safe. I will. They are my knickers after all." She attempted a smile, but the left side of her mouth let her down. "*Not that I want them back.*"

"You know what you said about your journalist friend, is that true?"

"Yes, I did that first year at Uni and made some good friends in the group. I still catch up with a couple of them. I made up the bit about the special drawer though." This time she did achieve a smile–one of the few I'd seen on her face. It made her look years younger and brightened my mood a little as well.

"We need to make us a bonfire," she continued, holding up the sports bag, "but maybe we should wait till dusk. "How about I stay here with you for a couple of days? Make sure things go to plan." She looked at me hopefully.

"Of course. I'd love it. I was wondering how I was going to manage to stay here on my own. Stay as long as you like."

* * *

The branches I'd cut down a few days ago were great kindling for our fire, which greedily consumed the array of graphic photographs that we fed it. It was blissfully unaware of whether they were pornographic photographs or photos of fluffy kittens–they were all the same fuel to the flames in the end.

As we threw in the last of them, I took a few steps away from the smoke, feeling the need to take a deep breath and let the relief wash over me. Sue joined me and put an arm around my shoulders. We'd already polished off two bottles of wine by three o'clock and then both had a much-needed nanna-nap. Neither of us had slept well the night before.

"We did it, mate. We fucking did it," she said and rested her head on top mine.

I covered her hand on my shoulder and gave it a squeeze, saying, "We're some team–that's for sure."

I enjoyed the moment but couldn't help but worry that her confidence might be a bit premature.

* * *

I was rostered on day shift the following day. As I donned my uniform and looked in the mirror a wave of guilt hit me. *Are you a hypocrite or what?* I said to my reflection.

I was thankful that at least women in the force finally had the option of wearing trousers. Up until a couple of years before, the A-line button front dress was the only option. The trousers covered the marks on my ankles, and I'd applied make-up to the yellow and purple bruise on my cheek. I then strapped some tape on my left wrist and slipped on a wrist support on my right. My cover story being that I fell down the steps going to the loo in the middle of the night and put my hands out to save myself–slight sprains the result.

When I emerged, Sue had cooked breakfast, so we ate together in silence. When I finished and moved to the sink to rinse off my plate she said, "It's kinda weird seeing you in uniform. You look good in it though."

"I *feel* a bit weird wearing it today, to be honest. I feel like a bit of a phony, you know? After what we did."

Sue came over to me as I wiped my hands on the kitchen towel. I turned to face her and she took me by the shoulders. "You were justified in doing what you did. I might've gone a bit far, but you weren't to know that ahead of time. You–we, were provoked and there were extenuating circumstances with fuckin' Bollington protecting him. We could have done a lot worse to him."

She followed me into the lounge where I gathered my bag and keys–offering me encouragement and attempting to brighten my mood, "Come on, chin up, chest out and go and catch those baddies."

I laughed and said goodbye, "Thanks Sue. And thanks for staying. I really appreciate it."

* * *

Rarely were two days the same on general police duties, so I had no idea what the day held in store. I could be faced with arresting someone for break and enter *(I'd been prepared to do that)*, or assault (*just did that*), or wilful damage (*yes, just did that one too*). I looked into my eyes in the rear-view mirror and faced the fact that I might be unable to maintain a façade. For the first time I wondered if I would need to resign.

When I arrived at the station, I half expected someone to say something about Geoff, but Don just said hello and asked if I enjoyed my days off. Then he enquired about my wrists and I trotted out my story. Noel turned from his typewriter and lifted a hand in greeting. Just a normal day.

Around ten-thirty that all changed. Noel came out of Bollington's office and straight over to my desk. "The boss just told me that *Geoff's resigned.*" He sounded incredulous and I tried to react in a similar vein. My heart was pounding, and I noticed that I sounded a little breathless as I asked, "Do you know why?"

"Not fully. He called up sick yesterday and apparently said he would be off for a while–and now this. Boss said he reckoned he'd just had enough of the job and needed a change. I wonder if I should go round and see him. You want to come?"

Shit, I hadn't thought of that. I opened my mouth to try and answer but had no idea of what to say. I needed to stall. *Did I need to try and talk him out of going to see him? Would it matter? Would he even talk to Noel?* So many questions galloped through my head in an instant before I came out with, "Ah, no, I'm pretty snowed under with reports. Did you run that past the boss?" I hoped the mention of the boss might make him at least reconsider.

"Well, he said Geoff didn't want any fuss but surely he wouldn't mind if I checked on him?"

"Well, it sounds like he's going through some stuff at the moment. Maybe give him a few days and then see if he wants to talk about it?"

I took my best shot at stalling him. The best I could come up with on such short notice.

He considered my advice and said, "Yeah, I suppose you're right–if he doesn't want any fuss, maybe I'll leave it a day or two." He turned and wandered off toward the meal room saying, "I need a coffee after that news."

Two days later, I heard from Ray that he'd been in Geoff's street that morning and spotted a removal van at the house. I maintained a neutral expression as I took in the news, bursting inside with relief and dying to get home to tell Sue. She had been so excited when I'd told her about his resignation. His exodus was going to be an even more welcome announcement.

* * *

"*So he's gone?* Oh man, that's so good." She placed her palms together and tilted her head back like she was sending off a prayer of thanks. "You wanna drive past, just to make sure?"

"I kind of do, but also don't really want to see that house again. It would be good to see for ourselves though–that it's empty, and he's really gone."

Just before dark, we took Rick's car and drove to 27 Highgrove Street. Sue slowed to a crawl as we passed the house. It looked suitably deserted and closed up, causing us both to allow a little smile. On the way home we grabbed a take-away Chinese dinner and made another stop at the bottle shop. That night we shared a strange kind of celebration–a little sombre but satisfying.

"Looks like I can safely go home to Rick now," Sue said as we said our good nights, reminding me that soon I would be all alone.

CHAPTER 35
The Call

He reaches up and pulls off the balaclava saying, "Not much need for this I wouldn't think." As he speaks, I feel my phone vibrate in my robe pocket. I slowly and as casually as possible reach in and slide my finger along the screen toward the bottom, hoping I have hit the right spot to accept the call–whoever it's from. Possibilities flash through my brain. Marta? Guy calling me back? Cinta or Dan checking on me? It doesn't matter, if they can hear whatever is going to be said here then surely they'll call the police. Please don't be someone trying to sell me solar panels or harass me about my mortgage, I silently pray.

"You must've known I'd turn up one day. You and your sadistic mate," he continues.

"What do you want? If it's the photos, I don't have them. They're probably still sitting in that drawer in some journalist's office."

He advances toward me saying, "They don't even matter any more. Leah's gone and my parents are dead. There's no one to care about some ex-copper and his pastimes. You met my little bro–he doesn't care, so now it's time for you to pay for what you did to me."

I hold up the can of bug spray, my only protection, and threaten to spray his eyes if he comes near me. As I do, I can hear a tiny voice in my pocket. It sounds like a man but I can't hear anything clearly or loudly enough to tell who it is. I hope and pray that Geoff can't hear it. I need to keep talking, to mask it, just in case.

"How did you manage to get in anyway? I've got cameras all around the house." I figure he'll enjoy telling me how clever he is in circumventing them.

My phone has gone quiet now, but I dare not chance a peek at it. I don't want him to know it's in my pocket, hopefully conveying every word we say to someone who understands the seriousness of this situation.

"Easy really, I only needed to put the camera on this end out of action and that's pretty easy with a laser light. So many people think their houses are safe and they forget about their skylights. Thought you'd be a bit more onto that after being a copper yourself." He sounds smug and arrogant.

"So you got your brother to go through that whole charade on the dating site? Just to make sure it was me?"

"Well, you'd hardly have agreed to meet up with me if I'd put a profile on there, so yeah, he did it for me. I've been watching and waiting a long time for one of you bitches to pop up on one of those sites. Plus, I had a long way to come and he's local, so made sense for him to check you out first. Anyway, enough of this chit-chat crap, what I want from you is the location of Sue Ryan. Bitch had to have such a common name, I'm sick of chasing false leads–where is she?"

"I honestly don't know. We didn't stay in touch." I know there is zero percent chance of him believing this, but I have to try. I have to stall.

"Wrong. Try again. Where's your mobile? I might just check out that contact list for myself."

Sue's number *is* in my phone, but not where he'd expect to find it. She's under 'R' for Rick. I wonder now if this is too close and he might work it out if he starts looking at 'R' for Ryan. I can't let him have my phone anyway–it's my link to the outside world and possible salvation.

Now he's two steps in front of me and I'm still holding the spray can at eye level. He covers his eyes with one hand as he lunges and grabs for the can with the other. Having diverted it from its position he now uses two hands to wrench it from my grip and throws it on the floor with such force that it bounces on the tiles, then rolls into the skirting board, the metallic clattering ringing in my ears.

He's tall and strong and fends off most of my attempts at kicking or punching him. One kick aimed at his groin misses slightly and connects with his thigh. He looks angry. I turn and try to run but he grabs my hair and pulls my head violently backwards onto his chest. My back is at an awkward angle and all I can see is the ceiling and the offending skylight. I reach blindly for his arms but just as I get a grasp on one, he transposes the grip, thrusting my arm painfully high behind my back. He releases my hair and slams his forearm onto my throat.

I cough, feeling like I'm about to choke. "*My arm. You're breaking my arm,*" I croak through the compression of my vocal chords. He doesn't back it off. I try to scream but he increases the pressure on my throat until I feel that the little bones in there will shatter at any moment. I scratch and claw at the fabric on the arm over my throat but can't grasp hold of anything. I try reaching upwards to attack his face and eyes. He evades my flailing hand.

"Phone. *Now.*" he growls into my ear.

"Bedroom," I whisper, thinking that if I get him close enough for Lola to smell him, she might go for him, but I didn't need to bother. The high-pitched sound of the can bouncing must have reached her poor old ears and now she comes gingerly into the room. I try to scream again and begin to struggle as hard as his grip on my arm will allow. I wave my free arm around madly, hoping this will let her know that I'm in distress.

She growls and shows her teeth, crouching down like she's about to spring. Then she starts barking. I struggle harder as I feel him loosen off on my neck slightly.

"Get that bloody dog under control. Call it off."

I croak in response, "She's deaf. I need my hands to give her signals."

"You think I'm stupid?" He squashes my throat even harder than before, and I struggle to breathe.

Lola can either see or sense this and decides that now is her time to attack. She shows her teeth again and runs for his ankle, latching onto his jeans and missing his leg. He kicks and shakes her off, inflicting more pain on my throat and arm with his jerking movements.

She doesn't give up. She lunges again and this time succeeds in latching onto his ankle. He groans and kicks, again sending new levels of pain through my body as he jerks around trying to dislodge her. Suddenly I feel him release his hold on my arm, but it's still pinned between my back and his chest. It feels weak and numb as I try to get it to move. He's also backed off the pressure on my neck and I can slightly turn my head to see what he's doing with the arm that he had been holding my wrist with.

It's emerging from his jeans pocket–holding a knife. I struggle with renewed strength, probably from the adrenaline that the sight of the knife has sent through my body. He's waving the knife around near Lola, not quite reaching because he's still trying to keep my arm pinned to his chest.

I yell at Lola, even though I know she can't hear me, using all of my strength to push my weight in the opposite direction so he can't reach her with the knife. Then I hear it. *Sirens.* He hears it too.

He pushes me away from him, hard, and I hit the floor face first. My useless, numb arm crumbling under me as I try to use it to break my fall. I feel dizzy. The room has contracted to a fish-eye view, but I can see him striking Lola with the knife.

"No!" I yell and struggle to get up.

She yelps and drops to the ground, blood beginning to stain her beautiful golden fur. My heart lurches and I make it to my feet. I hear banging on the front door and voices yelling, 'Police. Open the door.'

I try to move toward the door but he runs at me, knocking me down a second time. He continues to run, presumably for the back door. As I drag myself to my feet I'm torn between going to Lola and going to let the police in, but the thumping that has now started on the door makes me think they are about to break it down. I hurry to open it.

Four officers are gathered around the door and standing with them is Perry. My already fuzzy brain is now totally confused. I hear the officers saying something–I don't know what. I automatically point toward the back door and two of them head in that direction, the other two move out around the sides of the house. They're yelling and talking to each other and maybe to me, but all I can do is stare at Perry.

"Wh... what are you doing here?" I manage to ask.

He grabs my arm and steers me inside saying, "Come on. Let's sit you down. I heard everything on the phone. I tried to ring you about our picnic and then I heard you and him and I knew it wasn't good so I..."

I cut him off here as I remember... *picnic... dogs...Lola,* "Oh my God, Lola!" I bound out of the chair that my bottom has only just touched, my head thumping as I run back to the rumpus room and throw myself onto my knees to look at her. There's a wide patch of blood on her shoulder but no other signs of injury. I pick up her head and rest it on my thigh, patting her and crooning to her, or maybe myself, as she can't hear any of it. "You'll be ok girl. You'll be ok." I gently separate the fur and see that the wound is quite long but not too deep.

I straighten up enough to take my phone out of my pocket and shrug off my robe. I fashion it into a bandage of sorts and look up to find that Perry is beside me. "What can I do to help?" he asks.

"Would you drive us to the Vet?"

"Yes, of course," he says as two of the police officers enter the room.

"Got him," the policewoman says. "He was running for his car in Jelicoe Street when they caught him. Are you able to come down to the station so that we can take a statement? Or do you need medical attention?" she asks, looking at my forehead. I reach up and feel a massive egg emerging. I flinch at my own touch.

"I'm ok. I just need to get to the vet–quickly. I'll come in straight after. I promise."

She looks at Lola and gives me a sympathetic smile. "How about we get you there the quickest way possible? Come on, let's get her in the car." She pauses a moment and points to my pyjamas with a questioning look.

"Don't care," I say. "I'll grab a coat at the front door. Let's go."

I try to lift her, but struggle, so Perry takes over and ferries her out to the police car. When he places her gently on the seat with my robe wrapped around her, she looks so helpless. *My hero*, I think and then realise that my other hero is standing right beside me. I turn to him and throw my arms around his neck saying, "Thank you, thank you, thank you so much. I can't thank you enough, Perry."

One of the officers starts the car so I slide in next to Lola in the back seat and comfort her on the drive to the 24-hour Vet Hospital about ten kilometres away.

My heart bursts with pride for Lola as I explain to the Vet how she received the injury. The Vet tells me that she'll need stitches and that he'll want to keep her in overnight. All of the staff fuss over her and I don't want to leave her side but she's being hurried into surgery, and I can't go with her. I kiss her on the head and she looks at me with those loving honey coloured eyes. I allow the policewoman to coax me out to the car and back to the station where for the first time ever I tell my story–*all of it.*

EPILOGUE

Geoffrey Alwyn Watts was charged with *Break and Enter with Intent, Assault, Carrying a Concealed Weapon, Animal Cruelty and Conspiring to Commit a Crime.* Returning to the Courtroom after so many years, was a strange experience for me. I had always been the arresting officer, this time I was the victim.

He pled guilty and was convicted and sentenced to fifteen years in prison. His defence didn't try to prove provocation; there was no mention of his finger, his photographs or his fetishes. I wonder how his cellmates would treat him if they knew about those. He's going to have a hard enough time trying to hide the fact that he used to be a cop. If or when they find that out–his life won't be worth living. Maybe he and his brother can look after each other in there. Milton also charged with *Conspiring to Commit a Crime* and having breached his parole conditions, sentenced to five years imprisonment.

Perry Martin, my unlikely knight in shining armour, the mild-mannered accountant, is a firm friend and has a lot of new clients after his chivalrous dash to my rescue with the troops: Marta and Helen; Jacinta and Brad, who've opened their own café; Dan who's now engaged to his girl from the gym, and Nick, who's back from Canada and working in the café with his sister; more clients than he really wants as he's keen to start thinking about retirement. I am so thankful that he lied about his age, that he really was that little bit older. It meant that he still had a landline, and he could keep the connection to my mobile going while he rang the police on that dreadful night.

And Lola. Lola made a full recovery. She is eleven years old now and starting to slow down a bit on our walks. I try to avoid thinking about the day when she leaves my life, but I'm forever grateful it wasn't at the hands of Watts. She still has enough youthful energy to play with Guy's six-month-old staffy pup though–they're inseparable, which is great because they now live together.

Guy helped me so much after my ordeal, not in a professional capacity but as my rock. He was always there for me, and his support has become something I know I can rely on. After the incident, I opened up to him about my past and he knew he was too close to be the one to work with me, so he introduced me to his friend and colleague, Ned Hannan. A nicer and more understanding therapist I can't imagine, except maybe Guy–but I have other plans for him.

Ned and I have been going through the events and people that make up my life and this process has helped me to understand why I had so many trust issues. Almost every man in my life, with the exception of my kids, had let me down, starting with Russell and many of my colleagues in my early days in the police force, the disappointing outcome of my marriage to Bernie, and of course what Watts did to me. The work is still in progress–but the progress is good.

* * *

I considered trying to stick it out in Burmont but Bollington had other ideas. After I continually refused to denote my gender on my reports, he had me transferred out. At least I felt like I'd stuck up for myself and any other poor woman that ended up working there. In reality, I needed to go home anyway and start the process of getting over what had happened there.

Russell didn't come and try to win me back. He and Brooksie left for their trip three weeks earlier than they'd planned and only one of them came back to Australia after the six months. I stayed in touch with Letitia because she was the only one who checked on me after the break-up and we really hit it off. Apparently, Russell met a lovely Spanish girl and now has two strapping dark-haired, olive-skinned lads with beautiful sea-green eyes.

ACKNOWLEDGEMENTS

This book was almost three years in the making and whilst I wrestled with whether I could write it, if I should write it and where it would sit within recognised genre, there was always one person supporting and encouraging me. I've dedicated this book to you Hannah, not because of the topic or message but because it exists due to your unfailing willingness to read drafts, blurbs, bios; anything and everything and to provide such valuable feedback with love and a velvet dagger. Thank you.

My other willing (and incredibly well-read) reader, Tony, has been a constant sounding board and has given his time and valuable insight from the early drafts right through to publication. Thank you Tony.

My family has been behind me throughout, offering support and encouragement and I apologise for any discomfort at reading some of the revelations herein. When being read by a family member or friend it comes with the reassurance that I was not physically injured or in peril in any of the instances detailed throughout, and I did not inflict injury upon others.

Thank you to Marty for the incredible cover photo and for being ready to unconditionally support my many and varied crazy schemes and ideas. I always know you're there for me and your love is a rock.

To Bev Ryan from Smart Women Publish, thank you for guiding me through the publishing process and for supporting my ridiculous schedule with your meticulous professionalism.

To my early readers Marie and Brendan, thank you for believing it was worth reading and for your encouragement and love.

Lastly, apologies to my ex, who was definitely not a gambler.

AUTHOR BIOGRAPHY

Tess Merlin is an ex-police officer and writer. Her first novel, RANK, was written from her lived experiences as a policewoman and as someone who has struggled with the trauma of being stalked. She has written and published training resources during her earlier career as a trainer and facilitator and now also writes adult fiction and middle-grade fiction.

Tess is a mother of two, and a keen linguist in French and Italian. She has a love of the English language, which she has taught in various environments, to both adults and children. She has travelled extensively and lived in Italy and England, incorporating these experiences into her writing.

She writes from the peaceful shores in Gubbi Gubbi country, where she pretends to be a farmer, with several chickens and an impressive veggie garden. She believes in continuously attempting new challenges – most recently fence building and knitting.

www.ingramcontent.com/pod-product-compliance
Ingram Content Group UK Ltd.
Pitfield, Milton Keynes, MK11 3LW, UK
UKHW041634190726
13854UKWH00006B/2483

9 780645 664911